RISING

A **FOR THE STARS** NOVEL

RISING

O McCARTHY

ISBN (paperback): 979-8-9908446-3-6
ISBN (ebook): 979-8-9908446-2-9

Editing & proofreading by Caitlin Miller
Cover design & typesetting by Benita Thompson

*To anyone who's ever wondered what it means
to be truly accepted.*

Harsh, red, dust,
Mars.
An expanse of what was once
And what never was.

PART 1

1

I have light minutes to thank for my life. Light minutes—the intersection of physics, time, space, and the constraints of the human psyche—are the sole reason that I am alive. They gave me enough time to recode our mission from silent execution to rebellion. Light minutes provided a window to make a move before the government of Nation could counter it.

Now, I find myself in space, looking out into the vast expanse of blackness, speckled with light from distant suns, and despite perfect eyesight, I'm wearing glasses. My space mission partner Llama and I were both issued special glasses equipped with biofeedback monitors to use as we go about our duties on the spacecraft. Ever since I reworked the code for our mission, they have been flashing and whining alarms. They are no longer connected to the government of Nation, which means the "heartbeat of scientific progress" is no longer able to mine our bodies for data.

I rip the glasses off my face, throwing them in frustration at the constant warning flashing at the bottom of my periphery. The glasses float, denying me the satisfaction of watching them hit the floor. I roll my eyes before shoving the glasses into my space locker. When I look back at Llama, she's removed hers too.

Maintaining a spacecraft is critical to every space mission, and specific protocols exist to keep space travelers alive. Between diagnostic tests, cleaning, and running light science experiments, there's enough to keep us busy. The duties Llama and I are completing right now aren't the ones we were sent here for, though. Instead of following Nation's manual for space travel, we've changed the course from Station 51 to Mars. Unauthorized override, with a determination to find my father's people and convince them to take down Nation. No, these duties—cleaning, running diagnostics, and keeping busy with science experiments at our own discretion while charting a course to Mars—are the ones that make us rebels openly defying the corrupt government attempting to kill us for their own gain. Why *not* martyr two promising young scientists with traitorous heritage? The government loses two Hub-trained scientists, but gains the ability to unite a people on the brink of rebellion against a different, less nefarious cause: Martians.

Dr. Jog's final words before I left Earth were about Llama. His cryptic message plays on a thought loop. *She's more than what you know.*

I grab a calorie sluice from the food stores and steal a glance at Llama. My stomach drops as I turn to confront her. I fold my hands in front of my body, faking a calm I do not feel. "Llama, why did Dr. Jog say you were more than I knew? What exactly are you?"

Her response is unexpected. Instead of confusion or follow-up questions, Llama gives a Cheshire cat grin and says, "I guess it *is* time to tell you."

I sit with bated breath, wondering what other secrets my space mission partner could possibly be keeping from me.

"You know my parents' story," she says as she floats slightly off the floor and pushes a microfiber cloth over a knob on the climate control panel. The inky cosmos is visible over her shoulder. I can't stand to look at her after what she did, after what she showed herself to *be*. But I want to know. I probably *need* to know everything about her. This is the time in the game when secrets between the two of us are more likely to kill us than bring any advantage.

Llama looks directly at me, and I feel the heat of her gaze tingling over my spine. My fingers twitch, and I drop the prepackaged space food. I snatch it from midair, shoving it into my pocket, hating that she betrayed me, that she led to this, and that I still find myself attracted to her. *I'll need to work on that.*

She tenses, then inhales. For a moment, I think she won't say anything, but then she surprises me as a torrent of words rushes out. "My father was killed resisting arrest in Ward Eleven. My mother was already pregnant with me, so she ended up in Pen 1, where she lived the rest of her life as a high-security prisoner with inadequate care."

I nod, already knowing this information. I bite down the fury at all the other things I know about Llama and the deal she struck with Enforce. Llama's mother was killed despite the bargain. The idea was foolish at best, but Llama turned in my mother in exchange for her own incarcerated mother's freedom. It was all useless. Llama's mother is dead now. It was a lethally miscalculated move on Llama's part.

"My father resisted arrest because he wasn't an Earthling."

My eyes snap to her face as my jaw gapes open. I didn't know there was a colony on Mars until just before I was taken to Hub for training. In all my life, I had never heard of a Martian colonist returning to Earth. My mother met my father *in* space, on her own space mission. *How could a colonist return to Earth without Nation knowing? Does she mean her father is an alien? The same lie my mother told to protect me and give me a chance to live?*

Llama has the nerve to look bemused. I bite my tongue, but even the metallic taste of blood can't stop the torrent of words from spilling out.

"Your father was…wasn't? Isn't? I'm *not* half, but you *are*?" She still looks bemused. Anger at her courses through my body, hot and fluid.

She scoffs. "Of course not. I'm all human, just like you. But it's likely that there are some genetic differences between us and the general population, given that our fathers came from extreme conditions. Mars' genetics will have unfolded a bit differently than Earth's genetics. We saw what happened with my planimal experiment."

I continue gaping. I did not see what happened with her planimal experiment. Trying to force plant and animal cells to mutate into a combination of both was her experiment in cave training. I thought it was a blow off, something to do that didn't really matter. Maybe it actually did.

"Llama. Please tell me our fathers are not..." I trail off, unsure how to phrase this. "Please tell me that we have different fathers."

Her body stiffens and she bites her lip. "As far as I know, they were different. I just know that my father was sent to scout on Earth."

"Wait, you're older than me, right?" I prompt.

"Yes, according to the official records, I'm a year older. I'm twenty, and you're nineteen," she replies, and I watch her lips curve into a half smile. I breathe a huge sigh of relief because we cannot be related while I study her lips. Letting my gaze linger there is a mistake.

I've kissed Llama. I have trust issues with Llama. I do not want to think about kissing Llama, except now I *am* thinking about it, I am really glad she's not my half-sister. Except I still can't stand her, the lying, conniving sneak.

Llama breaks into my disparaging thoughts. "So we can't be brother and sister based on when your father met your mother."

I had already arrived at this conclusion. The story of my life began when my mother, a renowned scientist for the esteemed scientific community of Nation, served a space mission. While in space, she was contacted by a scout from a colony on Mars. The colony was full of the descendants of those who fled Earth just before the Scientific Revolution. My father, a man named Greg, asked my mother questions about Nation and life on Earth. She asked him questions about life on Mars. His colony wasn't full of power-hungry, corrupt leaders like the ones who ruled Nation.

The way of life in the colony was so appealing to my mother that she turned from a life of loyalty and service to the government to an active rebel. Greg and my mom fell in love, but he left to return to his colony before she knew she was pregnant with me. My mother had no way to contact him while still in space, so she did the only thing she could think of: she returned to Earth claiming that I was half-Martian and lived on Compound, a top-secret, government-classified science experiment base. To keep me alive and give me a chance at a childhood, she fudged data in experiments waged on me, along with Dr. Jog, who has been mine and Llama's mentor for the training and this mission.

The government let me stay with my mother until I was fourteen. Then they brought me to Nation Hub, where I began training for this space mission. Of course, my mother was an active member of the Resistance movement, which meant that I was inadvertently part of it too. In fact, without knowing it, I became the face of the Resistance movement. My mom had insisted I learn the game of chess when we lived on Compound. Every move I made at Hub was part of a bigger game for power, played against the Three Powers of Nation's corrupt government: Leader, Legislate, and Litigate.

Now, Llama and I are in space. Together. Despite the betrayal and romantic tension and downright loathing I feel for her, Nation launched us into space to gather data at Station 51, and along the way to it. Whatever data I send back is data Nation can use to further scientific progress.

Just before launch, Dr. Jog made it clear that Nation does not want Llama and me back. Nation sends people to Station 51 to get rid of them. No one has ever come back from it alive, except Dr. Jog. And he knows the terrible secret: There is no Station 51.

Station 51 is a silent execution. A way to get rid of trouble but give the people heroes who died. Martyrs to unite them.

This is why, for all our training, we used game theory against the government, waiting on the power moves of the government before we showed our hand. And this is why I'm in space and not heading to Station 51 with Llama to die.

Because of light minutes, I'm headed to Mars. *We're* headed to Mars to find my father, and maybe Llama's father too. The mental gymnastics I'm doing to keep everything straight are high-intensity. Thankfully, I'm very proficient at shoving my thoughts and feelings aside and getting work done.

"Reach?" Llama asks.

My focus turns from the wrench I was twisting against an instrument panel.

"You're going to break that."

I float away from the wrench, realizing that Llama is right. I'm over-torquing the equipment, and that's a sure way to make it snap.

Despite her being right, I'm defensive. She had information that could have made a difference to us on Earth, at Hub. "How long have you known?" I point a finger at her before remembering that it's rude to point.

"About my father?" Llama tips her head to the side a little to study me. Her mouth curves into a frown. "Not very long. Dr. Jog told me after his..." She trails off and bites her lower lip. "After his leg."

So not very long then. I don't know if I should be relieved or terrified. What other secrets have been kept from us?

"Is there anything else?" I ask, nerves trembling through my body. "Any other pieces of information?"

Llama shakes her head. "No, no other secrets about me or my past that anyone has bothered to tell me."

I sigh and turn away because isn't that the truth of everything? One day we'll have all the information we need, and maybe even people willing to simply tell us instead of making us figure it out and feeding us little pieces at a time.

When I reworked the code to travel to Mars, I thought time and space gave us the ultimate checkmate against Nation. Now, I'm not so sure. *Will Llama's family be on Mars? How will her heritage play into our goal of getting people back to Earth to fight against Nation? How does Llama's Martian heritage change the game?* The thoughts swirl through my mind as if they're circling a drain, but there isn't anything more we can do but wait.

Getting to Mars takes a long time, but we've trained specifically for a long-term space mission. And there are *people* living on Mars who will meet us at the end of it—people who will provide a refuge, and people we must convince to return to Earth and overthrow Nation.

There's two flaws in the plan, though. One: the people of Mars may not want to return to Earth. And two: an entire planet is huge, and I don't know how we'll find them when, historically, they haven't wanted to be found. The truth is, if we don't find them, we're just as dead as if I hadn't overridden the operating system. With these thoughts colliding with Llama's revelations, it's all I can do to keep calm.

I watch the stars and planets from my new perspective, just a tiny speck of insignificance in this vast, unfolding cosmos.

2

THEY CALL MARS the red planet. It doesn't look *that* red from a telescope on Earth, but up close, it's not so much red as it is crimson. I can't believe that primitive scientists gathered the *redness* of the planet from their early telescopes. Llama and I have been in space, existing together but mostly avoiding one another for several months. It's not that hard when I've buried myself in any data I could find in the systems about Mars. After an intensive self-appointed Mars seminar, I'm an expert.

It used to take years to get to Mars. It used to be impossible. It's still a longer journey than anyone would like, but it *is* possible. The technology Nation developed since the Scientific Revolution is the stuff of the early scientists' dreams. Back in the twenty-first century, no one could have imagined travel like this. Getting to Mars is possible now, but only for a select group of highly trained, specialized athletes. Months in space come at a physical cost to the body. No matter how good technology is, the body is your greatest asset in space. That's what Lift, our fitness trainer, told us while preparing for this mission. He was right. After months, I can already feel the effects of daily life without gravity weakening my muscles.

Today, we pass a navigational beacon, one that signals the end of our space journey coming near. The closest space station to Mars is Station 15. That's the one my mom was stationed at when she met my father. We're passing by the station tonight, and should reach Mars in just a few days. I can see the station, a distant speck of light reflecting off the metal in my viewfinder. I wonder who is staffing the station now. *Someone young and full of the ideals of Nation like my mother once was?* I wonder if they've been told what they will see, or if they will see us. I wonder about a lot of things.

The government knows we've gone rogue, but I can only guess at how they're handling the news. Have they warned the scientists serving a space mission about us? Have they instructed the space stations to watch for us? Or have they decided to let us be and told the people we're dead? It wouldn't take much to fake our deaths, not when they were already planned. And the government certainly has its share of secrets.

As far as I know, it was only Dr. Jog, and most recently myself and Llama, who've had the gall to defy orders and change our ship's course. It was hubris, absolute hubris, to think that we would just accept our fate, our silent executions. But the government has a tangled web of lies, half-truths, illusions, and an especial hatred for anyone who challenges the system. Or descendants of those who *did* challenge the system.

I watch Station 15 float past the viewfinder window and fix my sights on the end of our space sojourn. It looms ominously in the distance, stars twinkling around it. There's a hazy glow surrounding the planet—light, or dust, or its very thin atmosphere, or a combination of all three shimmering in the jet black that is not an absence of color, but of light.

I haven't tried to make contact with anyone on Mars yet. Dr. Jog didn't give many specifics before the launch. He was too busy dropping bombs of life-altering news on me. Mainly, that if I valued my life, I needed to go rogue. And going rogue would be exactly what he and the Resistance movement wanted from me.

Honestly, I'm tired of people wanting me to do things. The government wants me to send them data about deep space travel, then die, conveniently letting myself and my troublesome heritage no longer cause difficulties for them. Dr. Jog, my mentor, wants me to go rogue, travel to Mars, return to Earth, and lead a revolution. My mother wants me to live, which I'm grateful for, but also wants me to usher in a new way of life with a revolution. My head hurts and my anxiety flares.

If I could talk to someone, it would be easier. But it's been me and my wayward thoughts for months. When the only voice you hear is your own thoughts, it's easy to think you're insane. Llama's here, of course, but we hardly talk at all. When we do, it's business-related. We manage our parts of the spaceship and do *not* get personal. My walls are up. She tore them down and then left me to rebuild them with only the mangled debris. I have to protect myself. Unfortunately, my mind does not always get that memo. I find myself still stunned by her beauty. I need to find something else to look at. Space provides a decent alternative.

Llama has been timid around me, so unlike how she was when we were training at Hub. I suppose betraying your friend, who was also your romantic love interest, and then being sent into space together would be uncomfortable. If I was her—which I am not because I'd never do what she did—I'd tread lightly too. For the most part, she's quiet. She sticks to her jobs, murmurs a word here or there, and looks restlessly out of the viewfinder from time to time. She told me about *her* father at the very beginning of the trip, but we haven't had a real conversation since.

When Llama taps me on the shoulder, I startle, dropping the small wrench I was using to tighten a gear in one of the mechanical panels. "Reach. I'm sorry."

I stare at her. My mouth isn't working. She's standing there all beautiful in her gray waffle thermal shirt and orange pants, her long brown hair braided down her back and her blue eyes all mournful, but my mind is screaming *BETRAYER*.

"That I made you drop the wrench," she clarifies. I grasp the wrench in my hand again and shrug. "I think we're probably close enough to make contact with the colony, right?"

I suck in a breath. "Probably. I was thinking of trying tomorrow."

"Do you know what you'll say?" she presses.

"Uhhh…" I flounder, because I have no idea what to say. *Hey, I'm Reach. And this is Llama, and our dads are from this colony. Please come with us to Earth because it's bad down there and we want you back, but not just back—we need you to help us overthrow the government that you fled three hundred years ago. Good talk.*

"…probably. I should…" Llama trails off midspeech, staring at me with narrowed eyes. She was talking this whole time and I heard nothing. I'm embarrassed, but maintaining my muteness seems the best course of action. "Reach, did you hear what I said?" she asks bluntly. That's the Llama I remember from training. That's the Llama I know. Timid, shy, hiding Llama doesn't suit her.

"No. I didn't hear you." The words spill from my mouth before I register them. I hate how that happens with her.

"Yeah, I know," she replies in her typical, pre-betrayal dry voice. "I was saying that maybe I should be the one who talks."

"Why?"

"Because. They know about you, but they probably don't know about me." She breathes hard and fast as she says the words, looking lost, embarrassed, and a touch excited. "I suppose they should know about me. And I should tell them."

She makes a point, I'll give her that. But the only time any contact has ever been confirmed with the Martian colony was when they were talking about *me*. My mind whirls. Llama wants answers about her family just as much as I want answers about my own. My anger at her simmers just below my skin, and when my voice breaks the silence, it's harsher than it should be.

"Llama, I promise we'll find out what we can about you, but the only time contact was ever accepted was when *I* was discussed. It's possible Greg might be…alive. And your parents are both…" I pause, because as diplomatic as I try to be, there is no delicate way to say *you're an orphan.*

Llama hangs her head, but not before I see a fat tear roll down her cheek. It drips toward the ground, then slows, hanging there, suspended in midair.

Internally, I cringe. I have bungled this entire exchange. I swallow down my discomfort and distrust and try something more gentle because I hate the sight of her tears. More than anything, I hate that her tears move me. I bolster my courage and forge on. "You need to be with me when we make contact. I'll have to tell them about you. They will probably want to talk to you. I mean, we need to do this together." The words blur together. I have a headache. I haven't spoken aloud regularly for months. I feel like I've been drinking from a trickle and someone just turned on a high-powered fire hose. Now that we're conversing, it's clear that being in close proximity with Llama and not talking has been suffocating. She and I are *meant* to talk.

Llama swipes her hands across her cheeks and nods, giving me a small smile. "Tomorrow, then?"

"Uhh yeah, first thing?"

"That'd be great." She turns to her half of the spaceship, where her sleeping quarters are, and climbs into the hammock-like bed. "'Night, Reach."

And with those two words, we're back to something. Not quite friends, but not quite enemies either. Whatever we are, I still can't bring myself to say "goodnight" out loud—but that doesn't stop me from thinking it.

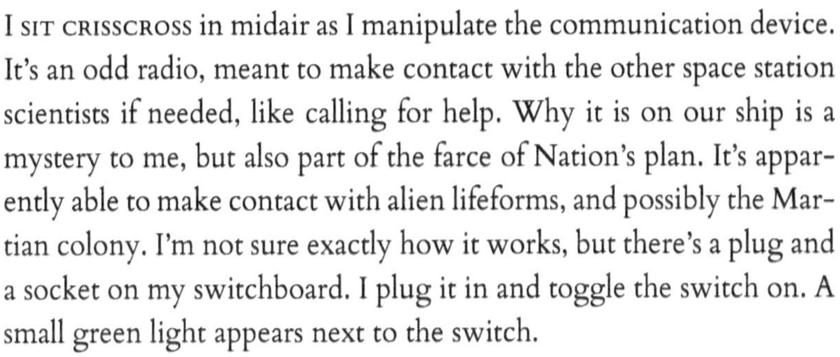

I SIT CRISSCROSS in midair as I manipulate the communication device. It's an odd radio, meant to make contact with the other space station scientists if needed, like calling for help. Why it is on our ship is a mystery to me, but also part of the farce of Nation's plan. It's apparently able to make contact with alien lifeforms, and possibly the Martian colony. I'm not sure exactly how it works, but there's a plug and a socket on my switchboard. I plug it in and toggle the switch on. A small green light appears next to the switch.

I press down on the only button on the machine. It's a large circle with a light inside. Text etched on the glass reads *COMs*, and when I press down, it lights up with a red glow. I am entirely unprepared with what to say, but it remains lit, even after I remove my finger from the button.

Llama elbows me, and I catch her raised brows. The look of indignation is enough to spur my speech. "Errr. This is Reach and my space mission partner Llama, and we are descendants of your colony. We come in…peace?"

She stifles laughter at the last phrase. Her laughter quickly fades to horror as absolutely nothing happens. She stares at the silent coms.

"Llama," I say softly. She doesn't look up. "They only ever acknowledged one attempt at communication." She still doesn't say anything or move. "In all the years of trying. One. It was only when my mother told Greg he had a son that there was a moment of visible connection. We don't know their technology. We don't know anything about them, except what maybe was true almost twenty years ago. We'll keep trying. We'll search. We'll land. We'll search some more." Llama's fists clench at her sides and her jaw ticks with worry. I'm worried, too, but this was the choice I made, to refuse to die on Nation's terms. At least this way, if we die, we die in the freedom of trying to survive.

The whole mission is not well planned. It's hard to plan a mission in meticulous detail when you have no idea where exactly the people you're trying to find *are*. I do have coordinates that Dr. Jog suggested based on the old landing sites used before the Scientific Revolution. That's the best guess I have, and it's where we'll land. In less than two days.

Llama bursts from her statuesque pose and impulsively hits the button, holding it down as she speaks. Her voice rises in pitch and she takes shaky breaths. "This is Llama, daughter of…someone who was sent to scout Earth years ago. And Reach, son of Greg. Greg! Do you hear us? Your son. He's coming to see you. We are coming to Mars. We will be there. Acknowledge this. We are on our way right now, and if you don't acknowledge this we…will…die…on Mars, trying to FIND YOU." Her high-pitched voice and shaking body reveal rage simmering just beneath the surface of Llama's skin.

"That's enough!" I grasp her wrist and pull her finger off the COMs button. I'm not as gentle as I should be, but she's hysterical. "Llama," I say. "Llama, we told them we come in peace." She meets my gaze directly, her mouth twisting into a scowl as her breath hitches. "That didn't sound very peaceful."

Defiance shines in her eyes as she responds with a raspy breath,

"Guess not." Then she folds her hands and places them in her lap. I move to press the COMs button again, aware that this is the very definition of insanity, but unable to think of anything else to do with our time except keep trying. My finger hovers over the button when a static crackle reverberates through the COMs device.

Llama shrieks and I pull back in surprise.

Static...static...static... The crackles are loud, snapping and popping. It hurts my ears and makes my brain feel like bouncing around my skull. *Static...* A deep voice fills the spacecraft. *Reach...land...-Jezero...Crater...static..static...peace...static...static...* The COMs device flashes twice and then resumes its steady light.

Llama's eyes flash with emotion. "They *responded*! They're THERE." She's suddenly a flurry of activity with no purpose. She spins and claps and jumps, which is hard to do in space, and then launches herself at my body for a celebratory hug. I freeze as she thuds into me, her palms on my chest. She stiffens. "Uh. I'm sorry." She backs away.

I grunt out the single word I can think of. "Yeah."

The rest of the day passes by in awkward silence. There are no protocols for landing our spacecraft on Mars. We're rogue. But, thanks to my intensive study, I have some idea of how to land. Mostly, I just have to hope we won't crash into a fiery explosion when we reach the surface.

I check the database maps of Mars only to find the Jezero Crater isn't that far from the projected landing site Dr. Jog gave me before our launch. In Martian miles, it's only thirty away. I'm able to shift our trajectory slightly in the code to within a mile of the landing site. I can only hope it will be close enough for whatever the Martian colony wants us to do. Jezero crater is large, twenty-eight miles across. We could land perfectly and still be twenty-nine or more miles from where we were told to land. Probability and statistics have never been my favorite, and in this instance, I'm reminded of why. These odds aren't great.

Llama and I have space exploration gear that will allow us to survive on the surface of the planet in short increments, but we don't have the equipment for a long hike. Some problems are best left for another day. I let out a bitter laugh at the thought of our gear. The government spared no expense in outfitting us for this mission. They actually did want us to gather data and send them information. They really did want us to make forays outside of the spacecraft and interact with space stations along our route. And then, after sending them data, they wanted us to drift off to the non-existent Station 51 to die. All because Llama and I are the progeny of rebels. And now, thanks to my ability with codes, we *are* rebels.

Code isn't that difficult once you understand how it works. It's also not possible for it to be changed and uploaded to us in real-time due to the lunar distance. Theoretically, the government could try to get us back onto their system, but light minutes save our lives again. The transmission system's original setup allowed for our data and notes to be inputted into a computer system and then relayed through different points—the space stations—and eventually back to Earth. I disabled that as soon as we were able to move about the spaceship freely.

"Why do they only acknowledge you?" Llama whispers from her workstation to my right as I begin to clear away my checklist of supplies. I watch her with narrowed eyes as she sweeps up dirt from a plant science experiment that needs to be secured before we can land. In this fragile environment, even the smallest particles of dust and dirt can cause problems with our equipment. I'm grateful she has been thorough in her cleaning, but I still can't come to terms with her choices. There's always the underlying thought that she's planning to sabotage everything about this trip to Mars. That she *could* sabotage this is a thought that keeps me up at night. It's not easy to be in space with only one person, and that person is someone you hold deep and lingering distrust for. It's its own kind of punishment.

I clench my jaw, feeling the tension between us, before I shake my head and answer her in as measured a voice as I can. "I have no idea."

"But I'm a descendant too." There's something lost in her eyes, something vulnerable and fragile. I shake my head to clear away the unhelpful thoughts about Llama, and when I focus again, the look is gone, replaced by something hard and stony.

I want to comfort her, and I hate that about myself. She's a liar, a manipulator, a traitor. Finally, words come to me, tinged with bitterness. "We'll be there tomorrow, Llama. I guess we'll just have to wait."

She grimaces at my harsh tone, but I can't be soft with her. She made her choice. And my choice is that I will never forget what she did.

"Yeah, I guess so." She moves away from the workstation to her sleeping quarters, where she stares out the viewfinder. Her station is clean, except for her notes. I would tell her to come back and deal with it, but I can't interact with her anymore. There's too much happening at once, and we land on Mars tomorrow.

Another problem for another day.

Why do I keep telling myself that?

4

Llama is up before me the next morning. She cleared her workstation and arranged her sleeping quarters. Now she bustles around in preparation for the landing, securing everything. Our landing should occur in four hours, if my calculations are correct.

We're hurtling toward the red planet. It looms ominously, growing larger and larger outside the viewfinder with each passing second. Llama searches the planet in front of us with keen eyes. "I don't see anything from here that might be a dust storm. But they are the major issue with this plan, right?"

"Right." I sigh. Dust storms on Mars are sudden and unpredictable. They can last hours, days, weeks, months, or years. The thin atmosphere and the tiny particles make a dust storm that really gets going hard to stop. We could do everything exactly right, and still a dust storm could blow us off course, or make it impossible to land, or cause us to crash into rock formations we thought we would avoid by miles.

I tap on the screen of my computer and find the maps of Mars. The trajectory looks good if we're counting plus or minus twenty-nine miles as good. An old weather station from Jezero Crater catches my eye on the map. For the first time, I feel something other than dread about this landing. Sometimes I can tap into old systems since the code is so basic. If I can tap into the station, I can find data about dust storms in the area. At the very least, I should be able to determine if there is a dust storm *now.*

I find the station, miraculously transmitting a weak signal despite being hundreds of years old, and open the code. I exhale a sigh of relief. Right now, there isn't a dust storm at the Jezero Crater. But this system is old, and the best thing we can do is look around with our own eyes.

"Will we start a dust storm when we land?" The nervousness in her voice is contagious. Biting down my fear, I try to think logically.

"I don't think so, but maybe that's why they want us to land in the crater. So that it's at least geographically contained."

Llama nods slowly, then turns away to complete more pre-landing checklist items.

Everything is stowed away and secure. We're only minutes from entering Mars' atmosphere. We've donned our space exploration suits and made our way to the couches custom-designed for our bodies. It's not easy to buckle in with the heavy space exploration gloves limiting our dexterity, but we manage.

I grip the arm of my chair so hard I think it will snap as we descend through Mars' atmosphere. Pockets of gas buffet our ship, causing turbulence that makes my teeth chatter and Llama groan. We may both have concussions when this is over.

Finally, after mere minutes, we pass through the buffeting and our ship begins descending smoothly. We enter into the crater, the rocky crags of the perimeter towering above us as we lower deeper into the ancient delta. The landing gear activates, and we settle onto the surface with a soft hiss and pop of the machinery as it stops its motion. Llama releases a shaky breath as we sit in the stillness, blinking at each other.

We're on Mars.

"We landed." She states the obvious, but I don't blame her. I can't think of anything to say. "Now what?" She unbuckles, so she has some sort of idea. I don't, but I unbuckle too.

My first idea is a bad one. I know it as soon as the words are out. I blame the potential concussion. "Maybe we leave the ship?" I suggest.

Llama scoffs. "Or, we could use the COMs device to try to get directions. Obviously they only want to talk to you, but I'm not being left behind here."

That is a much better idea.

"Oh, I could probably…"

Three swift taps at the hatch door of our spacecraft interrupt us.

I jam my space helmet onto my head and gesture for Llama to do the same. I hoist the oxygen backpack tank onto my shoulders and twist dials, causing the oxygen to flow. I signal to Llama, inquiring if she's ready for me to open the hatch. Our suits are connected with a communication system between helmets, but it's hard to hear over the oxygen hiss.

"Ready for this?" I ask, knowing that if I do open this door before either of us is truly ready, we will die a very quick, very cold death as our blood literally boils in the low atmosphere.

Her words are faint, but I hear, "Yes." When I look to her for visual confirmation, she gives a thumbs up. With that affirmation, I move my bulky spacesuit-clad body to the door and prepare to step into the unknown.

I twist the hatch gears and the door slides to the side. The first thing I'm met with on Mars is the rich iron-red of the planet and a woman in a spacesuit that looks nothing like mine. Mine is bulky. Hers is thin, like tinfoil, clinging to her body. Llama and I resemble overfilled inflatables. She has a clear helmet that lets me see her face; it's like a fishbowl on top of her head. She doesn't have the same advantage as Llama and me because our helmets are white with black-tinted visors.

The woman's hair falls down around her shoulders in twin braids. She gestures 'follow me' with her hands. I can read her lips through her helmet as she says, "Come with me," but I can't hear her voice. She steps away from the spacecraft and I clamber down awkwardly. Llama follows.

The mysterious Martian woman marches across the red surface of the crater with secure, firm steps, while Llama and I bumble along behind her like baby ducklings in our space gear.

I don't know what I expected to see when we landed on Mars, but the complete absence of signs of life throws me. There is nothing here but red rock and red sand. There are no dwellings, no signs of people. Still, the woman is here, and she marches on, and still, we follow.

The woman suddenly stops, bends over, and pulls up a hatch over a narrow hole in the ground. She looks at our heavy oxygen tanks, then down into the hole. She points at the oxygen backpacks and shakes her head no.

I understand immediately what the woman is communicating. In order to get down the hole, we'll have to go without supplemental oxygen. The backpacks won't fit on top of our bulky gear. We'll only have what we fill our lungs and flood our suits with right now. I can't see Llama's eyes through the space visor, but she shakes her head vigorously. She's not going down this hatch without her oxygen connected.

I try to communicate with her through gestures because the hiss of oxygen flooding my suit makes verbal intersuit communication impossible. The gestures progress into heated territory when the Martian woman taps me on the helmet. She points to a cloud rising in the distance, rolling and roiling like water boiling on Earth, then gestures toward where a watch might be worn on her wrist. This woman is adept at pantomiming. I understand what she's saying immediately. *We have no time to delay. Dust storm.*

I know from my self-directed Mars seminar that dust storms are fast-forming and brutal. They also can last for years. Suddenly, the idea of going into wherever this hole leads seems prudent instead of optional.

Exasperated at Llama, I point behind her to the cloud. She twists the dials on her suit to full oxygen before she drops her pack with a speed I did not expect. The Martian woman scoops up the oxygen backpacks and drops them down the hatch, then places both her hands on the ground and points at us. She wants us to go down that hatch first. There are a few things wrong with this, but the dust storm is already visibly closer. It's coming, and we have to move fast.

I place my hands on the ground and lower myself into the hatch, unsure of what I'll find. My feet find purchase on a ladder and I begin to descend, methodically moving foot, hand, foot, hand. When I'm several rungs down, I look up and see Llama's space boots above me, visible in the dim light from the open cover.

There is a sort of pattern to moving in space gear. Just when I think I've figured out the rhythm of going down, the tiny beam of light from above disappears. We are plunged into total blackness. My foot slips on the metal of the ladder, and I hang on with my gloved hands. I have no way of knowing how far it is to the bottom. I can't risk a fall.

I accidentally suck in a huge breath, tasting the oxygen that I flooded my suit with before I disconnected the supplemental oxygen pack. A swear word slips out of my mouth. The oxygen I'm using is running low. I'll have to hold my breath and hope for the best.

Clinging to the side of the ladder, I swing my foot around and grip the rung. I begin to lower myself again, slowly. Moving fast is a luxury I can't afford without supplemental oxygen. Already my head hurts and my vision, even in darkness, is fuzzy. My boot scrapes something—not a metal rung, but solid ground. I bite back a nervous laugh. My fear of falling off the ladder was unnecessary. It was only one more rung to the bottom.

I push myself away from the ladder and stand to the side. I can't see anything, but I can sense Llama approaching. When she and the woman touch the ground, the woman clicks on a lamp sewn into the breast pocket of her spacesuit. She points to the oxygen packs on the ground. I slip mine on my shoulders, then plug the hose into the port.

Immediately, sweet oxygen flows into my suit. My headache lessens and my vision sharpens. I sigh, enjoying the simple act of breathing.

When I look over, in the dim light, I see Llama has also reconnected her oxygen hose and pack. The Martian woman taps her wrist again and motions for us to follow. Bolstered by the oxygen, we obediently comply.

The woman leads us through a twisting tunnel of red rock. Even underground, Mars is red. The tunnels bring back memories of the cave training that nearly claimed our lives. My breathing picks up. Llama's voice sounds inside my helmet, the interconnected suits tethering us to each other. "Reach." Llama's tone is harsh, and I know she's thinking about the cave explosion too. "Think about something else. Focus on something *else*. Tell me about the rocks, Reach."

I swallow the panic rising in my chest and look at the rocks like a geologist. "The channels look as if they were carved by water. None of this is uniform, so nothing about this passage is manmade, but then *how* did these underground tunnels form?"

Llama's voice hums in my space helmet. "Hmmm. Lava?"

"Lava tubes are a possibility. Will you remind me to ask when we get there?"

"Yeah. Do you feel like this is a slope and we're going down? Or is this a complicated maze?"

I shrug. "Your guess is as good as mine. But I'm going to start counting turns, because…" I let the sentence hang there unfinished.

Llama must understand, because her response is, "I'll count them too."

I've just counted thirty turns along the passage when the last turn leads to a set of sliding metal doors blocking our way. It's a different version of what I've seen and studied during my time at Hub and when we completed space units in school, and it seems older, but I recognize it as an airlock. She punches a code into a keypad embedded in a rock pillar on the side of the door. The doors slide open, and the woman ushers us inside.

The three of us stand shoulder to shoulder in a small metal chamber. The doors slide shut and hoses appear, whooshing as they pump oxygen into the chamber. A gauge appears on the wall, blinking red while the text below reads PRESSURIZING. The colors in the gauge change from red to yellow to green. As the gauge shows full, the text changes to read PRESSURIZED.

The Martian woman peers at us as she removes her helmet. I'm stunned. Her skin is so white, it's nearly translucent. Gray eyes peer at me. If I had to guess, I'd assume she's around twenty-five. I can see her high cheekbones, the line of her jaw. Her hair is almost the exact color as the surface of Mars. I can't tell if it's dust, or if that's its actual color. She's slight, but her movements show confidence. She's not beautiful, but there's something about her that makes me want to watch her. *Maybe just too much oxygen.*

"You can take your helmets off now. We might live on Mars, but we still have to breathe, same as on Earth." Her voice is scratchy, but her syntax is oddly proper.

When I look at Llama, I discover she has already taken her helmet off and she's grinning. "I'm Llama." She sticks her hand out at the woman, and the woman stares at it with a blank look. "We shake them on Earth," Llama supplies.

The Martian woman squints at Llama's space-gloved hand. Llama's smile fades and she shrugs, turning away. At the last moment, the woman reaches out and grasps her hand. She clearly has never done this before, because to her,, shaking a hand means placing her palm over Llama's hand and jiggling her hand on top of it.

I laugh. *Definitely too much oxygen.* The sound echoes around the chamber now that my helmet is off. Llama and the woman snap their gazes to my face.

Llama joins my laughter. "Should we show her, Reach?"

"We do not have this gesture you speak of here." The woman's overly proper tone reeks of offense. I can't help but feel a twinge of concern. It's not ideal to offend the only person you've met on a foreign planet.

I shouldn't have laughed. I try to make amends. "I'm sorry. It's just that we have had quite the journey. And we don't even know your name. I assure you, Llama was just trying to be friendly."

The woman's features soften as she looks me up and down, then steps just over the line of personal space. I know I'm not bad-looking, but this level of perusal makes me uncomfortable. My jaw clenches as her eyes rake my face. "Friendly?" Her voice is a near purr, low and sultry. "We are friendly here." I hear an implication in her tone, but I don't know how to shut it down.

"What's your name?" Llama blurts out, and I'm grateful for her bluntness. We might not be friends, but we're in this together, and at least she's familiar. I don't trust Llama, but I don't trust the woman before me either.

The woman pulls back, blinks, and faces Llama. "I am Cait."

"And *who* are you?" Llama responds with a biting tone that tells me she did *not* like Cait's perusal of me either. I shoot Llama a glare, hoping to convey a 'back off' message. We really don't know what we're dealing with here. We have to tread lightly. We're in a chess game now, but we don't know how the pieces move.

Cait's lips purse as she turns her steely gaze to Llama. "I am the Commander of Jezero Colony Security. I'm taking you to see President McAllistair."

Llama must take this as a challenge because she does *not* back down. "Why?" she presses.

"To know what to do with you. He has a special interest in you." She lifts her hand in my direction, then continues. "He commanded it after your little radio snit. I'm following orders. And we should really be on our way."

The doors on the other side of the chamber open, and Llama and I are ushered into an entirely new underground world.

5

Cait steps over the threshold. Llama and I follow, side by side. We're in a type of city carved from the bowels of Mars. There is no sky, but overhead a curved red dome creates the same effect while also supplying a roof. A light source beats down from above, mimicking the sun and casting a red-tinged glow on the place. Square buildings ranging in size from squat and short to tall and impressive line the pathway Cait leads us down. The buildings closest to our entry point are smaller, closer together, and more decrepit than the buildings farther from the airlock. Many of the first buildings we pass are crumbling.

The first person I spy is a Martian child standing by a tall stack of smooth rocks about the size of my fist. He's wearing a spacesuit similar to Cait's, but it looks worn, overwashed, faded. I notice the patches on his knees and the dirt smudges on his cheek. At best guess, he's three years old. His thumb is jammed into his mouth, and he carries something in his hand. I squint to make it out. It's a blanket, just as worn and faded as the rest of his clothes. He scampers along, ducking into the cracked façade of the building. I hear a child's voice say, "Mama! Here. They here."

Moments later, two faces appear in the square hole of the red bricks making up the building. It's a window, but with no glass. There are no insects or pests on Mars that I'm aware of, so everyone's windows are just open, gaping holes.

The larger face must be the child's mother. She places two fingers from her left hand on her forehead and brings them up in a sharp line. The child mimics her movement. Cait's eyes are fixed ahead, and she makes no acknowledgment as she passes them. A shiver skitters down my spine. There is an eeriness to Cait's disregard for the gesture.

"Cait, what was that?" I ask after a few minutes of silent walking.

Cait looks back at me. "What was what?"

"The child and the mother, and what they did." I keep my voice even, my tone light. I'm trying to gather information, even if something about that interaction strikes me as wrong.

"Oh, that. It wasn't important. That's a greeting for military members. You might want to learn it, but I suspect it doesn't matter for *you*." Her response is cryptic at best, and I feel more unsettled than before. "There are some areas of our beloved Mars that have attracted less desirable residents. That area, near the airlock, isn't the best representation of what we've built here. It's not who we are. You'll see more as we continue deeper into the colony. Look around. I'm sure I can answer more questions after President McAllistair has seen you. His orders were for me to bring you in as swiftly as possible."

I chance a look at Llama, trying to understand how she is digesting this information. Cait's speech sounds entirely too similar to the Ward system we left back in Nation. Llama, raised in Ward Eleven, is the person who told me about Nation's determination to keep undesirables separate from the citizens. Anyone who couldn't further the progress of Nation in a scientific way was relegated to the Wards —to menial jobs and to a life of less. The separation wasn't about the best interest of the people, it was about the best interest of the state.

Llama's mouth sets in a grim line, but she plods on after Cait, determined.

My mind whirs with the unknown rules of this new game. Cait has already shown that she will talk, but it's up to us to ask the questions. I have many. *How does this place work? Why are those residents considered undesirable? Why didn't my mother tell me about this? Who is my father? Why does President McAllistair want to see me? Aren't all people valued here?*

I give Llama a bump with my elbow, which does nothing since we're both in our spacesuits. She must sense something, because she looks over at me instead of focusing on Cait's back.

"Follow me," I mouth.

She gives one eyebrow a quirk.

"Excuse me," I call. Cait turns around and stops. "How are we breathing?"

"I'm not supposed to tell you much, but since you asked, I'll tell you the basics. We have a closed circuit system that uses our technology to return carbon dioxide into oxygen."

I run mental calculations, but Llama beats me to it. "But what do you do with the leftover carbon? And, how do you have the energy to split the oxygen without creating more carbon dioxide?"

Cait looks mildly impressed, one eyebrow raised slightly. "On Earth, things are different. We're working with Martian technology in a Martian atmosphere. Our colony has been here for over three hundred years. Things are bound to have developed a bit differently." There's a small tone of condescension in her voice and a hint of something in her eyes, but I don't know anything about this colony. She's right—things developed differently here. That probably includes social cues. I used to think I could understand a person's body language, but now I know I was never great at that.

Llama is undeterred by Cait's stare. "But what about food? You have to be able to grow some things here, and I don't see any—"

"That's not really crucial information for you at this time. I assure you, you'll be fed here, just like all the other citizens of Jezero Colony."

She shut that one down. Why? I try a new tactic. "Could we share some technology with you?"

Cait narrows her eyes as she looks me up and down. I'm an over-inflated tube next to her sleek, slim-fitting spacesuit. I know the request looks and sounds ridiculous, but she hesitates. At this moment, I do have an advantage in the game. This woman is curious, and sharing knowledge is going to be the best way—and maybe the only way—to barter with her for information.

"I am curious about your garb," Cait says without a hint of irony. "Why is it so large?"

"I'm curious about yours," I retort, and then feel my ears flush bright red when Cait stares at me with a sly smile.

"Are you?" she asks, her voice husky as she meets my eyes with her piercing ones.

Llama coughs, breaking the awkward moment.

"Cait," Llama intervenes after shooting me a look that somehow conveys three messages simultaneously: *don't you dare, what are you thinking*, and *not going to work!* "What do people do for work here?"

"Each colonist is assigned specific duties for the good of the colony."

The vagueness of the answer bothers me. "How do the duties get assigned?" I take care to keep my voice even, and I do not look at Cait's eyes as I speak. I focus instead on a point just over her shoulder.

"It's really their own choice. Everyone here has free will. Some people do more with it than others."

"Like that woman?" Llama asks. "The one with the child we passed?" I notice her voice is sharper than usual; she's pressing back verbally with Cait. That wouldn't be such a problem if we knew anything about where we are and this society, but Cait and this entire place is still an unknown entity.

"Yes," Cait responds. "We need to go now. But we can swap technology anytime, Reach." I don't miss her singling me out. The omission of Llama's name leaves me feeling itchy. I do not want this woman's obvious coveting. I'm not a possession, but she's acting like I'm something that *belongs* to her. But since she is the Commander of Security, I should probably play along—for now.

Cait continues to lead us down a path of red dirt. It becomes obvious that hovels filled the area near the airlock. The path cuts a straight line from the airlock to the city center. The buildings increase in size the farther from the airlock we trek. The few people we spy from their windows wear better clothes, or at least shinier ones.

"Is the colony climate-controlled?" I ask.

"Yes," Cait says, still marching straight ahead and not bothering to look back.

I asked because my spacesuit is heavy, and Llama and I are beginning to lag behind Cait's persistent pace. I'd like to take my bulky spacesuit off and wear the base layer thermals issued by Nation's government, but that seems risky if we're going to flash-freeze to death.

Llama meets my eyes and wipes sweat off her forehead with the back of her hand. Cait walks on, oblivious, and Llama and I have no choice but to trundle after her, beads of sweat dripping down our bodies.

6

THE SPACESUITS ARE heavy. Mars' surface temperature is beyond frigid. If anyone stepped outside without proper covering, they'd flash-freeze. Not a pleasant way of dying, but it would be fast. This domed area has been made suitable for human habitation, but not knowing the parameters of the temperature means Llama and I can't risk removing our spacesuits. Every person we pass wears the same thin, shiny, flexible space suit material as Cait. Since Cait wore her spacesuit to the surface, I have to assume that these are necessary for survival—even underground in this place. I don't know how our faces aren't freezing without our helmets, but there is no telling what technology these people have developed. Maybe there's a heat shield that automatically controls the area around a person's face. It sounds preposterous, but so is an underground colony on Mars. I can't rule out anything at this point.

Cait leads us toward a towering building at the farthest edge of the gigantic dome from the airlock. The building appears carved into the side of the dome, but in the shadows from the overhead lighting, it's impossible to tell. A banner hangs from the structure next to the door, made of a red field with a single navy diagonal stripe. Dispersed along the red background are sixteen five-point white stars. In shimmery silver, the words 'Jezero Colony' are printed across the middle of the banner.

Cait stops in an open courtyard in front of the building. I'm dripping with sweat and exhausted from our trek down the manhole ladder and through the airlock. Llama looks like she's been tortured. Her face is pale, her brow sweaty, her eyes drooping. Cait is unperturbed by the ordeal. It's not every day *we* go to the surface of Mars and then walk for at least five miles in our spacesuits. Maybe it is an everyday occurrence for her.

Cait stands on a mark etched into the ground. I can't make out what the mark is, but it looks like some sort of picture. She stands rigid, at attention, her body completely straight. She glances back at Llama and me and then calls out, "I PRESENT THE EARTHLINGS."

There's a noise like a rushing wind, which is impossible since we're on Mars, underground, and there is no wind here. With Cait's announcement, people pour out of every building around the semicircle plaza and stand around us, whispering. They form a half circle at our sides and backs while the curved building looms in front.

An eerie hush falls on the group as a flicker of movement at the entrance of the large building catches my eye. I didn't know it was possible, but Cait stands even straighter as a man emerges from the building.

He's tall, slender, and his dark hair is speckled with gray. He wears the same silver, shimmery spacesuit outfit as everyone else, but he also has two navy-blue sashes across his body. They begin at the shoulders and loop to the opposite hip, creating an X on the front and the back. Along the sashes are a number of small white stars with a thin red stripe in between each. He stands on the top step of the curved building.

"Citizens of Jezero Colony!" the man's voice booms. He clearly has experience as an orator. Llama meets my eyes with a long, searching look. Anyone with our past would be wary of the word *citizen.* Knowing nothing about the structure of leadership here is disconcerting, at the least. At the worst, it might be deadly.

"It might not be as bad as home," I whisper to Llama. Her mouth quirks up in a flicker of acknowledgment before she turns her attention back to the man.

"We have the great honor, the great privilege, the great joy, of Earthlings joining our colony today. This is an event that we have never before experienced in our history, but have prepared for. You know the protocol. Follow it, and all will be well. Let us give our guests the proper Jezero welcome that they deserve!"

There's silence after his words. The man breaks it with a single clap, and then the people begin to sing. It's haunting, eerie, and chills my bones. They aren't speaking as much as using their voices to sing sounds. There are no words, just emotions—and not happy ones. Suddenly, the sounds change from sorrow and mourning to joy and exuberance. In the doorways and pathways around the courtyard, every person is part of a pair, doing a spinning dance as they make wordless music with their voices. It's mesmerizing. I'm lost in the dancing and the music until it abruptly stops, and the man begins speaking again.

"As President of Jezero Colony, I thank you for that wonderful welcome!" He smiles warmly, and I notice that wrinkles line his face, though he doesn't look *old.* "Business with the Earthlings will now convene in our Tribunal Hall. These are matters of safety and security, so the Tribunal Hall will not be open for this session. Records of our meeting will be kept sealed until such a time as should be deemed prudent to release these details to the general population. Only those elected and the Commander of Security will be privy to the transcript upon completion of the conversation. Remember your duty. Free will—"

"—to all!" the crowd roars back.

The President raises his hand, palm up, and lifts it above his head as if he is throwing something behind him. The rest of the people in the courtyard raise two fingers from their left hand and make a diagonal motion across their bodies, just as the woman and child by the airlock did earlier. Cait does nothing, standing in the same rigid posture until the President lowers his hand.

At this signal, Cait waves as an indication that we should follow her. She leaves the mark she was standing on and marches directly toward the President. We climb several steps, but stop when he is still one step above us.

"Your Excellency," she says, "I present to you the Earthlings. Reach, a male, and a female called Llama."

"Thank you, Cait," the President says in a much quieter voice. "Let us go inside, we have much to discuss. Cait, you know that, as part of your duties, you can attend but will not join the conversation."

Cait's gaze hardens, her mouth setting into a grim line. She stands aside, allowing Llama and me to pass.

"Hello," the President says to me, looking at me with soft bluish eyes. "I'm President McAllistair. I'm very interested to meet you, Reach." He turns and surveys Llama with a mixture of curiosity and something sinister. "And you as well, Miss Llama. Please follow me."

He leads us into the towering building. I read the words 'Tribunal Hall' carved into the red rock as we pass under the arched doorway. The inside of the building is made of the same red rock, but there are decorations on the walls. Mostly carvings, but many are painted, depicting scenes of trees, flowers, and also an image of men atop a hill that catches my eye. They wear strange hats and plant a flag on the hill. The flag has stripes in red and white, and white stars on a navy square. The colors and shapes are similar to the banner on the front of the Tribunal Hall.

"Do you find yourself studying history much, Reach?" President McAllistair's voice sounds directly next to my ear. When I stopped to study the image, he did too.

"I've never seen anything like this."

"Ahh," he says, scratching his chin. "Llama, do you know anything about American history?"

Her eyes flicker to mine before she answers. I can see the fear of the unknown in her pupils. "No, sir," she says before she coughs.

"Hmm. You've been kept in the dark, then?"

I don't know how to answer him. Honesty seems the best course of action. "Honestly, sir, we don't know…anything about A-mer-i-can history," I say in a scratchy voice. I'm parched and hot and desperate to remove my spacesuit.

President McAllistair looks from Llama to me with pity. He pushes through a swinging door made of metal and gestures us through into a small empty room.

"Here, you two must be tired and thirsty. Those spacesuits look terribly uncomfortable. Though they must be effective since you made it off the surface. Cait," he calls over his shoulder, where she trails behind us. "Please find an aide and procure more comfortable outfits for our guests. They also need some sustenance."

Cait nods once, then steps back through the door. The door swings back to shut, leaving just the three of us in the room.

"Reach," he says quietly, his eyes welling with tears. He extends a finger and touches my cheek in an oddly familiar gesture. "I've waited years to meet you."

My eyes widen. I have so many questions, but Llama beats me to one of them.

"Who are you?" she asks with the typical rashness I associate with her.

"President McAllistair of Jezero Colony." He smiles as he extends a hand in her direction. "President *Greg* McAllistair of Jezero Colony."

He knows how to shake hands. His name is Greg.

The pieces click into place, and I stand, dumbstruck, and stare at *him*.

Greg.

My father.

7

"G-g-Greg," I stutter as my heart beats double time.

"Yes. I'm Greg McAllistair. Which makes you Reach McAllistair, I believe," he replies with a gentleness in his tone that is unlike anything I've ever heard. *Is this what it's like to have a father?*

My mother was right: Greg's way of being *is* completely different than living under Nation's thumb.

"McAllistair?" Llama questions with narrowed eyes. "What does that mean?"

"It's my family name. A last name says where you came from, who you are." Greg's voice is kind despite the snark evident in Llama's tone.

"Family," I echo, a sense of belonging rising in my chest as I taste the unfamiliar word on my tongue. It's short-lived.

"Family," Greg replies firmly. His tone brooks no argument, but the word *family* spurs the only logical response I can think of in the moment.

My forehead creases as I stare at my father. "But I don't know you."

"You will." Greg's eyes shine as he looks me over. "You have a birthright here. There is so much to explain, so much to show you. I have no doubt you have things to share too. I need to ask that you keep our relationship private for now. There are things we need to do to protect...everyone. But that can wait. Cait is returning with more suitable garb for you. And then we must attend to official business."

Cait soon sidles into the room holding two cylinders attached to long straps over her shoulders. The cylinders are clear, and inside is the same shiny fabric of everyone's suits we've seen since arriving.

"Here." She thrusts one cylinder at Llama and then passes me the other one. She places the strap over my shoulder, allowing her fingers to trail down my arm. If I wasn't inside a giant puffy suit, the action would be provocative. For now, it looks like she's trying too hard. Which she is.

"Thanks," I murmur.

Greg watches the exchange with his head tipped slightly to the side and a pensive expression on his face. "Come on, Cait, let's give them space to change out of those preposterously giant spacesuits."

They move to exit, but Llama stops them. "Wait—we won't freeze to death when we take these off, right?"

Greg fixes Llama with a piercing gaze. "No. You've had your faces uncovered this entire time and are still functioning, aren't you?" Llama's eyes widen and round in embarrassment. Greg chuckles. "We thought you simply didn't have other clothes to wear. This entire colony is temperature-controlled. You'll find it is a lovely seventy-one degrees Fahrenheit during our daytime hours and a delightful fifty-nine degrees Fahrenheit during our nighttime hours for optimal sleeping. Your spacesuits are being loaned to you, so please care for them well. The technology in them allows for brief visits to the surface or out of our climate-controlled dome with proper ventilation gear."

"Thank you..." I venture. I don't know what to call him. Is he Greg? Is he President? I can't call him *dad*. I don't know him.

"Anytime." He gives a slight bow. "Cait." He steps outside of the room with Cait on his heel. Before she slinks out of the doorway, she fixes her dull gray eyes on me. I shudder.

"Someone's got themselves a…" Llama trails off when she sees my expression. If I had to guess, it would be that my face is contorted in disgust. I hate pushy people, and Cait *is* a pushy person. "Reach, come on, she's not that bad." Llama unfastens the cuff of her spacesuit glove with her teeth. Once her hand is free, she can maneuver out of the suit. I do the same. Taking off the spacesuit is like taking off a coat. A really big, really heavy coat.

I pop the top of the cylinder off and unroll my borrowed spacesuit. Inside, I find a different set of undergarments. They are silky to the touch and feel much nicer than the waffle thermal that's been sitting against my skin for months.

"Oh," Llama breathes as she unrolls her clothing.

"I'll just face this way and you face that way?" I suggest. "Besides, we're wearing our thermals underneath, so it's not a big deal."

"Or, I could ask about a different changing area…"

I huff. "Llama, I'm not going to look at you. Just get dressed, please. I'd like to learn more about this place. We can't forget the mission." I hold a glove in my teeth before dropping it to the ground as I undo a set of buttons. "We can't forget the whole reason we're here. You know, the *game*."

"Game theory, shame theory, crame theory, lame theory…" Llama mutters under her breath.

I turn away and begin changing. It's surprisingly easy to get dressed once I'm in the Jezero clothing. They are simple garments and far easier to put on than our Earth-made spacesuits.

"I'm done," Llama calls over her shoulder. I've been done for a minute or two, but kept staring at the wall while I waited for her to finish. Once, I would have been tempted to peek, but not now. She's still a betrayer, even if she seems safer than Cait.

There's no way to fold up our bulky spacesuits, so we leave them in the room. They sag like underinflated tires, but maintain their relative shape. The two suits give the appearance of astronauts slumping in the room after a harrowing journey. I glance back at them and burst into laughter. Llama looks back and smiles, too, then runs her hand down the shiny material of her spacesuit. I have to admit, the ability to move is incredible, and the temperature perfect.

Cait waits for us immediately outside the door. "This way," she barks and marches down the corridor before stopping in front of a different doorway. This one is an open arch with no door to close, just an entryway to step through. Llama and I step through it together when Cait gestures impatiently that we should go in.

Greg sits at the head of a long rock hewn table. Stools line the perimeter, made of the same reddish rock as everything else. Greg indicates the stools, and Llama and I sit. The taste of iron coats my tongue as a puff of red dust rises. The people around the edge of the room stand rigid, but Cait is the most stiff of them all. Varying insignia decorate their spacesuits. Some have a single sash featuring one color, others have double sashes in red or white, and the rest have a belt emblazoned with stars slung across the hips. My eyes dart around the room, trying to take it all in.

A small woman stands directly next to Greg. She holds a stylus and tablet, but it's her posture that concerns me. Her poise reminds me of Second, the second-in-command of the government, back on Earth. This Martian woman's tablet is round and balances on a triangular stand, like a spinning top. Greg begins to speak and the woman writes, curving around the tablet in circles. She must be a scribe.

"The meeting of the Tribunal Council has begun," Greg announces. "For the purpose of the security of our colony, the only attendees with license to speak are President McAllistair of Jezero Colony, Reach of Earth, and Llama, also of Earth. You are under the seal of the Jezero Colony government. Sharing what you hear in this room will result in the penalties of removal from your post and, in the case of treason, more extreme measures." Greg takes a breath and turns to us. "Reach, Llama, I am going to ask you some questions. Please answer honestly. We will endeavor to bridge any gaps in communication. For now, you are a foreign entity on our Jezero soil. Do you understand that this is a matter of the state?"

Llama lifts one shoulder in a small shrug of assent.

"Eh, yeah." I squeak out the words because the feeling of so many eyes silently watching me is more than disconcerting.

"First of all, Reach, Llama, how did you know our location?"

I blow out a breath. "We didn't know for sure. Our intelligence on Earth suspected the Jezero crater."

"Who *is* your intelligence? Or, rather, what are you loyal to?"

Llama jumps in. "The Resistance movement on Earth, against Nation." I shoot her a look that stops her from saying more. She is *not* loyal to the Resistance movement. I won't let her claim that label. I also can't say anything about it in front of this room full of strangers.

"Nation?" Greg prompts.

"Nation is the most advanced civilization on the planet Earth. It came to be three hundred years ago after the Scientific Revolution overthrew what had formerly been a conglomeration of states."

"Yes, we are familiar with that part of history," Greg deadpans. He shakes his head once and returns to his previous professional demeanor. "What I mean is, *what* is Nation? What does it want with us? Why are you here?"

Llama clenches her jaw so tightly I hear the scrape of bone on bone from her teeth.

"Errr—we are from Earth, from Nation…" I start.

"That has been established," Greg retorts.

"Right." I draw in a breath. This is complicated. My strategy was to get the lay of the land, to try to understand how things worked here, what their weaknesses were…instead, Greg is asking me to lay everything out on the table. I don't know the risk full transparency will pose. Once again, I'm playing chess, but without any idea of where my opponent's pieces are on the board. "So, we are from Nation… but we're not here on behalf of Nation. Llama mentioned the Resistance earlier. Things in Nation…aren't…good." Silence sounds throughout the room as everyone waits for me to continue. I take another breath. "The Resistance movement infiltrated the top levels of scientific progress and taught us what we would need to know to get here. Nation didn't send us to Mars, the Resistance did."

Greg's head tilts sideways. "Where were you supposed to go? Why put two teenagers in space in the first place when I'm sure they had other options?"

Llama's eyes flutter closed, then open with a fury as her mouth twists into a scowl. "We were supposed to send Nation whatever data we could from wherever we traveled in deep space and then die. Our mission was a lie. It was a silent execution."

A collective gasp sounds from around the perimeter of the room. Greg scans the people, then focuses back on Llama.

"They prepared children for space to kill you? Why?"

"The Resistance movement is making inroads," Llama says. "They want to blame our deaths on Martians, not you, of course, but little green alien men. To unite the people against a common enemy and let the government's powers remain uncontested. Since Reach and I are both the children of government traitors, getting rid of us seemed like the best way to end that legacy and rally the people to their cause."

"But why send *you two*?"

"My mother, I think you kn…" I respond, stopping myself before sharing my parentage with the room. "Served a space mission and was…"

"…put in an impossible position by being pregnant when she returned," Greg whispers, a look of angst on his face. There's a hiss around the room as the dignitaries, not permitted to speak, realize the implication that *I* am Greg's son. At least I didn't let the secret out. Greg holds up one hand to silence the room, then leans toward me, his voice lower. "What did she do?"

"She told them I was half Martian and bartered to keep me a classified experiment until I turned fourteen. Then the government took me for training at Hub. They always wanted to use my half-Martian genetics to get more information about deep space. But the fudged data and lies—" I will myself not to look at Llama. "It all came apart, just like she always knew it would. They sentenced her to death."

Greg's eyes close for a moment. "I…I'm so sorry."

"She escaped. She's not dead," Llama butts in like it absolves her involvement in everything, and my jaw clenches. "But my parents are."

Greg faces Llama and steeples his long fingers together. "I do know part of Reach's story, and more is becoming clear. But what's *your* story, exactly?"

Llama opens her mouth, then snaps it shut again. Her eyes meet mine with a question. I give the barest of nods, but she steels herself. She sits up straighter, opens her mouth, and pours out her story.

"My parents were leaders of a Resistance group that gained traction in a Ward in Nation. Wards are where people who aren't desirable live, because they're not citizens. If you're not a citizen, you don't get the best food, the jobs, the access to care, or anything. A government spy infiltrated my parents' group, posing as a malcontent. She passed all the tests, and my mother trusted her. The spy became second-in-command before she brought down the group. My father didn't trust her. He was killed resisting arrest. One reason he resisted arrest so hard is because *he* was from *here*."

The scribe stops her furious writing and the spinning tablet slows. A flash of something passes over Greg's face.

"To clarify," he says, "your father was from Jezero Colony on Mars?"

"What other colony on Mars would he have been from?" Llama huffs.

"Do you know his name?" Greg prods further.

"No."

"Do you know what year your father arrived on Earth?"

Llama shakes her head. "It must have been more than twenty Earth years ago, considering my age."

Greg shoves back from the table, urgency vibrating through his actions. "Everything discussed in this room is *classified*. Adjourned." Then he bellows, "CAIT!"

There's a scuffling and shuffling of feet as the people leave the room. Cait steps forward, her posture still oddly rigid. "We need Percy." Cait stands there, her face drawn and blank. Greg snaps his wrist at her. "GO!"

Cait salutes and leaves.

Greg slumps into his seat once the room is clear. The air in the room is dense with anticipation. "You two," he huffs while dragging his hand down his face and groaning, "are wildcards."

8

Llama and I remain still. I've avoided looking intently at her for a long time, but this weirdness triggers me. I stare at her, and we share a moment. It's not a romantic moment. It's a *what-just-happened* type of moment.

"What does that mean—wildcards?" My voice shakes with trepidation at our situational blindness.

Greg just shakes his head. "Percy should be here for…explanations."

"Who is Percy?" Llama cuts in.

"He's the head of Telecommunication Relations of Jezero Colony, and…ahh, here he is." A single knock raps on the side of the doorway. Then a man enters, followed by Cait. He's tall and thin, and his lips are curved into a deep frown. He is intimidating, but one detail about this man makes me think he might be a bit less uptight than at first glance. He has long brown hair pulled back into a bun. Cait stands stiffly.

"Cait, dismissed." Greg waves her away. She slinks out of the room, but I don't hear footsteps down the hall. Either she's light on her feet or lurking just outside the door, eavesdropping. "Percy."

"Greg." The man's voice is wheezy and unpleasant. He runs a hand over his hair, tightening the bun at the nape of his neck. "Why have you summoned me for this, but not the Tribunal?"

"Percy, you know the laws. Only the elected officials and the Head of Security have Tribunal clearance."

"And —?"

"And I can't break the laws, even for you. I have to uphold them for all of Jezero Colony."

Percy's blue eyes close in exasperation. I notice Llama studying him, her brows quirked slightly. Percy has made no acknowledgment of Llama or me, though he's clearly seen us and knows we were the reason for today's last-minute Tribunal meeting.

"So, what?" Percy snaps, turning his frigid gaze on Llama.

"Percy. This is Llama and Reach. From Earth."

"Yes, how extraordinary." He peers at us, a condescending smirk on his face. "Why do two children require my presence?"

"Percy, Reach is my son."

Percy's lips twist into a contorted frown while his nostrils flare. "Son? You have a *son*!" The blue veins are visible in his neck, and one especially prominent on his forehead bulge.

Watching the rage flow over him is comical at least. I can't help it, I give a little wave and smile while Greg responds, "Yes, and the laws will need to be taken into account. So consider this fair warning about that whole process, Percy. And while the succession laws are important and a matter of discussion, we actually have more pressing matters that require your assistance right now."

"More pressing?" Percy grinds through his teeth. His lips don't even move.

"It would seem that Miss Llama, from Earth…is…"

"Oh, for surface's sake!" Percy bursts out. "You can not also have a *daughter*." He spits out the word 'daughter.'

Greg's eyes widen and he scowls. "We will not curse in the Tribunal room, Percy. And no, Llama is *not* my progeny. But she has Martian lineage."

"From whom, and if not you, why does it matter?" Percy snarls.

"Llama, would you please tell Percy your story? About your father, specifically?" Greg asks.

Percy rolls his eyes, steeples his fingers together, and sits. As Llama begins to tell the tale of her parents, Percy's demeanor changes. He was angry before, but now he's tense. The air in the room thrums as he asks the same clarifying questions Greg did.

"Souterraine," he breathes, his eyes flashing.

"We *are* underground," Llama retorts. I forgot that Llama knows multiple languages. Her linguistic ability was one asset that Nation developed for space travel. I had assumed Souterraine was the name of a place.

Percy rolls his eyes again.

"Yes," Greg says, but it's unclear who he's agreeing with. He turns to Percy. "They need to know. Maybe we can convince them. When was the last transmission?"

"We discuss business once a week. The next transmission is tomorrow. I'll send an emergency request to discuss this with the Queen and King of Souterraine." Percy is all business now. He studies Llama with a new interest, clearly calculating. "You should be on this call."

The muscles in Greg's neck cord, but he nods. "All of us?"

Percy's nostrils flare. "Yes. Lends authenticity to have the girl speak." He shakes his head and mutters, "What a mess. I'll go prep the transmission team. Can you make it by three?" Percy strides to the door as he's talking. Greg just nods.

Once Percy is gone, Greg sits a little looser. I swear I hear him grumble the word "family" under his breath, but then he addresses Llama and me. "I know that was confusing for you." I shake my head in agreement. That was extremely confusing. "On Mars, we have our own complex history. You are aware that Jezero Colony exists, but there is another colony that preferred a different approach to government. Each colony is self-contained, but we do have to interact and keep the channels of communication open. The planet is only so large." Greg scrubs a large hand down his face. "Llama, I believe you are a descendant of the Souterraine Colony, not Jezero."

"Is that a problem?" I ask.

"Maybe." Greg sighs. "It also might be a wonderful opportunity for us. Souterraine and Jezero have found themselves competing for resources on Mars. The truth is that, as the colonies grow, we won't be able to sustain both of our populations. There's not enough liveable underground space or resources for people here. We'll run out in the next twenty years if things progress on their current trajectory."

"So?" Llama asks with one eye narrowed.

"So we've been thinking about what to do, and there aren't any good options."

"What are the options?" Llama presses.

"War. Or leaving Mars and returning to Earth."

I suck in air. "But that's what we need. We could help each other. Come to Earth, it solves all the problems…"

"No, Reach, it does not solve all the problems," Greg responds quickly, though not unkindly. "You have only been here for hours. We've been here our entire lives. Our legacies have been carved in Mars' soil. We are Martians. Returning to Earth would be a last resort."

Greg's ferocity is startling. Llama shakes in anger, small tremors causing her body to tremble as she asks, "What does *war* mean to you?"

"Believe me, both the King and Queen of Souterraine and I are trying our best to avoid it. But there are people who believe that war is the best answer to our problem."

Llama stands, splaying her hands on the red rock table. "Well, war on Mars is *not* the best answer. This is a stupid problem."

Greg's forehead crinkles and he sighs. It's clear his patience is wearing thin. "You've had a long trip. So far you haven't learned much about our way of life here in Jezero. I'll get Cait to give you a tour. But first, I suspect you need the opportunity to wash up and rest. Cait!"

Cait appears in the doorway.

"Cait, please take Miss Llama and Reach to a guest facility," Greg commands. "The embassy would be fine."

Cait nods but adds, "I don't think the embassy is fully staffed. We haven't had intergalactic travel in…"

"Noted, just get a cook and a housekeeper. I don't think these two are used to the finest of treatment from Nation anyhow."

I must be delirious from lack of sleep, but I snort and follow Cait out of the room, Llama at my heels.

Cait brings us to a small building outside the Tribunal Hall with the words 'Embassy of Jezero Colony' engraved on the lintel. We walk inside, greeted by a staircase inside the entrance. Cait leads us through the building. There are two floors, an upstairs, and a main level. The main level holds a kitchen, a room with a long table, and a room with puffy upholstered chairs, while upstairs is a set of several rock slab doors.

"Llama," Cait directs, "this will be your suite for the time being. There's a washroom attached. It's all yours. Enjoy." Her voice is flat and her facial features piercing. It is evident she does *not* want Llama to enjoy her stay.

Llama cocks her head to the side and then walks through the door. She snaps it shut, leaving me alone with Cait in the hall.

Cait steps forward and places a palm on my chest. "Reach? This is your room." She reaches behind her and turns a doorknob. The same red rock as everywhere else makes up the walls and structure, but a large bed in the middle of the room catches my eye. I would like to sleep in a real bed for the first time in months.

I grip her hand lightly with mine and lower it from my body. Dr. Etiquette did *not* explain how to deal with unwanted feminine attention in our Men's Manners course on Earth, but I'm making some guesses. I step back from Cait once her hand is off my body. Whatever she is implying, I have no interest. "Thanks, Cait. I appreciate it."

"There's a private bathroom…" she hints in a low voice.

Wow. This lady does not get it.

"Again, thanks. But Cait, I'm not interested."

Cait's eyes narrow as she surveys me from head to toe. I will my-self to stand tall and remain stoic in the face of perusal, but internally it's a different story.

"Not now, maybe. You will be." She bites her words out with a harsh edge. "Enjoy your stay. And that girl"—she indicates Llama's room—"is not worth your time."

"Goodbye, Cait." I step around her and into my room, shutting the door firmly before locking it.

When I turn around, I lean against the door and take in glorious, personal space. I'm alone for the first time in months.

I tread to the state-of-the-art bathroom. The shower is an expe-rience, with multiple jets and hot water that cuts a path into the grime months of space sponge baths have left on my skin. When I've toweled off, I pad across the red rock floor. The only downside is that the red dust accumulates on my bare feet. I slip into the bed, wearing nothing but the Jezero-issued underclothes.

As I pull the silky soft silver material of the sheets up to my chin, I briefly note how similar it is to the spacesuits here. I don't have time to wonder about it, though, because as my head sinks into the pillow, I fall into a sleep deeper than the farthest reaches of space.

9

Morning on Mars is unique. Or maybe it's afternoon. When I finally pry my eyes open, the lights are on outside my bedroom window. I curl into the silky, soft blankets and enjoy the feeling of being ensconced in comfort. It's a far cry from the feeling of hurtling through the universe on a rocket.

Without a communication device on my wrist, I can't tell the time. There are no clocks in my room either. After a quick trip to the bathroom, I meander down the stairs. The clatter of metal sounds from the kitchen. The rest of the downstairs is empty, so I head there.

"Ah great, you're awake!"

I stand, starstruck, in the entranceway to the kitchen as the most beautiful woman I have ever seen grabs a pan handle and gives the contents a vigorous flip, her long blonde hair secured in the back but flowing in waves from her head to below her waist. She focuses on stirring something on the stove, but she calls over her shoulder to me, "Are you hungry, Reach?"

Like an idiot, I stand there, gawking. She stops and raises one perfect blonde eyebrow at me while she stares back. She has the same pale skin as everyone else I've seen on Mars, but it doesn't make her look sickly. She's petite, but she doesn't look young. If anything, she looks a year or two older than me. If I had to guess, she's twenty-three.

I give my head a small shake to clear it before managing to force out a husky, "Yeah, I am."

"Great. I made pancakes. And eggs. You've been in space for a while, so you'll need protein to restore muscle mass." I watch her pink lips with fascination. *Are they as soft as they look?* They look nearly as soft as the blankets from the bed. She notices my stare, and her cheeks flush a bright pink. "So what do you want?"

"Er—eggs." I swallow, then remember my manners. Dr. Etiquette would be appalled that I forgot. "Please, Miss…" I leave the sentence open-ended, hoping to get a name to call this beautiful creature before me.

"Eggs it is, then. Do you know what Llama will want?" She grabs a large charcoal-colored dish with shallow, curved edges. It's a cross between a bowl and a plate. Soup wouldn't spill, but the edges aren't so high as to call it an official bowl either.

"What are the choices? Is there coffee?" Llama's voice, riddled with sleepiness, sounds from behind me. I spin around in surprise, embarrassment on my face. She surveys me. "What's with you?" Not waiting for a response, she marches into the kitchen and walks right up to the woman I'm thinking is made of stardust. "Hey, I'm Llama. Who are you? *Coffee?*"

I grimace at how she approaches the situation, but the beautiful woman smiles and laughs.

"Hi, Llama, yes, we have coffee." She hands Llama a steaming cup, which Llama cradles gently and sighs before taking a sip. "I'm Beatriz. I'm the chef assigned to you and Reach for the duration of your stay. What are some of your favorite foods to eat?" I'm struck by how Beatriz's voice sounds like music.

Llama lowers the coffee cup from her lips and searches Beatriz's face, confusion evident on her own.

"We don't eat food to enjoy it. It's fuel."

I nod along with Llama's statement. She grew up in the Wards back in Nation. I grew up on Compound in the care of Citizens. While I didn't have much to enjoy in the way of food, Llama had even less. Food has never been for enjoyment for either of us—except the three times a year I received celebration cookies as part of Compound's rations on Leader's Day, my mother's birthday, or my own. Food has always been about efficiency and productivity.

"Well what did…I mean, what *do* you typically eat?" Beatriz asks. Her brows knit together above deep brown eyes. At the mention of food, I reach into the pocket of my spacesuit pants and extract a pouch of calorie sluice. When I got dressed, I put a pouch into my spacesuit pocket for easy accessibility. I walk the sluice pouch over to Beatriz and hold it out, palm up near her. Her eyes blink rapidly and she blanches.

"Surely *not*," she whispers.

"Surely *yes*," Llama whispers back. "These have been our human body fuel for the past few months. Lightweight for space travel, but calorie dense for our needs."

"May I?" She indicates the pouch in my hand. I nod, and she picks it up. Her fingers brush my palm with a jolt of electrifying touch. She brings the pouch to her mouth and rips it open with white teeth. Then, she squeezes just a little bit of the calorie sluice into her mouth.

She gags.

"Blah!" She runs to a basin and spits vigorously, then turns on the tap and sticks her head under the faucet. She drinks directly from the stream of water flowing, drinking as if she will never cleanse her tongue of the taste.

Llama bursts into laughter. I would laugh, but I do not want to embarrass the woman. She's so beautiful it hurts. I don't want to break her.

"How do you…you…*live*…off…*that*?" Her eyes are wide, her mouth drawn in horror.

Llama shrugs. "When that's your only option, you can't be too picky."

"But what on the surface do you eat on Earth?" Beatriz asks.

I stifle back a laugh at Beatriz's use of a Martian curse word. The surface of Mars, so inhospitable, is a swear word here. It's odd, but her curiosity about food makes me like her more.

"That would depend on what you do, and who you are," I respond while trying not to stare at her. *Look her in the eye, but don't stare.* I didn't know I could find a woman so attractive.

"Ok, so what did *you* do, and who are *you* on Earth?" Beatriz presses. Tears spill from her eyes. *Did our space food really taste that bad?*

"Oh, um, we were…I was…" I stumble because I'm really not sure how to answer that particular question.

Llama saves me with her explanation. "We were special agents of the government. We trained for years to go to space. Our job was to go to deep space and make contact with Reach's alien father."

Heat rushes to my ears, and I feel my cheeks flush. I don't know if I should be grateful Llama just told Beatriz this or not. Something about it makes me uncomfortable.

"Really?" Beatriz's eyes widen as she turns her head from Llama to me. "But isn't your father…*human?*"

"It would appear that he is as human as both you and me," I try to jest. It sounds flat to my ears. Llama starts to say something, but I give her a quick 'no' with my head, and she stays silent on the topic of my lineage.

"So, you two haven't had real food?" Beatriz returns the conversation to safer topics. "Like pancakes?"

"What's a pancake?" Llama peers into an iron pan on the stove.

"A pancake, Earthlings, is a culinary delight. Best served on birthday mornings, or Sunday mornings, or holidays, or for dinner at any time. Pancakes are actually a type of batter that's then fried into a cake and often paired with sweet toppings. I have provided an array of choices that range from sweet to savory, since I wasn't sure of your palettes." She opens the oven door and slides out a tray heaping with golden brown, small, flat, round discs. "To the table!" she pronounces, then leads us out of the kitchen area and into the dining room. I follow behind Llama, noting the way her brown braid sways like the ticking of a pendulum compared to Beatriz's soft locks.

The dining area features a table and chairs carved from red rock. These chairs have backs to lean against, unlike the stools in the Tribunal room. I pull out a chair for Llama—it's shockingly heavy, but I manage to move it with a few grunts and heaves. When I turn to pull my chair out, I see that Beatriz has done so for me. A strange itchy sensation prickles over my skin when I realize that she saw me struggle with Llama's chair and moved mine because I am physically weaker than her. I don't mean to scowl, but I must because Beatriz smiles gently.

"Don't worry, I haven't been in space the way you two have. I'm used to our gravity and weight systems underground. You'll get your muscle mass back soon enough."

I nod, but don't meet her eyes. As I slip past her to sit in my chair, she leans down and whispers in my ear, her long blonde hair hanging over my shoulder. I have the strangest compulsion to run my hands through it. Her voice stops me. "Don't be afraid to let people help you." Then she begins placing the bread discs—pancakes—on plates along with a variety of other items.

"I'm making a little taste plate for both of you. I'll remember what you like and dislike so I can create dishes around your preferences while I'm cooking for you. Do you know how long you'll be here?"

I shake my head *no*, and Llama does the same.

The food is all foreign, but she hands Llama and me a knife and fork. It's not clear how to eat the pancakes, but I opt for cutting them into pieces and testing them with the toppings Beatriz placed on the edge of our plates.

They are, in a word, heavenly.

Llama moans as her eyes roll back into her skull. "What is this?" she asks with her eyes closed. "It's divine."

Beatriz smiles. "You're having a bite of pancake and candied bacon. It's sweet and savory at the same time." She looks at my plate. "Reach, you had a pancake with banana slices and strawberry jam. That's mostly just sweet."

By the time we've tried everything, it's become apparent that Llama and I both prefer the savory combinations. The sweet foods are full of flavor, but leave us feeling thirsty and jittery. It's like when something is *too* bright, *too* juicy, *too* sweet.

"Well, that's settled, then! Savory pancakes for breakfast tomorrow!" Beatriz proclaims with glee. Her exuberance is contagious, and both Llama and I grin at her.

A low buzzing sound reverberates throughout the room. Beatriz fishes in the hip pocket of her silver suit and extracts a small round device. She reads it before putting it back in her pocket. "Now that you've eaten, you are supposed to meet with President McAllistair for embassy business this afternoon. Your escort, Cait, will be here to guide you in thirty minutes. Now would be the time to freshen up and prepare for that meeting." She stands, gathering plates and utensils into a stack and carrying them to the kitchen.

I stand, too, staring after Beatriz even though she's disappeared from view. Llama leaves her seat, but she doesn't follow Beatriz. Instead, she comes around the table and grips my hand with hers. I startle at the contact.

"Reach," she says in her low voice.

"What?" I snap, the embarrassment of being caught staring at Beatriz frustrating me.

"She's lovely." I eye Llama skeptically. "Really. I like her too. Not like you do, but she's fun. She's pretty. You should probably go help her do the dishes if you don't have anything else to do to get ready."

My brow furrows. "Why would you…" I can't even begin to fathom the rest of that sentence, so I leave it hanging there, like dust motes in the sun back on Earth.

Her forehead creases and she frowns. "Because I messed everything up, Reach." She sighs and runs her hand down her braid. "I'm sorry. I know you won't ever trust me again, but we need to be able to…work together…here. I do want you to be happy."

My jaw clenches, and I bob my head just to make her go away. The sting of her betrayal is too fresh. I can't accept her well wishes for my happiness. We might be inching back toward friend territory, but wishing me happiness… That makes her seem entirely too good.

She releases my hand and walks around me. I don't bother watching her go. Instead, I steel myself and decide that though Llama might be a traitor, she is right: I should help Beatriz with the dishes. Men's Manners has made approaching women I don't know well a terrifying ordeal, but *at least Dr. Etiquette isn't here to critique.*

I shudder at the memories of the humiliation of the Men's Manners Seminar Nation made me endure during my training. Instead of focusing on the pain of losing friends, the sting of being told I was less than because of my gender, the anger at the systematic way in which every male was mocked, I admit that I did learn *some things* in that course.

"Beatriz," I call out as I walk through the doorway into the kitchen. She stands at the sink, dancing while water rushes over the dishes. I can't hear any music, but she is either ignoring me or can't hear me. "Beatriz?" I call again, louder. Still nothing. Hesitantly, I tap her lightly on the shoulder.

"Argh!" She shrieks and drops the plates into the stone basin before turning around, clutching one hand to her chest and holding a fork tightly in her other. When her eyes meet mine, she blows out a breath and lowers the fork slightly while removing a black disc from her ear. "Reach, you…" She inhales and exhales again. "You scared me. I'm sorry for reacting like that. What do you need?"

Her gorgeous brown eyes are so deep that I forget to answer.

"Reach?" she asks again.

Words stick to my tongue, but I manage to say one coherently: "Dishes."

Her brow furrows, and her lips pucker as she surveys me from head to toe. "You need dishes?" She tilts her head to the side.

"Yes. Uh. No. I mean—"

"Time to go!" Cait's voice breaks into the kitchen, along with her, causing me to jump back and flush with embarrassment. Beatriz offers me a small smile and waves before turning back to her dishes in the sink. I'm left with no choice but to face Cait again.

Llama stands directly behind Cait, a cross between a grin and a grimace on her face. While Llama said she likes Beatriz, it's clear she does *not* like Cait.

Cait's raspy voice assaults my ears. "Reach, Llama, you two are to follow me. This is important business we must partake in, so let's stop gawking at your chef and *get going*." She gestures to the door, frustration evident on her face and even more in her bitter voice. When she stalks out of the room, I follow.

Llama walks next to me. "Didn't go well, did it?" I can hear the smirk in her voice.

"I'm not great with…women," I snap. It's never fun to feel embarrassed. I especially hate it.

"Reach," Llama whispers in a low voice. "You're great with women. Have some confidence. Cait likes you." I shudder. Llama snorts. "See? You have a dry sense of humor and a great mind. And…" She looks me up and down. If she had been this open with her perusal of me back on Earth, a lot of things might have been different. "You aren't unattractive."

I frown as I look down my torso. It is true. I am well built from our Earth training, or at least, I was before spending months in space. My mother was very pretty, but Greg has a charming roguishness in his eyes. I don't know if I have that, but there is something pleasing about my face. There's nothing more to say, so I say the only thing I can: "Thanks, Llama."

"Any time." She bites her lip and looks away from me. I do the same, because I find that I can't look at Llama anymore. I know what she is, but this exchange, despite all the walls I've put up around her, feels dangerously close to friendship.

I harden my heart a little more against her with each step we take.

10

Cait leads us out the front door of the embassy and turns in a different direction than we went yesterday. We leave the larger buildings behind as we head back toward the airlock. We don't go all the way to the airlock, stopping instead at another building built into the curve of the colony wall. The structure is a half sphere, like a ball that has been sliced down the center. Surrounding the circular building are a number of square buildings with stacks of red Martian rock balancing off to the side of the front doors.

"What are the stacks of rock?" Llama asks Cait after we've passed several that look ready to fall, but are somehow balanced into a tower.

Cait grumbles, but answers, "Those are cairns. There's a rock for each member of the family living in that dwelling. It's an old tradition, but Jezero colonists like to keep things traditional."

"So the population isn't very big, then?" Llama asks.

Cait turns around and stares hard at Llama. "Why would you say that?"

"Because the cairns don't have very many rocks in each. I'm just doing some quick math here." Llama shrugs and starts to whistle as if proclaiming her innocence. Given how secretive Nation was about population information, it wouldn't surprise me if the numbers of people in Jezero were a state secret too. I work through reasons Jezero wouldn't want us to know the population numbers, and I cannot come up with a single reasonable explanation for the secrecy.

"What about you, Reach?" Cait asks in a much sweeter voice. "What have you perceived about Jezero Colony and our population?"

"Uh…" I stall. "I hadn't thought about it."

Cait gives a perfunctory nod and then marches us through the door of the building I've come to think of as *the ball building*. The same red rock as the outside paths continues inside the building. This time, the rock on the floor is etched in intricate designs. Deep grooves spiral and cut a dark line through the unrelenting red. I can't make out what it is, but I can tell it's something intentional.

"Reach," Llama whispers and jams her elbow into my stomach. I let out an *oof* and drag my gaze from the swirls on the floor to whatever it is she's looking at.

I'm glad I do. It's Percy, and he does not look happy. He comes down the sloping hallway, but his frown is nothing compared to the look in his eyes or his clenched fists. Greg is a few paces behind him. When he sees me, he waves and smiles, the perfect foil to Percy's demeanor.

"Reach!" Greg's voice is as warm as his expression. He turns to Llama and gives a small bow from the hips down. "Miss Llama. A pleasure."

Percy doesn't say anything in greeting. He huffs out a grunt and mutters a sharp "this way" before turning around to continue back down the hallway.

"Cait," Greg says with a nod, clearly indicating that she should not follow. Cait gives a salute and then stands with her back not quite against the wall, and impossibly straight. When Greg turns to follow Percy, I don't miss the scowl she flashes at being told to stay behind. "Miss Llama, Reach. Please, let's go attend to this business." He ushers us back the way he came, and now we're walking *up* the slope.

"So, Reach, Llama," Greg begins. Percy is significantly ahead of us. "I'm sure you have some questions. But first, how was your night at the Embassy? Were your accommodations satisfactory?"

Llama grins. "That was a lovely night's sleep. I didn't know sleeping in a real bed would feel so luxurious. I can't wait to go back to sleep tonight."

Greg smiles. "And you, Reach? Was *everything* to your liking?" There's a slight emphasis on the word *everything* which makes me think of Beatriz. But that would be absurd. He can't know that I found our chef attractive. Something about it feels off, but I can't determine what. I chalk it up to not knowing Greg. I simply don't know his speech patterns, expressions, or body language well enough to understand what he's implying. It's a problem for my game theory modus operandi.

"Yeah…yes. It was…very satisfactory."

Greg's face is open and looks trustworthy, but I don't know him. A fact that I keep reminding myself, even if he is my father.

"How was your food? I imagine that our chef's fresh meal was better than your space travel rations?"

Llama waits for a beat and then answers for me. My eyes narrow as she oversteps, but I don't interfere. I can't decide if I'm angry she's answering or grateful for the deflection away from Beatriz and food. That's what this was about: *food*. I know *nothing* about the structure of Jezero Colony. *How does romantic attraction between people even work here?*

"The pancakes were incredible. Thank you for sending the chef. We've been living on calorie sluices." Llama smiles up at Greg. He's clearly taller than she is, but still a bit shorter than me. I'm reminded of how pretty Llama truly is. My brain squashes that train of thought when it supplies a new one: *When she wants to be charming.*

Greg smiles back down at her. He cuts his gaze to me and must see my expression because his eyes flash a question. I look away, turning my head to stare at the relentless red rock that forms the walls, the floor, and the ceiling.

It would be reminiscent of the cave implosion Llama and I survived, except we are twisting upward instead of down. Thankfully, this time, there is no rushing water overflowing a reservoir while toxic gas builds up and causes a collapse. My heart begins an irregular staccato beat. *I'm safe. I'm safe. I'm safe.* I remind myself with each step.

Percy's nasally voice cuts through my thoughts. "Hurry up. Our transmission time is soon."

Greg mutters something incomprehensible to Llama and hurries off to join Percy ahead. Llama falls into step beside me. "It's like the…"

"Cave again," I snarl. I can't look at her. Heat gathers in my cheeks, red like everything else here.

"Reach…" she murmurs. I know I've hurt her. "I don't know what else I can say or do to tell you that I'm sorry. I regret everything. My mother is dead, and was dead long before they executed her. Your mother escaped. She's alive. You're alive. What I did wasn't right. I will regret it until I die. But please, Reach. You're the only thing familiar here." She swallows. "We need to work together. We need to make a *move* here, and I know I'm no good at game theory, but we can't forget what the Resistance needs from us."

I scowl because she's right. It's just so hard to let it go. Her betrayal is the kind that means I can't trust her ever again. And now she's the only thing familiar in a strange land.

The corridor twists upward for the next ten minutes. We reach a plateau where Greg and Percy stand outside of a glass box with a door.

"Is that…" Llama's eyes widen.

"Glass?" Greg answers. "Yes, Llama. It is glass."

"How? No one else has any."

"Ah. A scholar of the elements. We have developed some impressive technologies since our people arrived at Jezero. We are able to create a high and concentrated source of heat that reacts with certain elements of the Martian rock to create Mars glass. It has many of the same properties as the glass that you'd find on Earth."

"But why haven't we seen it until now?" she presses.

Percy rolls his eyes at their conversation. "Because we live underground. There are no insects or bad weather here. Glass is an expensive product to make, and we'd rather use it only when necessary instead of frivolously. It's a tool, not a status symbol." He opens the door and ushers the rest of us inside the small glass box. When he steps inside, we have no room to move unless we want to jostle everyone else.

Llama and I stand shoulder to shoulder, staring at our reflections against the panes. It seems strange to have walked all this way to be squished into a glass box.

Greg hands us each a pair of thick headphones.

In the dim, red haze, I can see there's a panel with switches and dials just behind Percy. He reaches behind himself and deftly flicks switches. A long tube descends from the glass above us.

"Transmission in 10…9…8…" He counts down to one. Greg meets my eyes and then Llama's while he places a finger on his lips in the universal 'shh' sign.

"Live," Percy whispers before he begins speaking in a louder voice. "Souterraine Colony, this is Jezero Colony. We have requested an emergency transmission because we have discovered something we think you will find valuable."

There's a crackle, static, and a loud whoosh. "This is Queen Eleanore of Souterraine. We received your transmission request. What have you discovered?"

"Well, we found something, or rather *someone*," Greg answers with a harsh, biting edge in his voice, and I'm surprised by his tone and demeanor. With Llama and me, he has been friendly and open; with this transmission, he is guarded and not as much agitated as he is terse. The entire exchange baffles me.

"I believe you might like to meet this person. It would appear you haven't been exactly truthful in your communications with Jezero throughout the past twenty-five years."

There's a hiss from the other end of the transmission. "You will not disrespect *my wife*," a man's deep voice replies. "Even if you are the President of a different colony. What exactly are you implying?"

Percy's wheedling voice joins in the conversation. "We've found out something—something that exposes your lies."

Greg puts up a hand to stop Percy from continuing. "We have been given the good fortune of receiving Earthling guests here at Jezero. One Mr. Reach and one Ms. Llama, of Nation. Ms. Llama's parentage is *most* interesting to us. She claims to have a father from Mars. Who returned to Earth. Since Jezero has sent no one to Earth in the past three hundred years, and would have informed Souterraine if this were the case, we find this *confusing*. Perhaps you could *clarify*."

"Alec?" The woman's whisper comes through the tube. "You...-found out—"

"Yes, we found out about *Alec*. How many more have you sent?" Percy snarls.

"This is hardly the time for this conversation," the man from the other side of the tube states.

"Actually, this seems like the ideal time for the conversation. Given that it didn't happen when, by Maritan law, it should have. There's no time like the present, especially when certain actions have been uncovered." Greg's brisk, business-like tone is intimidating. "How many more have you sent?"

There's a murmur on the other side. Finally, the woman called Queen of Souterraine speaks. "It was just Alec. We only had the resources for one to make it there and back. And when he didn't come home, and we lost contact with him, we knew Earth wasn't an option." She sighs. "We've regretted sending him every day, right, Alfred?"

"Yes, Eleanore and I were simply exploring options when our council devised this scheme two decades ago. It was thought best to keep it quiet, given that we have always wanted to avoid war between our two colonies. We depend on each other for survival here. Sending Alec was never ideal, but he was best prepared for the mission and knew what was at stake."

"And now?" Greg asks with a harshness in his voice I haven't heard before.

"Now we know that it was a mistake," Alfred responds with harshness in kind. "We haven't sent anyone else, nor do we plan to again. You know that your colony has the technological advances required for such an ordeal. For the past twenty years, we have focused our colony on agricultural needs. Surely you can see from our regular shipments of seeds and foods that we are not attempting to leave Mars, and that war is the last thing Eleanore and I desire for our people."

"Can you provide proof? Log books and such of *Alec's* mission?"

"Why would we do that?" Alfred snaps.

"Because we'd like to see the proof." Greg inhales and scans the room, his gaze skipping over Llama. "And because I think you'd like to meet your *granddaughter*." The words hang there, shocking to ears on both sides of the transmission tubes. Llama's face grows pale, but a smile breaks across her cheeks. She looks like a child who has been given extra celebration cookies for no reason at all.

Silence is broken by the low rumble of muffled speech coming through the tube breaks the silence, and then Queen Eleanore cries out, "Yes!"

"I'll arrange for her to come with our next shipment of technology. It's due when, Percy?"

"The tech truck with human transport capabilities will leave the base in two weeks."

"Good," Greg responds as he meets my eyes. "Be sure to provide the log books. A digital copy of the secure database will suffice if you have picture evidence of the physical copies. Don't forget, or she won't be coming."

The words are ominous, and Llama's face blanches. For the first time since we met Greg, I'm afraid for my life—and Llama's too.

11

Greg removes his headphones. Llama and I do the same. When we step out of the box, Greg faces us, his face shiny under the lights. "Dealing with Souterraine has been a headache since I took office. It's best to be stronger than they are, even if being tough is not my natural preference. It's really part of the political game."

I tense. Politics is a game I know well. My eyes track to Llama's involuntarily. She stands still, her hands curled into balls at her sides.

"I have grandparents?" she asks.

Greg looks at her, and I wonder if he sees the elation in her eyes. She's trying so hard to mask it, but if you know her, you can see it. "Yes."

"What are they like?" she whispers.

Greg's response is instant. "Weak."

Llama flinches.

Greg takes pity on her. "Weakness isn't an asset as a leader, but it isn't always a bad thing when you're family or friends." His eyes rove to Percy, who remains in the glass box, pulling cords and flicking switches off. "Friends." He sighs. "It's most important to our way of life in both Jezero Colony and Souterraine. It's a shame that so many things can come between people, no matter their relationship. War, money, material possessions, arrogance. We must always fight against arrogance."

Llama has regained some of her typical spitfire attitude. "That's quite a speech for someone who just called *my* family weak to *my* face."

I elbow her. "Llama!" I hiss her name between clenched teeth.

Greg's eyes twinkle with mirth. "I like you, Miss Llama," he says, laughing. "You're not weak. Now, we have two weeks to prepare both of you for a visit to Souterraine. Also, Reach, I'd like to show you more of our colony here on Jezero. I've cleared some time out of my schedule to spend with you. I know you…don't really know me…but I'd like to know you. Family is the most important thing here. Could I give you a tour?"

The question is directed at me, but I don't want to be alone with Greg. A protective instinct from deep inside must fire a warning into my subconscious, because despite Llama's betrayals and lies, I don't want to leave her with these strange people. I don't want to be with strange people. There's too much to see, too much to learn, too much to interpret. The logical part of my brain wars with the protective. Dividing and conquering our understanding of Jezero is one way to understand where the pieces are on the board. I remind myself that Llama's trying. And she's the only familiar person I have here. The adage 'keep your friends close and your enemies closer' could apply here, but I don't know where I stand with anyone on this planet.

"Yes, we'll take a tour, please." I look at Llama, who nods her head in agreement. "That would be enjoyable."

Greg's nostrils flare slightly at the word *we*, but he dips his chin. "This way, then."

We leave the red rock half-sphere building, stepping into the lights that line Jezero's domed ceiling. Cait stands directly to the left of the door. Her hands hold a small black button she pins onto herself when Greg is in her sight.

"Cait," Greg acknowledges. "These guests shall be having a tour. Can you arrange a motor vehicle?"

Cait nods and fishes something out of her pocket. She places it to her ear. "Motor requested by President McAllistair. Transmission building. ASAP."

While we wait, I study the façade of the transmission building. An old clock with Roman numerals is etched into the rock above the door. Three minutes and two seconds later, a vehicle draws to a stop directly in front of us. The vehicle is open, a box on four extra thick wheels and a steering wheel on the front left. Cait opens two of the half doors. Greg climbs into the driver's seat, Cait takes the seat next to him, and Llama and I scramble into the back.

"Reach, Llama. Welcome to the official guided tour of Jezero Colony," Greg speaks over the hum of the motor.

Greg wears two hats during our drive: tour guide and government official. As he winds the vehicle through the dusty red streets, I notice the way people stop what they are doing and offer the left-handed salute. Greg smiles and waves to them. The entire experience feels too casual for my liking. There's a farce somewhere in this drive. My only problem is that I can't tell who or what is being deceived.

Greg drives the vehicle—something he calls a MUV, or Martian Ultralite Vehicle—through the curves and twists of the colony, pointing out interesting landmarks as we go. The streets are arranged in concentric half circles, radiating away from the Tribunal Building, which is the pinnacle of the colony's design. There's also a pathway that cuts through the circles to the airlock, slicing through at exactly the halfway point, as well as smaller pathways that cut through the curved roads at different angles. A bird's-eye view would show a perfectly symmetrical half wheel and spoke pattern—a tribute to someplace once called Washington D.C.

Greg shares this tidbit of information about the colony, then waits for some response. I offer him a platitude: "It's very precise."

"What is *my*— Souterraine like?" Llama asks.

I shoot her a glare. She'll see it in two weeks, and she didn't even know it existed until yesterday. The immature part of me screams, *We're here to focus on Jezero Colony.* The empathetic part of me whispers, *She just wants to know her heritage, same as you.*

"You'll see it soon enough." Greg shuts her question down. "For now, let me tell you about Jezero. We're very proud of all we have accomplished here. This"—he points to a long red building—"is our hospital. We have had major medical advances here in the past three hundred years. We have a state-of-the-art wing for mothers and babies, and an impressive bone rehabilitation program. We don't have many accidents on Jezero, but occasionally someone in the tech labs cuts their fingers off." Llama shudders and Greg's rich laughter floats away from the MUV. "Don't worry. We can reattach them."

Greg explains how the colony is broken into sixteen different districts, which are wedges of the half wheel. Each district has a number and a representative. They took the idea of *democracy* with them from before the Scientific Revolution. I digest this information. Apparently one reason Hannah, the First Leader of Nation, succeeded in her reforms was because everyone who believed differently than her left.

Greg turns the MUV onto the straight path toward the airlock. We've seen the major government buildings, the bank that stores some sort of digital currency people earn through the government and then exchange for extra food or goods. The basics are provided by simply being part of the colony.

"This is where the people willing to accept a life with just the basics live," Greg says as we pull into an area that is decidedly more ramshackle than the rest of the colony. The red rock buildings have cracks, any cairns in front of the doors are haphazard or fallen over, and the people we do see appear embarrassed. They do salute, but their worn clothing stands out in comparison to Greg's, mine, and Llama's.

"What are the basics?" Llama asks softly, her gaze fixed on a little girl. Her hair is braided neatly, but her clothing could best be described as rags.

"Food. Clothing. Shelter."

"You provided *her* clothing?" Llama whispers as the little girl stares at us.

Greg follows Llama's finger and his jaw ticks. "Certainly not. But we provide an amount that is appropriate for the family's well-being that is in proportion to how much they assist the colony."

"So she wears *that* because…her family doesn't do more to assist the colony?"

Greg shifts uncomfortably. "There's more than meets the eye here. There are reasons we do things the way they do. Some people don't want to contribute. We can't help them if they don't."

"No, you just leave their children to…"

"Enough!"

It's the first time I've heard him snap, and it scares me. This man is like every other leader I've met. It's predictable how *unpredictable* government officials are.

"I understand what you're implying." Greg's voice quiets, but it's still just as firm. "You are obviously not a descendant of this colony, and do not hold the same values as Jezero colonists. As a guest, you will continue to receive our hospitality, but coming here and questioning our way of life is exceedingly rude."

Greg turns the vehicle around in front of a building shorn in two by a giant scraggly crack. Cait leans back just enough to fix Llama with a cocked eyebrow and a smirk before turning her attention forward.

It's silent for the ride back to the embassy building.

12

Beatriz stands in the kitchen of the embassy building, and whatever she is cooking smells tantalizing. Llama, stone-faced, clambered out of the MUV and disappeared into her room. I thought about knocking but decided against it, instead following my nose and my heart to the lovely Beatriz.

"You had a tour today?" she asks. Her wavy blonde hair is pulled back away from her face, and she bends to retrieve something from the oven. When she straightens and meets my gaze, I'm grateful for Men's Manners teaching me not to stare at ladies in compromising positions. Maybe that wasn't a total waste, because I can look at her and not blush.

"Yeah," I say. It's not much, but I don't know what to say because her brown eyes make me want to write poems.

"You sound unsure. Was it a tour? Or was it not?" Her voice holds a hint of humor that fires the attraction in my chest. Why do some women have such wonderful voices? Others have no impact on me at all, but Beatriz's voice is soft, and slow, and warm, and bemused. I could listen to it all day.

"It was a tour. But, Gr— What do *you* call him here?"

"President McAllistair?" she supplies.

"Yeah, him. I don't know what I'm supposed to call him because it's complicated. But he yelled at Llama. She was being insensitive with her questions, but I…"

"You have feelings for Llama?" Beatriz asks bluntly.

"What? No!" I blurt the words too close together and heat rises in my cheeks.

"What was she asking?" Beatriz smoothly transitions away from the topic of *my* feelings for Llama, and I am exceedingly glad. I do not want to discuss my previous attraction to her with the woman I actually am attracted to now.

"About the children's clothes. In the basics."

"Oh." Beatriz's face falls. "That is unfortunate. But we have to do the best we can with what we have. Everyone contributes to the good of the colony here. It's difficult when technology is our focus. We don't have as much in the way of renewable resources as you would have had available to you on Earth. I suppose that the clothing situation there would be shocking."

"But how do you get materials?"

"We have our ways. But the renewable resources issue has been more contentious of late. President McAllistair has been faced with some difficult choices. The children require less fabric, so they end up with the smaller clothing, and often it's been used by several other people before it comes to the children in the basics."

Beatriz doesn't sound sad. It doesn't sound like the idea of a child wearing rags bothers her. I begin to speak, but she interrupts, gesturing to the dish in front of me. "I made you a pie." Beatriz then sticks a fork into the still-steaming pie, extracts a bite, and extends the fork in my direction. When I start to take the fork from her hands, she whispers, "No, close your eyes. You can enjoy it better this way."

I have no choice but to obey. When she places the fork in my hands and I finally manage to taste the pie, I am overwhelmed with sweetness. It's too sweet. I don't want to offend her, so I chew it, pretending to savor it.

"What is it?" I ask, opening my eyes in search of a glass of water.

"Marsberry pie. It's a special treat here. We don't get to use that much sugar every day. I made yours with real sugar since you were given a full ration but won't be here for that long."

"Mmmm," I say, trying to sound noncommittal.

Llama chooses this moment to reappear. Her hair is braided neatly in a single brown rope down her back, and damp. "What's that?" she asks, pointing to the pie.

Beatriz's eyes widen, but she quickly recovers. "Llama, I didn't hear you coming. It's Marsberry pie. Made with real sugar."

This fact about sugar is apparently very important to Beatriz. "Oh, is it good, Reach?"

"Sure." Both women turn to look at me. "I mean, it's very good. We don't have much real sugar in Nation."

Beatriz beams, and Llama searches my eyes as if she can read my thoughts. If she could, she'd see the words *don't be rude again* flashing in front of her.

Beatriz serves Llama a portion of pie. I note that she doesn't talk in that husky, warm voice to Llama, and she also doesn't tell Llama to close her eyes for her first bite. Perhaps Llama could read my thoughts because even though I see the tiniest flicker of a grimace upon her first bite, she smiles and makes appreciative sounds. Beatriz grins.

"It's a little unorthodox, serving dessert before supper, but I made you a soup for your meal." Beatriz gestures to a tureen on the stovetop. "I need to head back home now, but I'll be here very early to make your bread and breakfast in the morning." She places bowls on the counter, reaching overhead to get the dishes. While her back is turned, Llama mouths, "I need to talk to you."

Beatriz gives Llama a small smile and me a larger one, and before she ducks out of the kitchen area completely, she says one final farewell. "Just leave your plates in the sink when you're done, and help yourself to as much of that pie as you'd like. It was fun to bake it." She turns and glides away.

Llama doesn't waste any time. She scoops soup from the tureen into both of our bowls. "We have to talk, Reach. Now," she hisses.

"About…" I prompt.

"About this *place*." She spits out the word *place*.

"What about it?" I hiss.

"These aren't the people who are going to help us," she whispers, and I hear an undercurrent of anger in her voice.

"Why would you say that?" I ask, but I suspect I know the answer.

"Because they *are* like Nation. This colony is about power and currency. The basics are…" She closes her eyes and clenches her fists. "The *basics* are essentially a *ward*."

Understanding dawns on me. "Llama." I say her name slowly and gently as the horror of being a child in one of Nation's wards dawns on me. "You've never told me much about growing up in a Ward. I know you never had enough…but…"

"Reach, it was horrible." She grips the edge of the counter so tightly I worry she's going to cause a piece of the stone to crack. It doesn't, but Llama does. She sinks to the ground and wraps her arms around her knees, laying her head on them and sobbing.

I stand by, unsure. The sobs intensify, and her whole body shakes. Finally, I crouch down next to her. "Llama?" My eyes scan the room for some type of towel she could wipe her tears away with. She puts out an arm and pulls me down next to her on the Martian floor. When she speaks, it's stilted and the gaps are full of sobs.

"It was…awful…always wearing rags…always feeling hungry…I was better off than most of the kids because I was in the Ward of the State school…and I was smart. I got more rations, and better things, but they were still always just…cast-offs from Citizens. Even the food was things that Citizens wouldn't want to eat but could be grown because…it had nutritional value…never valued…never seen…never…important enough to be noticed…never part of a family…this place is like…Nation…that little girl…she doesn't deserve to wear clothes like that. We don't even…belong…here…and we got…*these*."

Tears and snot soak the neckline of her borrowed spacesuit. I feel pity for her, for the little girl she once was, and the little girl she feels such pity for now. It would be against my better judgment if I considered it, but I don't consider it. I put my arm around Llama's shoulder and pull her into a half hug.

My contact snaps her out of her sobbing stupor. She wipes her eyes furiously with her sleeves. "You don't have to do this, Reach." She scoots away. "I know how you feel about me. I know I'm a traitor. I don't want your pity. That little girl might have no one who pities her in her entire life, except for me, and it's honestly better that way. Greg said Souterraine is weak, but I think Jezero isn't strong."

13

Beatriz arrives at the embassy building well before the Jezero lights change to the daytime setting. The smell of freshly baked bread is quite simply the most wonderful smell in the world. I believe I will become addicted to the taste of it, with butter and salt. It's not packed full of nutritional value, but Llama and I each devour an entire loaf. The Marsberry pie sits untouched.

Beatriz raises an eyebrow at the pie on the table. "Reach, you don't have to pretend you like things."

"Sorry," I manage around a mouthful of bread. "This is just my favorite."

"Mine too," Llama supplies.

"I have your schedules for today." Beatriz pulls a circular tablet out and places it on the inverted triangle that supports it. She spins it and reads, "Reach, you have meetings with President McAllistair. You'll go to the Tribunal Building after you finish eating. Llama, you're going to tour the hospital with…wait, that can't be right. One moment." Beatriz scoops up her device and walks away. We hear her voice a moment later. It's muffled, but I can understand

most of her words. "Schedule mistake…are you sure? Alright, then."
She returns, looking sober.

"Llama." Beatriz purses her lips slightly. "You're going to be touring the hospital with Percy McAllistair."

"Percy? Why?" I ask.

Llama's head snaps up from her buttery slice of heaven. "McAllistair?" Llama's voice chides. "Percy is related to Reach? "

My mouth drops open. How did I not see that? How did I not connect those dots?

Beatriz shrugs. "He's President McAllistair's second cousin and close friend. Percy will be here to pick you up in an MUV in an hour. Reach, you can walk yourself to the Tribunal Hall after you're done. I'll walk with you."

"Thanks," I manage, but a boulder-sized pit of dread drops into my stomach. I do not like the idea of Llama going on a tour with Percy without me there.

When I've finished my breakfast and prepared for the day, Beatriz bids Llama goodbye with a strain on her face and in her voice. "Be careful," she whispers before stepping out into the glow of the Mars daylight with me.

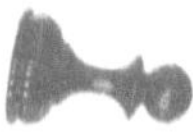

The walk to the Tribunal Building isn't far, and Beatriz is good company. She tells me an anecdote about the first time she ever knew she wanted to be a chef. Dissatisfied with the food served at the Jezero Colony School, Beatriz marched into the kitchen and "showed initiative." She found ingredients she liked and created her own lunch. I smile at the idea of her, a little child who would not accept something she could make better. Initiative is important in Nation, and Jezero apparently, because the adults took notice of her aptitude and interest. She was given instruction in the kitchen several times a week, and eventually studied under nutritionists.

When we arrive at the Tribunal Building, Beatriz stiffens. Greg stands just outside the entryway of the building, and Cait, as always, is a sentinel with a ramrod posture nearby.

"Thank you for accompanying Reach here, Beatriz," Greg says. "You're needed in the lower kitchen today. That's all."

Beatriz salutes with her left hand, just like the people all did on our tour yesterday. She disappears further into the building. I don't miss how her hips sway as she walks.

When I turn back to Greg, he's watching me with a knowing look. It angers me. He doesn't know me, and not only is he distantly related to Percy, but he calls a man I do not trust one bit a close friend. "She's quite lovely." His head jerks in Beatriz's direction.

"I hadn't noticed," I grumble.

Adding insult to injury, Greg throws back his head and laughs. The peals of mirth echo around the stone chamber. "I forgot what it's like to be…how old are you exactly, Reach?"

"Nineteen. How old are you?" I cut back, my words sharper than I intended.

"We don't experience the same time continuum as you here on Mars. If you'd like to know how old I was when I met your mother, in Earth years, I was twenty-five."

Something about that number feels comforting and also appalling. He was twenty-five, and left my mother helpless in space. He didn't know she was pregnant, but still—shouldn't he have known? Shouldn't he have taken responsibility for his actions? Condemnation rules my thoughts.

"I know you're…wondering," Greg says. "But I truly had no idea. I would have made other arrangements for things if I had known. That's actually why I needed to see you today—alone." He glances meaningfully at Cait who remains in her position by the door.

I resist the urge to roll my eyes. "I'm here."

Greg smiles as he looks me up and down, the light of pride in his eyes. I don't know why. I haven't done anything to deserve his regard other than show up on a foreign planet because my own government wants me dead.

"Come on." Greg leads me into the building and down the long hallway. The hall slopes down, and we descend. I shouldn't be surprised that there are levels below the main level, but somehow I am. I remind myself that the original defector colonists did manage to create and dig out a giant cavern to build Jezero in.

The temperature plummets as Greg ducks through a dark door. He rubs his hands together briskly. "We keep this very well preserved. Cold is the best way to keep this protected. But I will adjust it for your comfort." A lamp flickers on overhead, and Greg adjusts a button on the wall, sliding some sort of dial. Immediately a warm breeze begins to blow from a shaft above.

"Where are we?" I ask, surveying the room Greg has brought me to. It has a long rock table, and metal drawers create a filing cabinet system along the wall.

"The archives. This, Reach, is your history." He runs a thumb diagonally across one of the metal faces, and the drawer springs open. He extracts a file, handling it with delicate precision. Inked on the top corner is *Year 0*. Beatriz's words about renewable resources ring true. The file contains paper. I haven't seen a single tree since leaving Earth.

Greg gingerly sets it in front of me. "The original Jezero colonists wrote, by hand, some laws that we follow here. They are very exact and precise, and we honor the courageous spirit of those who came before us when we honor the way of life they prescribed. There are specific laws that pertain to you by virtue of your birth."

My body tenses. I've had more than enough *laws* related to my birth. Like the one on Earth that says I'm the descendant of a traitor so I deserve to be put to death.

"Our system is actually a partial democracy. A total monarchy was not advisable to the colonists, but a total democracy wasn't safe either. The colonists had to find a balance between the two. Some, like those who went to Souterraine, believed a total monarchy was the best way to govern. Others, those who stayed here in Jezero, understood that compromise is most efficient. Do you understand?"

I nod, because it's easier than saying 'no.' But really, I don't understand. *Partial democracy? What is that?*

Greg smiles. "Excellent. There is no king here in Jezero; there is only the President and the elected officials serving the colonists. But the laws clearly state that the progeny of the current President receive first choice for the Presidential office if the President is unfit or unable to fulfill the duties. It also states colony-wide that progeny receive material goods in the event of death of any parent. Reach, this means that when you arrived, you stepped into being second-in-command of Jezero Colony, and stand to inherit a fortune."

My eyes widen. "Is that why Percy was so upset?"

Greg's smile fades. "Yes. If I had no progeny in Jezero, or even on Mars, the Presidential office and the fortune the family amassed would go to the person named by me, which in my case is Percy."

"So this is about…your currency? And being next in line for President?"

Greg's voice is soft. "I've done well for myself. I've worked hard, been reliable and resourceful. You come from a long line of Jezero leaders. Leadership is embedded in your DNA. Reach, you may not have known it until you arrived, but you are a McAllistair. This family heritage goes back to the very beginning of Jezero Colony."

"What about Percy? He was…" I begin to utter a swear word, which probably means nothing on Mars, but stop myself. "…displeased when you told him I'm your son."

Greg's facial muscles twitch in a way that indicates he knows exactly what word I would have used, or at least has one similar enough on Jezero.

"Yes, if you aren't here, he gets first choice of the Presidential office if something happens to me. And he'd receive all my material possessions. He's been a good and faithful servant of Jezero all these years. He's quite a bit younger than me, so it stands to reason he thought he would take over once I was gone. In Jezero, we like tradition."

"But no one else knows I'm…" I stop because saying the word *son* feels wrong. "No one else knows I'm related to you except the people from the Tribunal Hall?"

"We can tell everyone in due time. For now, we need to let things play out."

It's too much to take in, so I open the file folder and begin skimming pages. *A family that contains both male and female offspring is considered a complete set. These families will receive access to DNA preservation materials and additional currency for the services a complete set of DNA will provide for Jezero. A family is only required to have one offspring of either gender to qualify for the inheritance laws.*

I scrub my hand down my face. "What does 'complete set' and 'DNA preservation materials' mean?" I ask.

"Oh, it's quite ingenious. In order to ensure that male and female offspring are considered equitable, families with both male and female offspring are compensated differently in the economy than families with exclusively male or female children. Our best asset here is our intellect, and since genetics play such a role in intellect, a complete set to carry on the genes is considered superior to only one gender."

I'm trying to make sense of what sounds bizarre to my ears when Percy's comment about Greg also having a daughter comes to mind. "Is that why Percy asked if you had a daughter?"

"Yes. You understand that Percy will uphold the law perfectly. He knows his place and has been preparing to lead Jezero for a long time. But it's jarring to have been here his entire life and then to have you show up. He doesn't know you. He didn't know you existed until you arrived." He looks away for a moment, abashed. "I was the telecommunications manager when your mother contacted us and said I had a son. And then, when your friend Llama messaged, I was in the COMs center discussing something with Souterraine. I never told anyone about you because I was…ashamed."

I fix him with a piercing look. *My own father is ashamed of me.* In my mind, that's all it takes to be ashamed of him. He interprets my condescension correctly and clarifies. "Ashamed that my only son was going to grow up oppressed and there was nothing I could do to change it."

It's weak, and I recognize that, but I long to give him a chance.

Greg continues. "Back to Percy. It was quite shocking and definitely made him rethink his plans for the future."

I can at least understand his shock, if not these strange laws about compensating people for male and female offspring. "I suppose that would be true of anyone. But I don't understand something. If you're President, that means your…parent…was President? So why did they send you to scout? How did you meet Mom?"

"Yes. Your grandmother was President before me. I was merely second-in-command, and Percy was the heir behind me. I was selected to scout because I had the aptitude and the courage to do so. Relations between Jezero and Souterraine have been tense for centuries. Scouting was one thing I could do to ensure that Jezero maintained a greater awareness of the area surrounding Mars. We had no idea that Souterraine had the technology to send someone back to Earth. Jezero is the technology hub on Mars."

"So how does that work, exactly—Jezero being a technology hub? Didn't you say there are shipments between the two colonies?"

"Yes, there are. We supply Souterraine with technology counterparts needed for their systems, and they supply Jezero with agricultural products. We need both to survive, but our rates of growth and consumption aren't sustainable. It's been a problem for at least the past fifty years, but our calculations show that we will outgrow our resource potential in the next ten years, so it's a much more pressing problem now."

Despite the warm air blowing over me, my breath comes in frost clouds and my teeth begin to chatter. Greg picks up the file folder delicately and replaces it in the cabinet. He closes the drawer and draws the diagonal line again with his thumb. "When you're President, you'll have access to these things. I suspect *my* chef will have made a delicious lunch. Shall we, Reach?"

I can't escape the morgue-like room fast enough.

14

Chefs are greatly revered in Jezero Colony. Greg's chef is an older man named Bill. He has tufts of white hair sticking out above his eyes, a crooked nose, and a flare for the dramatic.

"Mushroom soup with dill and cream," he pronounces with a flourish as he sets a tureen on the table, then he turns to me and whispers, "President McAllistair's favorite."

I smile politely, then he leaves. Greg ladles soup into bowls.

After leaving the historical archives room, Greg brought me to his private residence. His quarters are on the other side of the Tribunal Hall. The Presidential residence is an exact copy of the Embassy, so despite never being here before, I know my way around. The soup is a step above space food, but significantly less tasty than Beatriz's bread. I'm glad I have years of experience in eating unpalatable food. When I've finished my bowl and declined a second serving, I decide to ask Greg some questions.

He seems to be expecting it, steepling his long fingers together and waiting with pursed lips. "Yes, Reach?"

"Why exactly can't you tell anyone about me being your progeny?"

Greg's eyes widen and he blinks twice. His fingers tap together. "The leadership situation here is…complicated. I thought you understood that."

"Not really. Percy was set to be the next leader, but then I showed up, and now he's not. And that makes things complicated for the rest of Jezero, how?"

Greg's shoulders rise as he inhales. "Because the people *know* Percy. He's been here his entire life. It's a bit like a usurper to have you come along. They *like* Percy. He *likes* them. He believes in the good of Jezero, and has been a trusted advisor. He has helped alleviate tensions between us and Souterraine, at least at a surface level. The people see him as an asset to strengthen Jezero. You're unknown. You'll need to prove yourself before we can freely share your relation to me."

His words about proving myself irk me. I don't want to be heir to the Presidency. "What if you became incapacitated tomorrow?"

He breaks eye contact. "That's why I told Percy. He needed to know so he could…handle the transition if anything did occur." He slaps his hands on his legs and stands. "It's unlikely anything will happen here. I'm healthy, I'm young, and Jezero Colony knows its needs. If you don't mind, I'd like to ask you some unofficial things." He looks at the door for a fleeting moment before turning his attention back to me. "This level of interest I have in you is reasonable because of your arrival from Earth, but the questions I ask that are personal are…" He pauses and considers, scratching absently at his temple. "Confidential."

He is my father. He's curious about me. A sensation drips from my brain down to my chest, filling me with warmth. It's nice to feel wanted. Just as quickly as the sensation came, it fades.

What if he doesn't like me? What if he's not what he seems? "I'll answer your questions, but only if you agree to answer mine too."

"Deal."

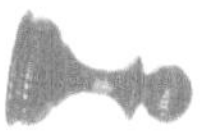

I leave Greg's personal residence with a greater understanding of my father. I still can't decide if I like him. He asked questions about growing up. Those were easy enough to answer, and they helped my objective. Compound and Hub and the totalitarian government truly are awful. The other questions he asked were harder to answer. Questions about Mom, questions about what I *like*. I'm not sure anyone has ever bothered wondering about these things.

I learned that Greg rose to the Presidency because he was the only child of the previous President, my grandmother. I learned that before becoming President, Greg was a scientist with an interest in what he called space economics. He actively studied the possibility of an Earth-Mars economy, and what that would mean for Jezero Colony. He also had to consider Souterraine.

The prospects were not very good.

Greg enjoys painting, but doesn't have much time for it now that he has an office to run. He studied American history. I'm still not clear on what that means, but he said it is relevant to what I've been sharing about Nation.

The Mars daylight fades into the twilight setting as I sojourn across the plaza and pass the Tribunal Hall. Red dust kicks up in little puffs as my feet hit the ground in my shin-high spacesuit boots. There was something reserved about Greg as he answered my questions. My attempt to balance personal inquiries with ones that would help me determine the next move seemed to be expected. *Was Greg holding back because he's hiding something? Is he guarded because he's the President? Is he reluctant to confide because it's awkward meeting a son whose existence he's hid for nearly two decades?*

The thoughts rattle around my brain until I reach the door of the embassy. I step inside, not bothering to wipe my feet since the inside of the embassy is the same material as outside. The red is monotonous. I'd like to see a plant. One thing you don't realize about Earth is how beautiful the palette of colors is.

I'm lost in thought when a hand grabs a fistful of my spacesuit and yanks me into a dark corner near the staircase.

It's Llama, her blue eyes blazing. She stands on her tiptoes and comes very close to my face, so close I'm certain she's going to kiss me. I start to back away, because this is beyond strange, but she pulls me closer. She stops, millimeters from my lips. I can taste the mint on her breath.

"Reach. There is something I need you to know. I'm going to do something that looks crazy, but it's for a reason, ok? I learned something today. Something about the *game*."

My eyes are wide, but I nod.

"We're romantically involved," she whispers harshly as her breath puffs against my lips.

I swallow and start to protest. This is not true, even if I wished it were at one point. Even if we could have been, there's no way I trust her. "But I already…they know we aren't."

"They know only what we tell them. They have to figure us out, the same as we do them. We're going to have a fight. I'm going to break something. I'm going to look unhinged."

"More than this?" I gesture at the dark corner she's pushed me into. To anyone passing by, it would look like we're in the midst of a romantic and lengthy kiss.

She grabs my neck and angles my ear closer to her mouth. "Just trust me," she hisses before she backs away. She climbs the stairs toward her room, and I'm left staring after her.

A soft sound comes from the opposite direction. Beatriz stands, mouth agape, her eyes wide and brimming with tears.

My shoulders deflate as I understand what Llama just did.

I can't make this better.

I will *never* trust Llama.

15

BEATRIZ MEETS MY eyes for a flash of time, a mere moment, before she disappears. I will never forget the sight of her tears or her pain. I hadn't been certain if she had romantic interest in me, but the look on her face made it clear that she did.

Furious at Llama and her ability to interfere in any circumstance of my happiness, I stomp up the stairs to her room. She's going to answer for this. She *knew* I liked Beatriz. She *said* she would help. She *said* she was trying to make amends with us, even though she knew it could never be the same.

Leopards don't change their spots. Once a liar, always a liar.

Llama's door is closed. I want to barge in and confront her, but the door makes me stop. The luxury of personal space isn't something to be trifled with. We both know this after years without doors to our private spaces at Hub. I settle for three hard raps. The knocks are so hard that a cloud of dust puffs up from the surrounding red rock walls.

A bemused Llama opens the door. I can't begin to formulate my anger at her in words. Rage makes my blood boil.

"Did she leave?" Llama asks, putting one hand on her hip as she leans against the doorframe.

"Yes," I hiss. "Thanks to you. *WHAT was THAT?*" It's only years of extreme mental and physical training that keep my tongue from forming swear words.

Llama doesn't say anything. She grabs my hand and pulls me into her room, shutting the door behind her. If what Beatriz saw was incriminating, this is even worse. I back up, bumping into the door, the knob jamming into my spine.

Llama throws a pillow at me. I don't react. I watch the pillow fall to the ground. I hope it gets coated in the relentless rust-colored dust. I hope it makes her nose itch all night long. I hope…

"She's a spy," Llama hisses as she hunches down to pick up the pillow and hands it to me. "She's not interested in you. She's Greg's pawn. He's using *her* to get information from you, and *you're playing into his game.*"

My mouth opens. Closes. Opens again. Venom drips from my words when I stop gaping and grind out a reply. "Takes one to know one."

Llama startles at my tone, shrinking away from me. I don't care. I continue. "Is it really so bad to think I might be worth someone's notice, not because I'm something special to any government, but because I'm a person? A person who *maybe* is worth getting to know without all this political intrigue? Just because you committed the crime doesn't mean you have to drag everyone else down with you."

"Reach." Llama's hand stretches out, and I recoil as far away from her touch as I can. It's difficult with the door behind me.

"No." I manage to find the doorknob and flee from the room as quickly as my legs will carry me. It's only when I sink into the comfort of my own bed that I begin to wonder if Llama's words carried any truth.

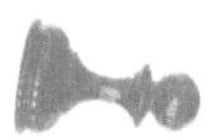

Beatriz is in the kitchen the next morning. I slip out of my bed early, hoping to find her, to explain that Llama has lost her mind. That I wasn't kissing Llama, and that if she was interested, I'd like to…do whatever Jezero colonists do for romance, and with her.

Her back stiffens as I walk into the room. There's a grim determination on her face as she removes a tray of bread rolls from the oven.

"Beatriz?" I say softly, wanting to tell her everything and knowing that's impossible.

"You lied," she says, her tone harder than lead.

"I…didn—"

"Yes, you did. Don't lie again," Beatriz snaps. "You told me there was nothing going on between you two." Her eyes brim with tears again, spilling onto her cheeks. "I asked, because I knew better than to think I could be…interesting…to someone as brave as you."

Her words sting. I shrink back. "Beatriz. Please, may I explain?" I lower my voice, keeping it as soothing as I can, pleading with her. I need this chance to fix what Llama broke.

"I don't see that it will help much." Her face is a mask of ice.

"Llama and I do have a history." Beatriz bites her lip but doesn't interrupt. "I have not had a romantic relationship with her beyond a brief moment, really a blip in time, back in Nation. She was using me."

Beatriz raises one delicate eyebrow. I take the gesture as my sign to continue.

"She betrayed my mother to the…"

A crash sounds in the dining area. A dish or a glass shattering stops my speech. Beatriz rushes out of the kitchen, concern etched on her pretty face.

Llama stands by the table, shards of broken dishes on the ground, a gouge in the wall. She has a cut on her hand that's bleeding profusely. She'll need stitches. Her other hand is clenched into a fist at her side.

"Are you alright?" Beatriz asks stiffly.

"I…I…think so." Llama wavers slightly both in her voice and on her feet. Blood streams down her spacesuit pants and puddles at her feet. She pitches forward, and I leap into action, catching her in my arms. As I do, she presses something small into my pocket.

"I'll go get a doctor," Beatriz says.

I lie Llama down away from the pool of blood and the shattered fragments of a plate. Grabbing a napkin from the table, I use it to wrap her hand. She's actually unconscious.

Beatriz reappears with a female doctor. The doctor doesn't say anything, but pours something over Llama's wound, and then produces a roll of fabric the same color as skin. She cuts a strip and sticks it over the cut before opening a tube of something that smells like musk.

"What is that stuff?" I ask, gesturing to the skin-colored material.

The doctor nods slightly at Beatriz.

Beatriz says, "That's skin tape. It was created here years ago. It's more durable than stitches, the skin regenerates around it more quickly, and it doesn't leave a scar."

"What's the smelly stuff?" Llama mumbles. She stirs and attempts to sit up, but the doctor places a hand on her stomach to keep her down.

Beatriz answers again, "That's a smelling salt. It's old-fashioned, but effective. I'm surprised you don't recognize them. They are an Earth thing."

"Nope," I say. "Why isn't the doctor talking?"

"Clearance," Beatriz replies.

The doctor checks Llama's eyes with a flashlight, then moves away from Llama. She summons Beatriz over to the far corner of the room. Her voice is high-pitched, but I can hear it from my spot next to Llama. "She needs rest. Nothing strenuous for several weeks. She lost a significant volume of blood. She'll need iron-rich foods and more liquids for the next several days as her blood restores. Keep her tape clean."

Beatriz murmurs a reply that I can't quite make out. I'm still sitting on the ground next to Llama. "What happened?" I whisper to her, but she's grimacing.

"Pocket," she whispers.

I slide my hand in my pocket and feel something smooth and small. A quick glance at Beatriz shows that she is walking the doctor out of the room. When I extract the object from my pocket, I realize I'm holding a tiny camera, or perhaps a microphone. Maybe it's both. I'm not familiar with all the technology here in Jezero.

"Where?" I whisper.

"They're everywhere here."

"The plate?"

"Just a distraction. To get your attention. And something was there. I've found several things under the furniture in my room too. Microphones, I guess, since they wouldn't see anything, but there's a video-based one in the hall. Reach, I tried to make it seem like I was kissing you because I was certain that…"

"Someone would appear right then, even though we were being quiet," I finish for her.

She shakes her head, then grimaces. "Reach, could I have some water?" I stand and pour her a glass, then help her hold the glass to her lips. "Thanks."

Llama was right. Beatriz was spying on us. I'm rattled that she saw what I didn't.

"I have horrible taste in women," I murmur.

Llama's eyes flash before she sighs and sways forward. "I guess so."

The sound of footsteps echo down the hall, and this time it's not just Beatriz. Greg and Percy stand at the edge of the room.

"I think it's time for you to go, Miss Llama," Greg says. "Percy has arranged to send a transport earlier. Souterraine will be more to your liking."

"But the doctor said that she needs rest, and nothing strenuous…" I begin to interject.

Greg holds up a hand. "She goes. We have no room in this colony for people who engage in acts of subterfuge and endanger our people."

"She didn't endanger…"

"Enough!" Percy roars. His bun vibrates as the rage simmering in him boils over. "She. Goes."

I don't know why Greg and Percy are so angry at Llama, but it doesn't make her a safe person either. And yet, she's my space mission partner. "I'm not leaving her."

"Then go with her." Greg's eyes won't meet mine, but any hint of shame he feels doesn't stop him. "She's not welcome here, and as long as you consort with her, you aren't welcome either."

PART 2

16

ONE MOMENT LLAMA and I are in the embassy, enjoying home-cooked meals by a personal chef. The next, Cait, Beatriz, and a burly man I've never seen before load us onto a transport truck, along with special technology components that Souterraine requires in their agricultural systems. I learned at Greg's private residence that Jezero focuses on supplying the technological needs of all the Martians, while Souterraine supplies the food. Trucks deliver the goods back and forth across the planet through a lengthy tunnel formed by lava tubes. It's narrow, and it's difficult to traverse. Multiple trucks exist to serve the two colonies, and some even offer seating for dignitaries needing to visit the other colony.

We are forced to march to a small airlock in the curved wall of the colony, where we see the transport truck. The truck is a large tank, essentially a balloon of oxygen hauled on rover wheels. Cait offers us a sarcastic smile before she shoves Llama inside the tank. "Enjoy your comfortable ride through the lava tubes. This one has the perfect accommodations for people inclined to espionage."

Llama's face is still pale from loss of blood as she leans against the side of the tank. I'm worried. She shouldn't be forced to move so soon. She shouldn't be left to possibly die back here. Looking at her shivering, weak, and pale, I know death is a very real possibility.

I boost myself into the tank behind Llama. The truck is not designed for human transport. There are no seats in the tank. Llama crumples to the floor, rests her head on her knees, and moans.

I slide down next to her. "Are you all right?"

There are no lights in the tank, so all I can see is what the light from the open hatch reveals. The technology pieces are packaged securely. I take in the gloom, the straps and foam around the boxes telling me that either the pieces are extremely fragile or it's going to be a bumpy ride.

Cait pokes her head in and tosses us the supplemental oxygen tank backpacks we wore from the surface. "Might need these. Might not. It's a long ride. At least twenty hours. Here." She throws a loaf of bread and a canteen in before she slams the door in the hatch shut, and we are plunged into total darkness.

"Llama?" I ask again.

"Reach. I just…" She blows out a forceful breath. "I think that was a lot of movement."

"Do you…" I want to ask if she needs anything, but that's a ridiculous question. She's shut in the back of a tank after losing an obscene amount of blood. I opt for a different tactic. "Why did you break that plate?" It's easier to ask her in the pitch dark. "What were you thinking? Surely you could have found a better way to show me."

I feel her sigh. "Reach, it's the game. It's always the game. You were distracted. Also, I thought there might be something embedded in the wall."

"Was there?"

"Yeah. I put it in your pocket."

"It's right here." I hold it out, extending it until it touches Llama. I can tell from the angle of her body I'm touching her bent knees.

"What is it, Llama?"

"I'm not sure," she whispers, her voice weak. "But it's something for espionage. I noticed it blinking once, but I needed something jagged to dislodge it."

I'm amazed. I missed so much. I was so distracted by Beatriz. "How did I miss so much?" I whisper to myself. Llama doesn't respond. "Maybe we can ask about it in Souterraine." Llama still doesn't respond, and anxiety claws its way into my throat. "Llama?"

"What?" Her voice wavers.

"I think…" I feel contrite, but I don't know how to say I'm sorry. Llama was playing the game, and all I was doing was imagining having a real family with Greg, a life that didn't center around a complex political game of chess, and feeling attracted to a woman I knew nothing about.

"I'm okay, Reach," Llama murmurs. "But it helps if you talk."

"Ok." It's so dark, I can practically see my thoughts. "Why did…" I correct myself. "How did you know Beatriz was spying? How did I miss it? Why would I only see her as the chef who makes delicious bread?"

"Mmm." Llama's reply comes out muted. "She clearly reports to someone. Probably Greg or Percy. I mean, look who showed up after I cornered you in the embassy by the stairs, and then again after the plate incident to kick us out of the colony. But really…" Llama sighs. "You might not like this. It was the way she looked at you. It looked like how Enforce used to look at me. But she didn't look like that when you were watching." She draws a shaky breath. "She was subtle, but I saw that she was shifty. And I know you. You don't see what you need to see when pretty women are in the equation."

I'm grateful for the darkness of the truck because my jaw falls open, and it will take a crank to close it. Llama just spoke a truth about me that I would never have realized by myself. It's a truth that's as earth-shattering as it is terrifying. And above all, it's the *truth*. The prettiness of a woman impacts my judgment. She's speaking of herself, too, and I don't miss the self-deprecation and loathing in her voice.

"Reach?" Llama says. I feel her shiver. "I'm very cold."

The truck isn't climate-controlled the way Jezero Colony is, and in our short time there, we had gotten used to the comfortable temperatures. The low temperature conditions, combined with the loss of blood, and Llama is absolutely freezing. I have nothing to offer her except my arms. Her factual approach to my character flaw and her refusal to omit her own treachery in our story cleaves my heart, tiny fissures expanding from the crack her words have wrought.

I haven't forgiven her. But she hasn't forgiven herself.

Some truths are hard to hear. She just told me one, and I can feel that what she needs more than anything in order to forgive herself is for me to forgive her. Forgiveness is a choice. It's one I can make for her.

"Llama," I say, scooting closer. "I'm going to put my arms around you to help you stay warmer. Just lean against me, ok?"

I slide my arms around her and wonder how much longer we'll be in this truck. She nods off to sleep, her head on my shoulder. The ride is bumpy and cold, and despite being stuck in one uncomfortable position for hours and ensconced in inky blackness, I can't help but feel that holding Llama in my arms is right.

17

There is only so much to do in a dark oxygen tank for twenty hours. Eventually, I also fall asleep. The grinding of gears assaults my ears, and my eyes fly open to find that there is still nothing to see in the pitch black.

Llama shifts. "Reach?" she whispers.

I prop myself up on my elbows. I have no idea where she is.

"Reach?" The whisper sounds from the ground on my left. It's futile, but I can't help it: I turn my head.

"Llama?" I squint, and there is just the barest flicker of movement. I hold out my hand and find her in the dark.

"Reach, I think we might be almost there." Her voice is hoarse. I can't see her face, but I'm worried.

"We might be. It seems like this sort of journey is unpredictable."

"No," Llama says. "Listen." I do. There are noises outside. It sounds distinctly like human voices. The voices sound closer. Metal strikes metal, reverberating throughout the tank and making the technology component boxes shake.

The door in the hatch opens, and backlit in the sudden glow of bright light is someone wearing a satchel across their body. Their eyes must adjust to the darkness before ours can adjust to the light because a voice roars out, "What is the meaning of this?"

It's a man; he approaches with heavy footsteps. He's lean and wiry and rather tall.

I squint against the harsh light. I can't think of any way to explain our situation, so I blurt out the first thing that comes to mind. "We need to see the King and Queen of Souterraine."

The man's facial expression changes. His eyebrows pitch up sharply while his nostrils flare and his pupils dilate. "*You* look like stowaways, *you* come from Jezero, and *you* want to see the king and queen?"

Llama scrambles to stand up, but she's weak and can't do it on her own. I stand and offer Llama my hand. She can barely stand, so I slide my arm around her waist, supporting her.

"Please," I say. "She's…" I almost launch into the entire tale, but then think better of revealing secrets like that the reigning monarchs have a granddaughter visiting from Earth and just got thrown out of Jezero Colony, and stop. "She needs medical assistance."

The man looks Llama over. "Did the driver know you were back here?"

I shrug. I have no idea. I never saw him.

His gaze bounces from my face to Llama's. It's impossible for me to see how pale Llama truly is, but his features flash concern. "Ok. Let's get you out of this truck." He backs out of the hatch and stands on the ground. Beads of perspiration dot Llama's forehead as she stands in the open hatch. The man stretches up and places his hands on her waist, lifting her to the ground, where they stay wrapped around her waist as she leans into him for support.

I don't like it. I don't like it at all.

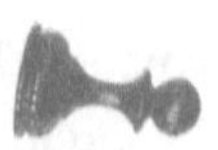

The ground in Souterraine is different. The colony is underground—that is obvious by the domed ceiling above us—but the ground is not sparse red rock. The most surprising thing about Souterraine is that the ground is covered in vegetation.

The man removes his arm from around Llama as soon as I stand next to her. I take over supporting her. She slumps against my shoulder, and I'm half dragging her as I walk. I try to take in all of this new colony, but in the end, the only thing I can do is scan the ground to make sure I don't trip and bring Llama down with me.

The man leads us to a small vehicle. It's similar to the one we rode in with Greg on the tour of Jezero. I lift Llama into a seat, where she collapses as I climb next to her. The man, who I can now see has curly brown hair and dark skin, revs the engine to life and takes off. There aren't many other vehicles on the pathway, but there are some. He honks, and every other vehicle lets him pass.

Now that we're sitting, I get a good look at this Martian colony. Souterraine is more like Earth than Jezero. In between willing Llama to survive this, I see trees with great massive trunks, moss, and a river winding along through the vegetation. The buildings are not laid out in an organized pattern like Jezero, but each building is clearly well cared for. People are out tending gardens that look full of vegetables while others are minding their children. An entire group of children stands in a grove of trees near the river. A woman and a man sit nearby on a fallen log, watching over the children with easy smiles. Everything is idyllic. The air tastes pure.

A quick glance back at Llama reveals a face contorted in pain. She's tough, and thank goodness for our physical training sessions with Lift, but I don't know how much longer Llama can sustain this. The doctor in Jezero did say to take things easy for a few weeks while she recovered. Beatriz, Percy, Greg, and Cait all put a stop to that. I still don't fully understand why.

The buildings we pass are simple, well-tended, and made of wood and rock. The roadway doesn't stay straight for long; it seems to wind around the trees, and perhaps it does. We emerge from a maze of trees with wispy leaves onto a bright, open plain covered with clover. In the center of the clover is a house at least twelve times larger than the other buildings.

"I've brought you to the castle. Honestly, I'm skeptical, but I don't know what else to do with you," the man says, his white teeth flashing against his dark skin. He gestures for us to exit the vehicle. Llama leans heavily against the side of the vehicle, her knuckles white as they grip the half door. "Wait here and I'll get someone to attend to you."

He hurries off and runs inside the large wooden doors. When he returns, he's surrounded by an older man, an older woman, and a younger woman. The three people all wear crowns of twisted wood atop their heads. The women have crowns with flowers and ribbons and wear dresses; the man wears a pair of tan pants and a black shirt that buttons down the center. I get a good look at the man who drove us. It's similar to the man with the crown. His pants are a tan color and his shirt is a soft green.

"What on the surface?" The older woman's voice is flowy like the river. She peers around the vehicle at Llama and me. "Jerome. Please, would you get the physician? He's at the school doing some education, but I suspect this is more important."

Jerome, takes off at a run, heading down the river and disappearing under the shade of the trees.

Llama's face has turned a putrid shade of green.

"Just close your eyes, Llama," I whisper. "Help is coming."

Her eyes flutter shut as I wrap my arm around her shoulders, trying not to worry about her raspy breaths and the way her chest rises and falls weakly.

Six expectant eyes meet my own.

"Who might you be?" the man with the crown asks, his gray hair falling below his ears and a short beard covering his chin.

"Reach," I say, then think I should add a title on, but I can't remember what you call kings, so I tack on, "Sir."

The king's golden brown eyes twitch as something comes over his countenance. He resembles a thundercloud. The queen speaks next, her face looking horrified. "Then this is…" She gestures to Llama.

"Yeah," I say with some bitterness about everything we just endured. "This is Llama."

"Why did they come like that, Mama?" the younger woman asks. Her deep brown eyes are wide, and her hair is as dark as night. Something about her speech isn't quite typical. She's grown physically and has the stature of an adult, but her words sound like a child's.

"I don't know, Pippa. But we will certainly find out." There's a tinge of iron in her voice, something that says these two rulers are not to be trifled with. Greg called them weak, but I see something strong, and I've known them for less than two minutes.

Jerome and another man come bursting out of a grove of trees and sprint across the clover to where we stand.

The new man, who wears all white with a red X on his collar, takes one look at Llama and asks, "What happened?"

Llama tries to answer, but her voice is a hiss. I take over. "She lost a lot of blood. The doctor in Jezero said she should take it easy and not do anything strenuous for a few weeks while she recovers, but President McAllistair and Percy were insistent that we leave Jezero immediately."

A clap of thunder crosses the king's face and he nearly spits in anger. "They did what?" Despite his rage, his voice is quiet, and I'm impressed with his control.

"We need to get her inside," the doctor says quickly. "I can help her, but she should *not* have endured that twenty-hour ride in this condition. She will need rest and care." He looks at the queen while he speaks.

"Of course. She is clearly ill. Pippa, run ahead and please tell Bernard to ready the Willow room."

The younger woman scampers ahead. I watch her for a moment, noticing that her limbs aren't totally coordinated as she walks. I'm fascinated. I've never seen anyone like her before.

"You." I snap back around at the doctor's voice. "I need you to help me carry her in. I doubt she can walk." He turns to Llama.

"We're going to carry you inside where you can get some rest," he says to her, though her eyes are still closed. "It won't feel good. You may become unconscious. You need to know, though, that you're in Souterraine and are going to get better."

The doctor and I lift Llama, carrying her limp body across the clover field, while the King and Queen of Souterraine walk by her side. Our driver from the vehicle is ahead of us, opening the huge wooden door to let us in. As soon as we cross the threshold, the queen takes over leading our odd procession. She walks down a long hallway, past a space that must be a kitchen based on the aromas wafting by, and finally into a small landing with three doors off to the side. There are just two steps between the hallway and the landing, but carrying Llama this entire way has been difficult. She's not heavy, but she's also not carrying any of her own weight. I glimpse her face, white as a sheet and dotted with beads of perspiration. She's not unconscious, but she's biting down on pain. *I've never known anyone so brave.*

I slip on the step, knocking my shin into the wood. I let out a curse word that would have earned me a reprimand on Earth, but no one even blinks at my language here. Shoving my own pain down, I manage to get both feet on the landing.

The queen opens the door to one room and gestures for us to lay Llama on the bed. The doctor and I do, and then he begins finding instruments and tools. I stand back, unsure what to do now. The queen gives a quick flick of her head to the side, and the king's warm hand lands on my shoulder.

"Reach?" the king says. I look up at him and am suddenly exhausted. I don't say a word. "I think you could use a rest too. We'll take care of her, and we promise we will hear the full story when you're ready to tell it. We aren't in the habit of harming people here in Souterraine, least of all our granddaughter."

I nod, understanding and oddly trusting this man who's no more than a stranger to me.

"Come," the king says. "I'm going to show you your room. It's just across the hall. You'll have the oak room." He steers me out of Llama's sickroom and through the door directly opposite Llama's. He gently guides me onto the bed. I don't resist. He gathers up blankets that have been folded at the edge of the bed and lays them over me.

It's the most loving thing anyone has ever done for me.

18

A GENTLE HAND strokes my brow. A warm weight lands on my chest. Something fuzzy hits my cheek. My eyes flick open. A black cat is curled into a ball over my chest, and sitting on a chair next to my bed is the Queen of Souterraine. She has a crown on again today and wears a light green dress. The green of her gown highlights her bronze skin and long dark hair that falls loosely over her shoulders. In the light, I notice streaks of gray. She stoops and pets the cat on my chest. I push up on my elbows, trying to sit up.

"Hello." The queen's voice is soft like a breeze. "It's been quite a while. We left you to sleep after we had the doctor look at you, but it's been two days, and you must be hungry by now."

I attempt to speak, but my voice is rougher than the grit that floated in the air on Compound. "Llama?" I choke.

The queen gives a small smile and passes me a glass of cool water. "It's good you're here. Llama is still under the doctor's care, but she is recovering. The doctor has her eating iron-rich foods and resting. She's going to spend some time in the meadow after lunch; perhaps you could join us?"

I nod, and my stomach growls louder than the rocket thrusters we used to get to space. The cat hisses at the noise, swipes a disgruntled paw at my belly, and hops off with its tail haughtily in the air. The queen's shoulders shake with subdued laughter. "I'll take that as a yes. Wash up first, dear, and there are clothes for you in that wardrobe. Come down the steps of this landing and you'll find the kitchen."

I shake my head as the queen leaves. A quick whiff of my own scent lets me know why she told me to wash up. I stink like someone who hasn't showered in… I do the mental calculations. I think it's been nearly four full days. I ignore my protesting stomach as I tread to the bathroom. The shower is colder than I'd like, but by the end of it, I'm clean and invigorated. When I find the kitchen, I'm ready to face the ruling monarchs of Souterraine and Llama.

My heart stutters for a moment when I think of Llama. I've been worried about her, but what happened between us on the way to Souterraine is the sort of thing that could be nothing or could be *something*. I need to figure out what that all was, but the fact that Llama sees me, *the real me*, and understands my weaknesses has me off kilter.

I hesitate for a moment before I duck into the kitchen. A kind man introduces himself as Bernard before he ladles a thick goop into a wooden bowl. "Stew. Doctor's orders. Lots of iron in the meat, and the broth, and the greens." He then hands me a wooden spoon. "Eat!" He points with his own wooden ladle to a planked table.

I sit obediently and take a bite. It's rich, it's savory, it's delicious, and I practically inhale it. When I've drained the bowl, I leave the table, dishes in hand. Bernard is there, swooping in with a scowl on his face. "This is Souterraine!" he proclaims. "We have staff to clear your dishes. You are visiting! We treat our guests well here!"

"Oh," I mumble, chastised. "I just wanted to…help."

"You can help the queen and king in the meadow. It's just through this door." Bernard gestures to a small door on the side of the kitchen. Like everything else I've seen, it's made of wood. My footsteps tap across the wooden floor, and the door squeaks ever so slightly when I open it. I step out into a bright green space. It's full of clover, but there is a kitchen garden growing near the castle.

My eyes track over the meadow and find three people sitting in wooden chairs, bathed in what can only be described as sunlight. I squint. *How is there sun?* We're underground, on Mars. I have questions.

I approach slowly, noticing that Llama's chair is on wheels. An odd pang floats through my chest as I remember Dr. Jog. I thought of him often when we were in space, but since arriving on Mars, I've been distracted. *What happened to him when we went rogue? What about Hero? Lift, Dr. Geo, Sty 8—the people who were good to me in Nation?* Their memories press against my throat as I imagine the pain Enforce would relish inflicting on those I've called friends.

"Reach!" Llama's voice calls out, and she waves me over. I approach slowly, trying to give myself time to school my features. It doesn't work. "Reach?" she says when I'm closer. "What's wrong?"

I give a small smile and cut my eyes to the queen and king. "Nothing, I'm just…taking it all in." I turn to study Llama after making awkward eye contact with the king and queen.

Llama is a sight to behold. Her brown hair is loose and long, cascading over her shoulders in silky waves and blowing gently in the breeze. I have a nearly uncontrollable desire to touch it, to touch her. Her skin stands out, starkly white against the darkness of her blue dress. Her eyes are bright, framed by her thick lashes, but most importantly, she's smiling. It's bright and genuine. I know Llama well enough by now to know when she's acting.

The King and Queen of Souterraine stand when I arrive. "Reach." The king's warm voice settles over my ears. "Sit, please." He holds out a chair next to Llama. I don't know what protocol is, but so far, the ruling monarchs of Souterraine seem to stand on less ceremony than the President of Jezero Colony. I sink into the chair, not exhausted by my walk through the meadow but from the weight of concern for the people left on Earth.

Llama stretches out her hand and touches mine. Seeing her in a wheelchair is jarring, and I clasp my hand tight around hers. She blinks in surprise, gives a small smile, and shifts her chair a bit closer to me.

The king and queen watch on with interest. I feel too vulnerable to say anything, so I don't. I sit still and wait, Llama's hand in mine. The silence doesn't last long.

"Reach," the queen says in her melodic voice. "We are hoping that, now that you and Llama are well enough to sit in the meadow, you could tell us how you came from Jezero to here."

"Oh." There's a lot to unpack here, and I don't know who to trust. I'm also certain that I'm stuck on Mars and do not trust the leadership of Jezero Colony. In terms of game theory, the King and Queen of Souterraine are my best bet for the entire story.

Llama bites her lip but squeezes my hand in a gesture that's reassuring and comfortable.

"Yes," I deliberate. "I guess that's important for you to know."

"Son," the King of Souterraine says in his rumbly baritone, but my brain glitches at the word *son*. "It is extremely important."

"Where would you like me to start?" I ask, keeping my eyes on the clover below my feet.

"We are anxious to hear of your entire journey to Mars, of course," the queen replies. "But for now, it would be best if you explained *what* happened that led to President McAllistair sending you away from Jezero Colony the way he did."

Llama frowns when I glance at her. I don't know exactly what to say to the queen and king, but I remember that Llama is their granddaughter. The political intrigues of foreign government systems on a planet that isn't Earth are too much to make sense of.

I scrub my hands down my face, feeling the slight stubble that's grown on my chin.

Llama's eyes flash with a challenge as I debate what I need to tell the king and queen. It's too complicated a story to purposely omit anything. I'm at the point where the truth serves us better, simply because I can keep it straight.

"We were welcomed at Jezero because I'm Greg McAllistair's

son." A sharp intake of breath comes from the king, and a startled "Oh!" escapes the queen's mouth. "I knew my father's name was Greg, but I didn't know anything about Jezero or his role there until we arrived. Greg asked me to keep our relationship quiet because of something about succession laws. I don't really understand it. It made his friend and cousin mad, and then we found out in the transmission room that Llama is your granddaughter."

"That's right." The king's eyes move to Llama's and hold her in warm regard. His actions exactly match the tone of his voice to his words. He's not full of any artifice.

"Err— anyway, we were staying at the embassy in Jezero." The king makes a dignified sniffing noise. "And then…" I trail off, unsure how I want to explain this part. Llama's eyes slide over my face, and she gives the smallest of nods. "I liked the chef they assigned to us. She was very pretty." The faintest of shadows crosses the queen's face, but her eyes remain focused on me. It's hard to look at her when she's watching me with this intensity. I fix my eyes on Llama. "But Llama noticed things I was too distracted to see. She suspected that Beatriz, the chef, was trying to get close to me to…use me. I don't know what she wanted to gain. Llama found devices in her suite, at the dining table, and gouged something out of the wall with a plate. When she did that, she cut her hand and lost a lot of blood. They had a doctor come to look at her, but then Greg and Percy handed us off to Cait, and she forced us on the truck, and now we're here." I pause for a breath, but realize there's nothing more to tell, so I stay silent.

The silence around me tells me that everyone else is digesting my words too.

"So," the king says. "The fine President of Jezero Colony has a son who's lived on Earth for the past…" He studies me. "Twenty years?"

"Nineteen," I say.

"Nineteen years. And this son shows up on Mars with the granddaughter of the rulers of Souterraine, and his response is to shove you *both* into the back of a truck?" He clicks his tongue. "What a leader."

"Well," Llama inserts, "I pointed out that they were spying and gouged something out of their wall and then accused Beatriz of being a spy to her face, which was actually true…"

My turn to interject. "And I was still welcome in Jezero, but because Llama wasn't and because of how they were treating her, I wouldn't let her go without me."

"Interesting." The king steeples his long fingers under the short gray beard that covers his chin. "What was this thing you extracted from their wall, Llama?"

"I actually don't know. It was small and black and round. Reach had it."

"You have it now, Reach?" the queen asks.

"It was in my Jezero clothes' pocket," I say.

"Very well, we can certainly get it from the laundry." The queen's response is all business. "We should run some tests, Alfred."

"Of course, Eleanore, dear." The king stands from his chair and bends down to brush a tender kiss along the queen's lips. "I'm sure they have questions and that you can answer them without my help. I'll go attend to the laundry. How grumpy will they be today, do you think, dear?" He smiles and Queen Eleanore rolls her eyes.

The King of Souterraine ambles away across the field, his odd shoes clapping along after him.

19

"So my dears." The Queen of Souterraine arranges her skirt around her legs. "You must have many questions. We thought it best not to give you an open opportunity to ask things until you were together."

Llama's gaze shifts to mine and I shrug. I do have questions. I try to think of the order I should ask them for the sake of the political chess game, but Llama surprises me by launching first. "What was my father like? Why was he on Earth? Why was Jezero so mad about that?"

"Oh, my. Going right for it. That's just what Alec would have done too." Queen Eleanore presses her hand to her heart, the faintest hint of a smile mixed with an expression of sorrow on her face. "Your father went to Earth to see what conditions were like there. We have a thriving colony here on Souterraine, but it will never thrive the way an Earth-based colony would. There is too much artificial here. Our trees, our resources, would not survive on Earth because they have never experienced the stress that makes things stronger."

"But why?" Llama presses, leaning forward in her chair.

"Alec was always putting the good of the people of Souterraine above his own needs. He trained for years to return to Earth. Our limited technology resources meant that we had to depend on Jezero's technology and make amendments to their pieces in order to get the spacecraft ready to return to Earth. Jezero doesn't like the idea of us having technological power. Perhaps you came to this conclusion, but we have two very different ways of life between the two colonies on Mars. We've managed to exist somewhat peacefully for three hundred years, but it's become apparent to leadership in both colonies that we cannot both stay here on Mars and maintain our current ways of life."

I scan the horizon, noting the trees, the clover, the greenery, the river. It's all so Earth-like. It's so much more pleasant than Jezero. I never want to leave.

"Why?" I blurt out. "It's perfect here."

The queen sighs heavily. "We have terraformed Souterraine into an Earth-like colony, but it requires technology to keep the components running. While we were focusing on the agricultural needs of terraforming, Jezero focused on the technology. But each colony has limited resources, and as our colonies grow, there are fewer resources to support our growth."

"So..." I hedge, already knowing the answer.

"We needed information about Earth, because we may need to evacuate our colony. Jezero has no intention of doing so. When Alec was on Earth, he made three transmission calls to us. The first told us he had arrived. The second informed us that Nation was hostile. The third was something like a goodbye, but we never could be sure."

Llama's eyes are misty, and her jaw clenches. I press my hand into hers, and she latches on like she's drowning and I'm saving her. "My father sounds like a good man," she says. She rolls her lip under her teeth. "I know the rest of the story." She looks at the queen. "Do you want to know?"

The queen's eyes brim with unshed tears as she nods.

"He was killed resisting arrest in Ward 11 of Nation. My mother ran a Resistance group, and her second-in-command was a government spy. My father didn't trust her, but she kept passing every test. When he finally confronted her, she told him he was the smartest of them all, and he was right. Arrests were made, but my mother was already eight months pregnant with me. She had me in Pen 1—Nation's high security prison—and then I was raised 'care of the state' in Ward 11."

"And no one told you about your history until…"

"Until I needed to know. I didn't know about my father being from Mars until just before the space mission. Dr. Jog told me, but I don't think he knew about…Souterraine. Both my parents are…were considered…" She draws a sharp breath. "Nation tried to keep me in line, to remind me that I'm the daughter of traitors." Her voice breaks on the last word, and I know why.

"Llama." The Queen of Souterraine leaves her chair and crouches in front of Llama's wheelchair. "Llama, you are brave. You are not the daughter of a traitor *here*. You are the daughter of a hero. Llama, you are a *princess here*."

The Queen of Souterraine kneels on the clover meadow next to Llama, gently cupping her hand around Llama's cheek. Llama's eyes betray her vulnerability as tears gather in the corners and bead down her face.

"Thank you," Llama breathes. "No one has ever…"

"No one has ever been your family," the queen inserts. "We are family. I can see so much of Alec in you."

"Do you…have any pictures?" Llama whispers, and it occurs to me that *this* is why she didn't give up my picture of Greg and my mother to Enforce when she betrayed me. She knew what it meant to me to have a link to my past because she was missing the same pieces I was.

"Yes, dear. We do have photographic technology here. I imagine things have developed differently than on Earth, but I can find a photograph of your father to show you."

"Thank you!" Llama's voice is soft, but her actions are loud. She flings herself into Queen Eleanore's arms, the wheelchair toppling over behind her. The queen rocks unsteadily on her knees as she adjusts to Llama's sudden embrace. I'm not sure if I should help, so I hover, until the queen gestures to me with her hand.

I place my hand in hers and she yanks me into the hug.

I'm off-kilter, and in more ways than one.

Llama is weak and can't walk more than a few yards before she tires, which explains the wheelchair. After the longest embrace I can remember ever experiencing breaks apart, I right the wheelchair for Llama. The queen steadies it as I help Llama sit down. Llama smiles gratefully, and there is something entirely different about her. Nothing has changed physically about her in the past few minutes, but she has a glow around her face, and her pale cheeks stretch wide in a…smile.

Llama's smiling. She's genuinely happy. I'm taken aback by the realization that I've never seen this version of Llama before.

"Reach?" Queen Eleanore prompts. "Would you please push *Princess* Llama back to the castle? And I suppose you have some questions for us here too?" The emphasis on the honorific is startling, but I accept my role as Llama's chauffeur, placing my hands on the handlebars.

Llama stretches back and places one cool palm gently on top of my hand, giving me a beam of a smile. I don't think I've ever seen anything so intriguing. Not Beatriz with false beauty used to ensnare and entrap, not Llama when she was still Llama but playing a double agent. It's Llama, the one who's a mere breath away, that makes my heart thrum as I push her through the clover.

Queen Eleanore coughs, and my gaze jerks sharply up to her, amusement dancing in her eyes as she raises one delicate eyebrow. Llama can't see the gesture, but I can.

The King and Queen of Souterraine are extremely likable. That doesn't make a person good, I know that. I don't want to be used or to use them. But I like them.

"So, Reach," Queen Eleanore says as she falls in step beside me. "What are your questions?"

"How is it sunny here? We are underground. On Mars." I push the first question in my brain out through my mouth. It's probably not the most important question I could ask, but it's what's perplexing me most at the moment.

"Ah. Excellent question." The warmth in her eyes reaches my own body like a comforting hug. "Our ancestors developed a stronger spectrum light technology for growing plants. We've since perfected it, and now have a thriving ecosystem similar to the one on Earth, but both underground and on Mars. The idea of our ancestors—the ones who began Souterraine—was to terraform the entire planet. That would require too much manpower and cooperation, so Souterraine was created with borders."

"Jezero Colony didn't want to terraform?" I ask, surveying the picturesque scene before me. The trees, the greenery, the blueness of the dome above.

"No. They did not. They were focused on other components of life on Mars. Worthy in their own way, but not what the ancestors had envisioned."

"Why is the top of Souterraine—is it a dome?—blue?"

"Yes, we're in a dome. That's the benefit of our technology. We are able to project different lengths of light to different parts of the dome. I'm sure you'd like to see it. Perhaps you'd like to see all of our operations." The queen gives me a knowing look that is borderline meddlesome, but also paired with a mischievous glint in her eyes. It's clear she's playing matchmaker. "When Llama's well enough to visit, she must see everything, learn everything she can about her people. You should definitely come with her. Now, other questions?"

My mind draws a blank. It's as if there's a white wall in front of me and I cannot formulate a single thought because she is clearly implying something romantic about Llama and me. *Or is it Llama and I?* I'm too tripped up in my thoughts to answer.

Llama's voice joins the conversation. It's still quiet, but it sounds more like her. "What do I call you?" she asks the queen.

"Grandmere, of course." Queen Eleanore smiles down at Llama. "And Reach, you are welcome to address me as Eleanore."

I blink. This is not what I expected. It does draw out a question, albeit a poorly formed one. "How do things work here?"

Llama turns around, her lips pressed together and her eyes sparkling with mirth. I sigh. The past few days have been a lot to take in. She should excuse a few poorly worded questions.

The queen—Eleanore—cocks her head slightly to the side. "Could you be more specific, dear?"

The term of endearment sounds so natural coming from her lips that I can't be upset about it. Heat rises to my cheeks as I realize what a ridiculous question that was. "I mean..." I stumble. "I meant the government structure."

"Ah. That would be important to you after what you saw in Jezero."

"And Nation," Llama mutters.

"Yes, you must tell us everything about Earth and Nation. We will make sure we have that conversation with our advisors, and when Alfred is present." The queen straightens her crown slightly, and a purple petal floats to the ground. "Our government is quite simple. The people of Souterraine are ruled by a king and queen who share equal duties of government leadership. We have advisors, which we select based on different factors, such as experience, knowledge, and, of course, our ability to work and trust these people."

"What do you do with people you don't trust?" Llama's voice turns stone-cold.

"Llama, dear. We are not barbaric here. I suspect you have experienced a lot of mistrust in your life. In Souterraine, if we do not trust someone, they are not given a position of power."

I cut in. "That sounds too easy."

"Yes, well, when a family has been the ruling governing body of a colony for several hundred years with minimal conflict, I think we have something of a system. Besides, the people who came to Souterraine in the first place came to have a simpler life, not a more complicated one. Power and ambition are not nearly as important here as in other government structures. You'll find that many people who cause trouble simply want to *advance*. We have projects for those people. When people feel useful and are contributing to a good cause, conflict is reduced to an almost nonexistent status."

I have just been lectured by the Queen of Souterraine. "Oh," I breathe out, but it's not enough to squash the embarrassment. A double inhale helps before I empty my lungs completely. There is too much emotion in this air. And I want the king and queen to like me, although I'm not entirely sure why that's important to me. I just know it is.

"Reach." The queen places a hand on my arm. "I am sorry if that sounded sharp. We have been trying to avoid conflict for so long. I sometimes forget that not every place is like Souterraine. That not every leader is a good leader. I know from Alec's transmissions that Nation was not a friendly place. I'm sorry for what you've experienced."

There's wisdom in her eyes, and I can't meet them for long. I feel an odd sense of shame. Shame for being from Nation. Shame for Greg being my father. It's clear that Jezero Colony and Souterraine aren't cooperating well, and I like it *here* far better than I liked Jezero.

The queen is kind, but distant after our talk. I don't think she's angry but rather giving me some space. Back inside the castle, we sit around Llama in a room that's full of light. Wooden floors, wood plank walls, and furniture made of wood make for a welcoming space. I try to take in the beauty of the room, but I can't stop my eyes from drifting over to Llama at every opportunity. She carries the conversation, asking questions about her father, but what's most startling is the way that Llama is lighted up from within. A glow on her cheeks, a smile tugging on her lips. I marvel at all she's been through, and the way a family has given her a sense of purpose. The king and queen respond kindly, laughing at warm memories of their son. When it's time for the evening meal, Bernard appears, followed by the other woman who also wears a crown. Pippa, I think.

"Pippa, dear. I'm so glad you could join us. How was learning this afternoon?" Queen Eleanore asks.

"It was good, Momma," Pippa replies, but her words are a bit stiff, like she has to think before she can summon them, and that speaking takes some effort.

"I'm so glad, darling. Come, let's eat." Queen Eleanore takes Pippa by the arm and sweeps out of the room, their dresses swishing behind them.

I don't mean to stare at Pippa, but something is different about her. I've never seen another person with her physical features. The king, who notably has *not* given me permission to call him by his first name, clears his throat. I meet his eyes, his hands resting on Llama's wheelchair handlebars. His eyes flash a challenge at me, but I don't understand why. My mouth opens, then closes.

"I think I'd like to try to walk," Llama whispers.

The king's expression softens. "Of course. I'll help. Unless you'd prefer…"

"Yes, please." Llama blushes. "I mean, I'd like Reach to help. We've known each other, and he knows my body." Llama's flush turns darker and I nearly laugh. "I did *not* mean that." The king snorts and gives me a glare, which Llama observes. "We trained for space together. Reach is familiar with how I move, and my athletic ability, and…we just have a lot of time where we've been forced to be around each other, and I think he knows…my…body…"

"Llama!" I whisper-hiss, my amusement turning to mortification as her words keep tumbling out.

The king stands, arms crossed over his chest. His close-cropped white beard does not conceal the frown he has on his face. "Young man." His voice is deep and rumbly and commanding. He sounds like a leader. He sounds like a *king*. "You will tell me your intentions with my granddaughter this instant."

"Woah." Llama holds a hand up, her tone suddenly biting. "That's not fair. I came here with Reach. You didn't know I existed until we were at Jezero. I've known Reach far longer than I've known you! I'm just more comfortable with Reach because I've known him for years. Please don't make this something. It's not. It's nothing. It's…nothing. Please."

The king startles back slightly, his brow creasing. "Apologies," he says, his deep voice reverberating around the room. "I have been very protective of Pippa since she was born. And Llama, you are…unexpected. Truly, when we lost Alec, we mourned for so long. Pippa was born after that, when we were quite old by usual standards. She has a genetic disorder. Things are harder for her, and she will never have the same experiences as other people her age, but she is still our ray of sunshine. I will endeavor to trust you as an adult, Llama. But I will always regret not knowing you as a child." He turns and pierces me with a scowl that begins at the top of my head and travels to my toes. I will myself not to flinch. "Reach."

The King of Souterraine exits the room after his unexpected soliloquy, and Llama and I are alone together for the first time in days.

"Reach?" Her voice is soft, tentative. "I'm sorry."

I smile at her because it *was* funny, until the king made his feelings clear, but now she's looking at me, and I know she *sees* me.

"Would you help me?" she asks. "I feel ready to walk."

I extend a hand to her and she grasps it. When she's standing, I start to drop it.

"Don't," she says. And I don't. Despite her protests that there is

nothing between us, we arrive at the evening meal after an agoniz-
ingly slow walk down the corridor, hand in hand. The king gives me
one quick glare, but no one says anything about it.

21

Souterraine lives and breathes trees. Everywhere we go, there are trees. When people pass by the trees, they often place their hand gently on the bark. Touching the trees is as familiar to the people of Souterraine as bestowing affection on their children.

Llama is regaining her strength quickly due to our iron-fortified diet, so we've been given license to explore. Her skin is no longer ghostly pale flesh stretched taut over her cheekbones, but rather a warm, almost golden, color. The king was called away on urgent business to an agricultural sector, and I haven't seen him in a few days. The queen has always been gentler, and I've been grateful to interact with her, but she also has kept her interactions with me to a minimum since she and the king chastised me.

Llama has been given time to rest and heal. I've been given time to wander. At first, I wondered if there was a schedule or person I needed to report to. I found myself glancing at the floor and wishing for an arrow to map out my every move—just like when I was at Hub—several times. Finally, after pacing for half a day, I could not take it. I went and found Bernard in the kitchen.

"May I help you?" Bernard asked, mid-stir of something in a large pot.

"Is there something specific I need to do? Any rules I need to follow? Any place I need to be?" I asked.

Bernard's broad shoulders shook with laughter. "Why? Are you intending to break the rules? And you are here, so learn. If you'd like to be someplace other than here, try walking the river awhile. You'll find you need to be where you are, exactly when you are there. The river is like that."

This is why today, one week after the King of Souterraine made his feelings regarding his newfound granddaughter perfectly clear to me, I am out, away from Llama, away from the meadow, away from everyone, exploring.

I left through the massive front door and walked across the meadow of clover, cutting over a wooden footbridge that crosses a small stream on my way to the wider river. The river meanders back and forth, cutting through the greenery, as I notice several other people out for a stroll, reaching out and stroking the trunk of the trees they see growing along the river.

I recall Dr. Jog's words about a river and a riparian habitat. So much has happened, so much has changed since that day, it overwhelms me. Thinking of Dr. Jog brings an ache to my chest, so I place my hand on my heart and rub like it will remove the pain. Thinking of Dr. Jog, my mother, my friends—it's something I avoid if I can. Today, I cannot.

My eyes dart upward into the branches of a large tree covered in green five-pointed leaves. There's a flash of color up above. Pink. My eyes narrow as I try to determine if it's an animal, though so far the only animal I've seen on Mars is a cat. Perhaps it's a bird? Another flash and a thud as someone drops out of the tree in front of me.

The someone has a pink dress on, the same sandals I wear, and a crown made of woven wooden pieces and yellow flowers upon her head. It's Pippa.

"Hi," Pippa says after studying me. She shakes her hands vigorously at her sides before blinking at me.

I'm startled, but I manage to find words. "Hi, Pippa." I recall her genetic condition and her own father's words about her. "Should you be out here?"

Pippa considers my question for a moment, then responds in a stilted way. "Momma won't mind." Then she surprises me by asking, "Will you walk with me?"

I look around, unsure of what to do. I've never met anyone like Pippa before. Llama once told me that the Wards of Nation were full of people with odd bodies and unusual minds, but Hub and Compound were *not*. I have no experience with any person like her. Pippa is full-grown, but she doesn't seem to understand that. She slips her hand into mine and then begins to run. I'm pulled along after her, watching her jet-black hair stream behind her.

"Pippa!" I try to shout, but she's running too hard and too fast, and won't let go. When we approach a curve in the river, she stops running and drops onto a wooden bench. She releases my hand, and I gratefully stand a few feet away from her. I ease my shoulder up and down, trying to work out the tenderness from the way her sprint pulled me.

"Why did you run here?" I ask once I've recovered my breath.

"Like it here," she says in reply. "You like too?"

I take a moment to see the beauty of the river, the way that it bends and curves, the way the current pushes leaves and branches downstream, the way the riverbed looks pink. *I do like it here.*

Pippa is unexpected. She's good, she's pure, she's childlike in her trust. From the few interactions I've had with her, it seems that asking her direct questions slows her responses, but I wonder if she can talk about the river. It is beautiful.

"I like the way those branches touch the water," I say, pointing to a group of trees on the opposite bank, their feathery fingers dancing lightly above the water and every so often jostling close enough to the surface that one breaks the surface tension and creates miniature ripples.

Pippa nods in appreciation. "I like willows. Those are weeping willows. They don't seem sad, though; they are happy willows. What does a willow do when it's happy?"

The question surprises me, but I find I have an answer for her. "They dance. Dancing willows."

Pippa's smile is brighter than the sunlight technology shining down on us from overhead. It's brighter than a sunny day on Earth. "Dancing willows." Pippa gets up and leaves the bench, wandering away down the river bank. I don't feel comfortable watching her walk away. I don't know what she's supposed to be doing right now, but on the first day, Queen Eleanore said something about school.

"Pippa?" Pippa looks back over her shoulder. "Pippa, wait!"

Pippa's response is to hike her skirts above her knees and run, her arms akimbo as her legs lead her down the river and disappear into a hole in a strange structure.

The structure is made of twisted branches with four *dancing*, not weeping, willows anchoring each corner. The branches above form a sort of ceiling, but the entire effect is like stepping into shade after being in the sun.

I follow Pippa, but the moment I step inside, I realize I shouldn't have worried. Pippa might be different, but she's not in-capable.

I duck inside the entrance, and it takes a moment for my eyes to adjust to the dim lighting. A man stands at the front of the large room. Children sit cross-legged on the floor, some in chairs, and some at long plank tables.

"May I help you?" the man asks.

As my eyes take in the new surroundings, I recognize that this man is close to my own age. He has a hint of reddish stubble across his chin, reddish hair on his head, and piercing brown eyes. The sleeves of his pale green button-down shirt are rolled up to his el-bows, and his tan pants are exactly like what every other man wears here, including myself. Shades of green seem to be the favorite color for shirts, I note. My own shirt today is a soft green with a bit of a reddish undertint. Even the children have miniature versions of the clothes, right down to the odd footwear.

"Hi, yes," I breathe, when I realize that every single eye in the large room is trained on me. The familiar dread of meeting new people creeps up, but I shove the anxiety back down my throat and force my words to work. "I'm sorry to interrupt, I was walking when Pippa—"

"Princess Pippa," the man interrupts.

"Yes, sorry. When Princess Pippa began running, I was worried about her, so I followed her. I didn't know this was…"

"This is the school for the children of Souterraine."

"Oh." My shoulders sag. Princess Pippa wasn't running into danger. She was running into *school. But why was she out of school?* "I didn't mean to interrupt. I'm…" I trail off as I consider what to say. "Visiting."

The man barks out a laugh. "We know, Reach. And welcome to Souterraine. You're not interrupting anything at all. Class, please say hello to Reach. He's visiting Souterraine from Earth."

The hush of awe that follows the word *Earth* makes me smile. I can only imagine if someone had appeared at the Educational Facility on Compound and said they were from Mars.

The younger children are the ones sitting on the ground by the teacher's feet. One of them pops up. She's wearing a blue dress and, I notice, only one shoe. "Did you *REALLY* come from Erff?"

I bite my lip at her pronunciation of *Earth* to keep from laughing.

"Emily," the man reprimands. "Let's let Reach share what he wants to share."

"Oh. Yes, I'm from Earth." I look at the man and he nods. "Would you like to ask me more questions? I could answer a few if you'd like me to."

Every single student in the large room raises their hand. The teacher smirks as he inclines his head once and leans against the woven branches at the front of the room.

I'm out of my depth, but I'll give it a try. "Yes?" I point to a boy sitting cross-legged with the younger students on the floor.

"Did you come here on a rocket ship? What's a toilet like in space?"

Valid questions. "Yes, I came on a rocket ship. And you use the bathroom just like everywhere else, but you have to follow all the protocols, or else people could get sick." The younger children nod in understanding while the older students watch on. I answer many questions about the rocket ship, and being in space, and zero-g, space toilets, and gravity. Finally, I'm exhausted.

The teacher jumps in. "Last question, class. We have to send you home for your afternoon jobs."

I point to an older girl. "Yes, in the purple dress?"

"What is a storm like?" she asks. "With *lightning* and rain and stuff?"

I blink. Out of all the questions I'd answered today, I had not anticipated that. Suddenly, the fact that we're underground on Mars is stifling. "Err," I hedge. "Maybe I could tell you about that another day." It's a lame answer, but she doesn't complain.

"Right," the teacher says. "Students, gather up your things. Remember that your learning extends into your afternoon jobs, so go, do your best, and know that I'll be getting a report from your parents and caretakers on your afternoon work. Have a wonderful day, and remember to use your manners. Souterraine needs you."

Each of the students stands and files out of the structure with a polite head bob at both me and the teacher. When the room is empty, the man extends a hand.

"I'm Phil."

"Reach," I say, taking his hand and shaking it. "How did you know all that?" I jerk my chin at the handshake, remembering Cait's confusion back when we first landed on Mars.

"The King and Queen of Souterraine gave an address and let us know that you and Princess Llama are visiting from Earth."

I frown. That must have happened when I was asleep for literal days. *What else did I miss?*

"Yeah, but at Jez—" I stop myself, unsure of how to say the next words. Am I supposed to talk about being at Jezero?

"Reach, we know you and Princess Llama were at Jezero first."

"Oh, good," I breathe. "Well, at Jezero, they don't know what shaking hands means."

Phil smiles at this, making the skin around his brown eyes crinkle. "Jezero has a lot of differences from Souterraine, one of which is studying other cultures. Our ancestors thought it important to preserve some traditions. Jezero's ancestors preferred to create their own."

"Oh." The fact that two colonies exist on Mars and have handled everything so differently from the very start strikes me as odd, but major philosophical differences have a way of dividing people. "So this is a school?"

"Yeah," Phil says. "It's a good one, too, but I'm biased." He laughs, and I laugh too. I like him. I like the people of Souterraine. "Now that I've put you through your paces with my students, could I answer some questions for you? I'm sure you have some. I'm walking to the castle for a lunch meeting today. Are you headed back that way?"

"Yes, I am."

22

Phil laughs easily and has a refreshing self-deprecating sense of humor. He is tall, but lean, and makes me think of Lift with his long, purposeful strides.

"So, what do you think of Souterraine's educational system?" Phil asks.

I respond with the question that's been burning in my brain since he dismissed the class. "Where are the students going this afternoon? Only learning in the morning would never happen on Earth."

Phil gives me a long look before answering. "On Earth, things are different from Souterraine, naturally. But here, learning takes an experiential course in the afternoons. The students rotate through different jobs, learning new life skills every few months. We see education like a spiral. Book learning is important, but so is learning to contribute. The students might be assigned to working in an agricultural sector their youngest year, and would have age-appropriate tasks. Then, as they are older and rotate back through, they are given more difficult tasks. Perhaps the first-year students learn about and manage compost while the tenth-year students are actively managing the plants of a plot."

"I'm surprised by the amount of vegetation here." I let my eyes run over the groves of trees beside the river. "It's very different from…Jezero."

Phil gives me a sad smile. "I've never seen Jezero, but I've heard about how they've integrated their colony into Mars with no terraforming. It's a different way of life, to be sure. Especially when Souterraine's terraforming is our most impressive feat. We know that nature on Earth is one of the major indicators of health, both for the planet itself and its inhabitants. Trees have always played a vital role in Souterraine."

"How?"

"I can show you if you don't mind a short detour." I shake my head and shrug. I don't have anywhere in particular to be, and he's the one offering. "Great."

He leads us down the river bank for a few more minutes. When we arrive at the footbridge I crossed this morning, Phil turns in the opposite direction of the castle and leads me into a grove of trees. He points to the behemoths.

"These are the first trees planted on Mars. They are ceremonial and special. Look closely."

I do look. A small metal plaque is affixed to a wooden post next to each tree. I see the words *maple, beech, oak, sequoia, willow, jack pine, cypress, white pine, elm, birch, palm, coconut, hickory, cedar, hawthorn, walnut,* and others.

"Each person in Souterraine has their name carved into the tree their ancestors planted on the day they are born and named," Phil explains. He stops beneath the birch tree and runs his hands over the bark. "The bark heals itself eventually, so you can't see all the names, but they are there. It's a way to preserve our history. Birch is the one that my ancestors carried from Earth to Mars. These are our family trees."

Phil's awe and gentleness with the tree strikes me as extremely sentimental, and also ignites a longing in me. He has a family, a history, that he's proud of. I swallow and think of Llama, of how happy she is here, and of how peaceful it is. There's a current of jealousy that swirls in my stomach. I want peace, I want belonging. I want to know, to understand, to be a part of something *good* for once. These family trees, they feel like wholeness and goodness personified. Thoughts of Llama make me want to know something about her, something that maybe I could teach her one day.

"Which tree does the royal ruling family use?" I ask.

Phil's response is to walk to the tree with reddish bark, the furrows on it running up and down. The sign next to the tree says *maple*. Phil puts his hand on the tree. "This one. It was the happiest day when Princess Pippa was added to it." The sadness in his voice floats away on the gentle breeze the trees gift us. "What a delight," he says, "to be her teacher."

I'm not sure how old Princess Pippa is, but she seems nearly as old as Phil.

"How is it possible that *you* are her teacher?" I ask. When Phil's eyes cut to me, I realize that I sounded insensitive. "I'm sorry. I meant, she…has a genetic condition, doesn't she? The king told me that. And you don't seem much older than her."

"Ah," Phil replies, nodding in understanding. "Yes, I'm only a few years older than Princess Pippa, but her intellectual disabilities require her to take longer in her learning. She's achieved half the levels of schooling now. Her condition doesn't make her incapable, it just takes time and creativity."

"You seem like you enjoy teaching."

Phil is quick to smile. "Yes, I enjoy it now, but it wasn't easy to get here." He turns and leaves the grove of trees, and I trot along at his side.

After regaling me with stories of his first year of teaching, he directs the conversation back to me. "So, Reach. What brings you to Souterraine?"

"Llama," I say simply. I don't know how much I'm allowed to divulge. The chessboard continues to add facets, and no one tells me enough to make the entire puzzle clear.

"Ahhh, Llama. She's your…"

"Space mission partner. We trained together and were supposed to be sent to Station 51."

"What's that?" Phil's eyebrows raise as he searches my face. He really doesn't know about Earth, or Nation's space stations. "I thought there were only a few manned space stations that belonged to Earth."

"I think that's true." I hedge my response. "But Station 51 is the farthest from Earth. Or so everyone in Nation has been told. I found out recently that it also doesn't exist."

Phil's brow creases. "They were sending you to a station that doesn't exist? Why? What does that mean?"

"It means that they were trying to get rid of us while giving the people of Nation a common enemy. Llama and I both have a rather..." I blow out a breath. "Rather complicated history with the government of Nation. They were using us and disposing us."

"That's terrible. How did you know? How did you end up here?" Phil's interest in this conversation feels purely academic, but I'm nervous about it just the same.

"There are people on Earth who do not like the government of Nation—"

"A Resistance? How fascinating."

"Yes, a Resistance, and they had gained enough intel to warn me, but also to help Llama and me train in ways that overlapped with how Nation intended to use us. My aptitude for maps and geography and charting courses was especially useful."

"I do love to look at old maps of Earth. We have an entire unit on geological features for our year-six students."

I don't know what I expected Phil's response to be to the word *maps*, but it was not to offhandedly offer up that he has access to *maps of Earth*. That's something the people on Earth don't have access to. "You have maps? Of Earth?" I can't keep the disbelief out of my voice.

"Of course." My jaw hangs open and I stand still, staring, while Phil continues walking. When he realizes I've stopped, he turns. "We do have maps of Earth here, Reach."

"Yes," I sputter. "Yes, but maps are classified in Nation. Most people never see one. I only saw practice maps until I got clearance. What do you *have*?"

"I have maps from the pre-Scientific Revolution, and more modern ones."

"Of Earth? You have *modern* maps of Nation?"

"Reach, I have maps of Nation and the rest of the countries that reside on Earth."

"There's *more countries* on Earth?"

Phil's eyes narrow into a squint. "What do you know about Earth? And countries? This feels like a conversation advisors should be present for. How do you not know about other countries on Earth? Do you know about landforms? Islands?" Phil's words come in rapid fire. He's clearly talking more to himself now. "Never mind. We definitely need to have this discussion with the advisors. There's a massive amount of information you're missing, and I can't explain it all properly."

Phil picks up the pace. His long strides cover more ground, and I find myself jogging to keep up. I'm reeling inside. I'm on Mars, and there are *other* countries, which means *other* people, which means *other* governments on Earth. *What am I doing on Mars?* The entirety of my life is redundant.

When we reach the wooden doors of the castle, Phil turns to me. "One thing I would be remiss not to say to you, Reach, is that while there is very little ceremony in Souterraine, there is still some. You must address the royal ruling family by their titles in public. *Princess* Pippa, *King*, *Queen*. For everyone else, a first name only is fine, but this is really important to everyone here. That's why I corrected you earlier at the school."

"Yes, of course. Thank you."

Phil pulls the door open and steps inside. I follow him, feeling more and more lost with each step.

PHIL KNOWS THE castle better than I do. He turns to me at the bottom of a staircase I have never seen before. "You have a lot of questions, and I think I need to talk to the advisors about what you don't know. Maybe you should make yourself comfortable, and I'll request a meeting for you. I'm a junior advisor, so I have some sway."

"Oh," I breathe. I'm being dismissed, kindly, but I still recognize it. "Yeah, I can go back to my room and do something…" I trail off.

"I think you'd enjoy the library, Reach," Phil suggests.

My eyes widen. A library? *Yes.*

"Yes, that would be…" It would be wonderful, but I don't know where it is. "Where is it?"

Phil's eyes twinkle. "An educator can always tell a life-long learner. It's the turret."

He disappears up the stairs, his shoes flopping along against the polished wood steps.

I retrace my steps and return to the front of the castle. I need to find the turret. The castle is sprawling, and I've only seen portions of it. Walking through the inside won't help me, but I can walk around the outside and find it. Half an hour later, I spy a spire rising off a back area of the building. I'm not sweating, but I do feel invigorated. I had a directional problem to solve. My mind feels fresh, my limbs happy from the exercise. I'm rounding the corner when I smash into something. It's warm and somewhat solid and definitely surprised, if the shriek is any indication.

"Reach!" Llama's voice hits my eardrums while I'm still looking for the turret. I've spent the entire time I've been outside looking up and away, and not noticing what's in front of me. I have good instincts, but I'm not sure how I ended up crashing into her.

I look down and grin at her, her wrinkled nose making me smile. That, and the fact that she's walking on her own. My hands are on her waist, steadying her, and she's leaning into me after our collision threw her off balance.

"I'm sorry, Llama," I whisper. "I was looking for the library." My hands are still on her waist, and I don't want to lower them. No one else is around, least of all the king, so I don't. I enjoy the feel of her dress against my palms.

"Reach," Llama whispers back. "This place is…amazing. And I'm glad we bumped into each other. But we need to talk."

I clear my throat and reluctantly step back. My hands fall to my sides. Those words are ominous. I swallow hard. "Where? I have time now."

Llama reaches out her hand and grasps mine. I'm startled, but don't pull back. "Could you come with me to someplace private? My room? I haven't seen any indication of spying devices here, and I've been looking."

"Ok," I say again, still reveling in the feel of her hand in mine and the fact that she doesn't need me to help her but is touching me. "Let's go there. But I think we could talk here too."

Llama looks around. There's clover growing beneath our feet, and the castle is so large that most people wouldn't be out walking this way. If anyone needed something in the castle, they'd walk through it. "Yeah, but I need to sit, I think."

I offer her my arm and help her lower to the ground. She spreads out her long red skirt, and I get a glimpse of her shoes, the same sandals as mine before they are covered up again.

"Reach, Jezero was…I'm sorry. I know that it's your father's colony, but it is a bad place."

I blink a few times. I didn't anticipate this being the topic of our conversation. "Yes, I kind of figured that out when they forced you onto a truck not designed for human transportation after losing liters of blood." Llama shrugs. "Why do you say that though?"

She crinkles her forehead and she hangs her head. "It was…the hospital tour. They…showed me the 'state of the art maternity ward'." I wait in silence as she clenches her jaw. "Reach. It's not…people in Jezero don't want to have babies. They are trying to *make* them." I snort. She swats my hand away. "I mean, they are trying to *manufacture* people." Llama pushes her hand into the ground cover, digging in with her fingers like she's trying to anchor herself here. "It was disgusting, Reach. People can put their…specifications into a system, and there's a machine, and then it makes…a baby…that's got everything exactly the way they ordered it. It takes months, and defects happen, and so there's an…" Her breath hitches. "An entire area they have dedicated to the babies and children that will have defects that no one wants."

I frown. "What do you mean? What do they do?"

Llama's swallow indicates that what they do isn't good. "I'm not sure, but I wasn't supposed to see it. I went…off the tour path. I think they keep it secret from the general population too. It's hidden in the basement."

"But what about *normal* babies?" I ask, confused.

"They showed me the machine where you input the specifications. The doctor told me this is a new and experimental technology, but it's easier to…have the hospital do it for you. He said it's expensive." She tenses. "I…excused myself to use the bathroom, but when he said it was experimental technology, something felt wrong, so I wandered and found the area labeled 'defective maternity' hidden in the basement. It was empty, but it's ready and waiting for…defective people. Just like Nation and the Wards. That's where the doctor found me. Percy was so mad when he picked me up from the tour, but I said I got lost, and there was nothing he could do to prove that I was snooping."

My mind whirs with thoughts of money, babies, and power. Why are those things interconnected in Jezero? I drag my fingers through my hair, tugging and feeling grounded by the motion. "I did not understand the economy there, but after seeing how they handled the succession laws, I'm not surprised that money has something to do with it." A new thought crosses over my prefrontal cortex like a shadow. "Do you think Souterraine knows?"

Llama bites her lip as she picks at the greenery on the ground. "I don't know. I don't think this place would be like that though." She slumps. "Reach, I like it here. I don't think I could bear it if they were…" Her hands fly up to her face and she buries her head in her palms. Her hands can't hide the tears as drops of water stream steadily onto the red fabric of her dress and leave stains.

I don't know what comes over me, but I can't stand seeing her look so broken. "Llama." It comes out commanding. I didn't know I had a commanding voice. She breaks her fingers apart and looks at me, her digits casting shadows like bars on her face. "I like it here too."

My hand lands on her arm in a gesture meant to comfort her, to tell her she's not alone, and to tell her she's not wrong about this place. Llama interprets my gesture differently and, with surprising agility for someone who has been struggling with the basic task of walking, launches herself at me. She wraps her arms around my neck and leans into me.

I can feel her tears dropping onto my neck. Her hair isn't braided, and it dances on the slight breeze that seems to be constant here. The fact that her hair is loose and unbound—that she's *free*— undoes me. Before I know it, my fingers are running through her hair, and then my lips are on her forehead, planting a soft kiss on the broken woman beside me. The woman who's been abused and found a place she'd like to call home. I want that for her. But, selfishly, I also want her to want me.

Llama tilts her head up, her blue eyes ringed with red, but such a deep hue that I'm drawn in. I always have been. I can't *not* kiss her.

Llama's breath hitches. "Reach," she breathes, leaning closer.

My lips are on hers. She's solid and warm and somehow still soft, and I'm not really thinking at all about anything except the fact that I'm kissing her and she is kissing me back. I have no intention of ever stopping. She feels right, and I could do this forever. I *intend* to do this forever.

But a deep baritone voice interrupts. "Nothing. What an interesting development."

Llama pushes herself away and leaves me firmly in the crossfire of the King of Souterraine's glare.

24

THE KING OF Souterraine isn't alone. Phil stands slightly behind him, his eyes downcast, but I can see how wide his pupils are. I don't think public displays of affection are common here, or at least not the kind Llama and I were engaging in.

"Reach," the king's gravelly voice booms. I do not flinch. I will not flinch. I did *nothing* wrong. "You are aware that you said there was nothing between you two. I trusted you."

My eyebrows raise at the irony of this statement. He did most certainly *not* trust us. Or at least, *not me*. Kissing Llama has emboldened me. I don't answer to this king. I'm a guest here, and Llama is a princess, and Llama *likes* me.

I meet the king's eyes. "There was nothing between us recently. We have a complicated history that you're unaware of. If Llama and I both agree to be romantically involved, what concern is it of yours?"

"It is my concern," the king retorts, "when my granddaughter is a princess and I know *nothing* about *you*."

"What do you want to know?" I ask, steel in my voice. The king and I are locked in a staring match.

"There are other people who need to ask you questions too. Phil and I have been looking for you for half an hour. Both of you, come with us."

I stand and extend a hand to Llama, who takes it and pulls herself up. Her eyes are puffy and swollen, and her lips are too. I want to grin, but I also am quickly losing my façade as a tough guy who isn't bothered by the king's demeanor. Anxiety starts to flare up again. What if they have laws here about princesses and who they can be with? I know so little, and here I am…consorting with Llama, even after I was warned away. I think the warning was wrong, but I have no sway here.

Llama doesn't say anything to the king, but links her fingers in mine and says, "Are you ready, Reach?"

"Yeah." My is voice gruff with tension.

The king observes our exchange with something that borders on disbelief, or perhaps disgust. But Llama, whom the king continually acknowledges as a princess, has made her feelings on the matter clear. She *wants* the king to see it, and he does.

Maybe Llama has gotten better at game theory.

The king and Phil lead Llama and me into the castle. They march us down several corridors and finally into a large room with vaulted high ceilings. There are windows everywhere, and wooden benches border the perimeter of the room. People stand in clusters of two or three, talking together. A fireplace in the center of the front wall holds a blazing fire that warms the space. The Queen of Souterraine—I probably shouldn't address her as Eleanore, given the circumstances—stands when we enter.

"Alfred? What's wrong?" she asks.

"Perhaps you should let him tell you," he says, jerking his chin at me.

All eyes turn to me, and somewhere around twenty people wait for me to admit to something, but I didn't do anything wrong.

Llama stares the king in the eyes and answers, "Reach and I have spent a lot of time together, and our feelings for each other have grown. The king, unfortunately, witnessed us in a moment that was ill-advised, and that won't happen again." She lowers her voice and looks at the ground as the queen and king look at each other. "In public," she murmurs, her voice too low for anyone else to hear but me.

I don't miss the way she doesn't apologize for it. Her defiance makes me want to swoop down and kiss her again, but I refrain. There are a lot of people in this room, and the King of Souterraine is rather frightening.

My gaze shifts to the queen, who has the look of someone solving a complicated problem on her face. She stands and calls out, "Attention, please, everyone." All eyes turn to her. "We called a special assembly today because there are many missing pieces in all of our knowledge, and it's only by working together that we can see the path forward."

There's a murmur of agreement, and then some people take seats on the benches while others stand. Llama and I remain standing near the king and queen, unsure of what to do.

I am surprised when Phil and the king bring chairs over for Llama and me. The king sets a chair down behind me. "Sit," he orders.

I comply.

"We need to understand something about you two," a tall, reedy man says from a corner by the fireplace. "We understand that Princess Llama was considered a problem by the government rulers of Nation due to her lineage, but why are *you* a problem, Reach?"

All eyes land on me again. I'm being sized up, and I'm not a fan of the tingly, itchy feeling that it leaves. Fine. They want to make me uncomfortable. I suppose I'll just tell them the truth, something Greg warned me against saying.

"I am the son of a scientist who, years ago, was sent to Nation's Space Station 15. While there, she met a man from Mars who was scouting for his colony." I wait, appreciating the intake of breath as my words hit their ears. "He and my mother fell in love. She was soon pregnant with me, but the man from Jezero Colony left before she knew of the pregnancy. There was no way for her to contact him, so she did the only thing she could think of: she returned to Earth and told a number of lies to protect me and give me a chance at life. The main lie was that I am half-Martian."

The air in the room is fraught with tension. Llama places her hand on my sleeve. I place my hand on top of hers before I continue. "I was, without knowing it, a symbol for the Resistance movement against Nation. With the help of other head scientists, my mother was able to falsify enough data that my origins were unclear to everyone but her. The government didn't totally buy it, but they did want to use my alien genetics to advance their knowledge of deep space. The people of Nation are growing discontent, though they'd never tell you that directly. The government wanted a common enemy for everyone to unite against—an enemy that wasn't them. They sent Llama and me into space to gather information, and also to execute us. We are nothing to them but the children of traitors, and they planned to use our data for their own knowledge and pin our deaths on alien activity. When we die, the people can unite against alien activity instead of finding fault with the Three Powers who rule Nation. We're only on Mars because the Resistance movement was a step ahead." I pat Llama's hand with my own and offer her a small smile.

"Reach," a woman who has been sitting under a window and wrapping a ball of string around smooth sticks inquires. "Do you know the name of your father—the man from Jezero Colony who met your mother while she was stationed at…15?"

I scrunch my eyes tight. "Yeah. Yeah I do," I breathe. Llama's hands tense in mine. I have the very real sense that the words I am about to utter will change everything. "I am the son of Greg McAllistair."

I swear I can feel the air whoosh straight up to the tall ceiling as everyone, every single person in the room, stares slack-jawed at me.

All but the queen. She jumps up and surveys the room brightly.

"This is perfect!" she announces.

"No," the king says.

"Alfred." She draws out the *d*. "You know and I know what this means. They are of age. Llama is twenty and Reach is nineteen."

"No. I just— I don't like it," the king growls.

"Alfred!" she chides quietly. "You are the King of Souterraine. You are a good king. But don't be blinded by your prejudice against Jezero. Llama is not Pippa. You don't have to protect her the same way." She turns to the other people in the room. "Trusted advisors, Reach's story rings true. And provides us with the solution we've been looking for. A diplomatic marriage will preserve the peace between Souterraine and Jezero Colonies. Since both Princess Llama and Reach already have romantic feelings for each other, this shouldn't be a burden on either of them. I propose marriage!"

I would very much like to marry, or unionize, or whatever it is actually called, but I only just kissed Llama today after months of distrust. This is fast. I don't look at Llama. I can't look at Llama.

"Marriage does seem the easiest solution. And very convenient," a new voice chimes in.

"Are we certain he's McAllistair's son?" another voice adds to the din of people discussing mine and Llama's relationship without our input.

I can't help it. I look to Llama. She's looking at me, her eyes wide enough that I can see myself mirrored back in them. My eyes are also wide. My mouth is agape. Our linked hands are taken as a sign of acquiescence.

The queen takes over the conversation. "Now then, Llama, you had something you needed to tell us about Jezero?"

Llama drops my hand as if it's suddenly scalding. I involuntarily stretch my fingers out, my digits seeking hers. An advisor gives a pointed look at my hand, and I curl my fingers back into a fist.

Llama gives me an apologetic look, and I think she's going to protest our betrothal. In a clear voice that's entirely too calm for someone who's just been engaged to someone else by an entire party of people you don't really know, she speaks out. "In Jezero, President McAllistair was doing something with Reach. During that time, I was given a tour of the hospital, specifically the state-of-the-art maternity ward. I don't claim to be the best at following rules…" Her eyes track to mine, and a small quirk of her mouth hints at a smile. "I evaded my tour guide and saw things I wasn't supposed to see. That's why they made me leave Jezero. They knew that I understood things when I pulled that out of the wall in the embassy."

An advisor holds the small black bead out in his hand. The king made good on his promise to remove it from the laundry. Several other advisors come close, inspecting.

"What is it?" a few ask.

"It's an espionage device, but it's more advanced than anything we've ever seen."

"How?" another advisor asks.

"We believe this is directly connected to the brain of a Jezero agent. It's unclear exactly how it works, but this technology makes it impossible to interfere with their espionage devices without them knowing."

Llama grimaces. "That wasn't all I saw." Every head turns to her. "I pulled that out of the embassy, but what was concerning was what I saw in the maternity ward. I noticed a bead thing, like this, embedded in the wall there. But I was shown their new technology, which they were proud of. It creates things." The air in the room is still, everyone collectively holding their breath while they wait for Llama's answer. "They are going to manufacture babies—and they have a plan for defective ones."

25

Once, long ago, there was a massive organism of fungi on Earth. Dr. Geo showed me when we were studying different landscapes. Individual stalks connected by roots, existing as part of a whole. The collective response of the advisors of Souterraine reminds me of this fungus. Each individual seems to be connected to the others, like they've been given some sort of telepathic message through a root system, because each individual advisor makes the same face at the same time.

First, their eyes widen, then their mouths hang open.

"B—babies?" a woman advisor stutters.

The queen balks, taking a step forward and then two steps back. With clenched fists at her side, the Queen of Souterraine who, moments ago, betrothed Llama and me, asks in a voice so low that I would not have been able to hear it if it wasn't for the silence in the room, "What else did you find out?"

Llama says, "The doctor giving the tour found me after I wandered into the place they didn't want me to see. He was...upset. As was Percy."

Again, the entire organism seems to be controlling the individuals because each person collectively shudders. The king's eyes have hardened, and though I've tried to avoid making eye contact with him since my incident with him and Llama, I meet his steel eyes. "This—*this* is what you want to unite Souterraine to by *marriage?*"

I blink. I've been a lot of things in my life: half-alien, half-Citizen, promising young scientist, unknowing figurehead of a Resistance movement, son of the President of Jezero Colony. But I'm not really part of Jezero Colony. I'm certainly not a part of decisions to hide 'defective' people away.

Before I can speak in my own defense, the queen interrupts. "Alfred." Her sharp tone turns the king's face sheepish.

"It's just, he's one of them. And they have always been obsessed with the newest technology, the latest things, the most currency. It's so *different* from our way of life. How could someone with roots in Souterraine be happy with someone who has roots in Jezero?"

"I hardly think my happiness is worth worrying over right now," Llama interrupts. "They are *proud* of the technology. They wanted to show me that they would be manufacturing people. They told me it was going to be in a testing phase soon, that they would begin creating, and it would allow…" She closes her eyes. "More economic freedom and productivity for their women if they didn't have to actually carry the children." Llama's voice cracks, and her hands rub her stomach where a pregnant woman would carry a baby. One by one, each woman in the room does the same, no matter their age. Llama's whisper floats into the air amid the crackle of the fire. "What can be done to stop them?"

"That, my dear," the queen says softly, "is the question." She claps her hands together and turns to the advisors. "We have much to think about now. Would Elaina please begin the process of gathering more intel on this? There's quite a bit of thinking we need to understand behind their decision to have this technology, and also to show it to Llama when they knew she was coming here."

A wiry woman in a dark red dress with a pile of curly brown hair atop her head slips from the room. Phil steps forward after she leaves.

"Yes, Phil?"

"It came to my attention earlier today that Reach and Llama are unaware of the other…entities on Earth. I think it might be best to enlighten them."

The queen purses her lips. "Ah, yes. Thank you for reminding us, Phil. Have you had a moment to collect the reports from the experiential learning sessions?"

"Not yet, Queen Eleanore." Phil's eyes remain downcast slightly as his shoulders slump.

"Please, don't worry about it, Phil. Truly, you do so much for the future of Souterraine." Queen Eleanore smiles softly at him, then turns her attention to a different advisor. This man, with close-cropped black hair, large eyes, and the same bronze skin as the queen, steps forward.

"Go ahead, Lyle," the queen permits.

Lyle turns golden eyes on me, then Llama. "Reach, Llama." He inclines his head toward us. "I understand you are unaware of other entities on Earth. That would imply all you know about is the continent in which Nation resides. Would that be correct?"

Llama looks at me. Pieces of information shuffle through my mind at a rapid pace. Phil told me there was more to Earth, but I can't figure out how that's possible. I stand there, confused, as all the things I know about Earth fly through my brain.

"Nation, which resides on the continent formerly known as North America, is not the only population center," Lyle says. "I am curious, what were you told regarding other peoples? How could they hide other continents from you?"

I'm still unable to form words, but now I understand the implications of Nation's geographical secrecy. I understand that *this* new information changes the chess game we've been playing.

"Do you play chess?" Llama asks, startling my mind out of its spiral and back into the present.

Lyle looks slightly taken aback. "We are aware of the game, yes. But it hasn't been very popular in Souterraine. I think that's more of a Jezero type of game."

Well that tracks.

I regain my speech. "Chess is about game theory. Thinking about how your move impacts your opponent, and how your opponent will look for weaknesses in your moves. Nation kept all geographical information and maps classified. When we learned map reading skills in school, they were *practice* maps, which were falsified."

A collective hum sounds as the advisors all consider my words.

Lyle speaks up again. "So you are unaware of the vast...continents Earth is home to?"

I think he's made the point a few times now. "Yes." My voice is razor-sharp. "The Three Powers of Nation do not believe in letting their people know the geographical features of Nation, let alone anywhere else. They want absolute power, and geographical secrecy is one way they maintain it."

"Yes, I see. I'm just wondering what I need to show you."

My blood boils. Llama seems to sense it, too, because she places a hand on my arm, effectively grounding me and reminding me not to snap.

"We need to know *everything* you know about Earth, Lyle." How her voice can be so calm is beyond me. But then again, Llama wasn't as quick to understand game theory as me. She seems to have gotten better at it lately though. And she's right, we need to know everything. Every piece of information can be the difference between the Resistance movement's success or failure.

"So, you do not know anything about the landmasses on Earth, let alone the people?"

"All we know, Lyle," Llama says with an authority that sounds eerily like Queen Eleanore's, "is Nation. And even then, what we know is bound to be different from what you do."

King Alfred's bushy eyebrows furrow. "I think this meeting is adjourned. Lyle, Phil, will you please begin a course for Princess Llama and Reach? Phil, you can collect the experiential learning reports in a month. I doubt we'll have the pleasure of Reach's company that long since he's set on vengeance, so a delay won't matter much." The sarcasm drips from his voice, but I can't figure out why he said that. Or why he looks at me with sadness in his eyes and then shifts away. "We'd appreciate your reports and insight into these matters by the end of tomorrow."

"Yes, Your Majesty," Phil, Lyle, and the other advisors respond in kind. The advisors all file out of the room, a few of them stopping to chat with Queen Eleanore and King Alfred. Everyone skirts around Llama and me. There's a tension in the room that I can't understand.

Llama's hand falls off my arm, but as I'm watching the plethora of advisors leave, she reaches up and plants a soft kiss on my cheek. I blink, surprised at her boldness in front of the king, and look down at her.

"Sorry," she whispers. "It's just that you looked so sad. And, I guess we're…betrothed now?"

"Llama," I whisper back. "I…don't understand the game here."

"Me neither, Reach, but they have the resources to get us back to Earth. Let's play their game a little longer. I can *help* here. It's *good* here. Maybe we can do something good for Mars and Earth."

The way her eyes focus off into the distance is a dead giveaway for the fact that she has something specific in mind.

"What do you want to do, Llama?" I can't help how her name rolls off my tongue like a caress. It's so easy to say. She's been so different here. She's happy, and she deserves to be a princess. All her struggles on Earth, the broken girl she's been, the way she's tried so hard to beat Nation at their own game and failed, and yet she's here, working with me to beat them yet again.

I'm staring hard into her eyes when she answers, "The king is right. I want vengeance. I want to take down Jezero, and I want to take down Nation."

26

THE KING ESCORTS Llama from the advisory room. He gives me an appraising look before offering her his arm and asking her to come see the royal gardens. The Queen of Souterraine approaches me, a hard glint in her eyes. The black cat slides in through the open door and trails at her feet.

"Do you know what we're going to ask of you?" she says, her voice rising and falling like waves.

"In addition to marrying Llama?" I retort.

"Is that really such a hardship?" she counters.

I can't respond to that. I do like Llama. But I don't appreciate the choice being made for me.

"Llama and I have a complicated history together."

"So you've said." The queen's eyebrow arches into a sharp carat. "Care to enlighten me?"

"There are some..." I think about what I need to share. "Trust issues there."

"Trust of *you*, or trust of *her*?"

I have to give her credit, she's astute. I don't want to explain what Llama did. I also don't want to taint her only living relative's opinion of her, so I grit my teeth and shake my head. "It doesn't matter really, does it?"

The queen smiles. "No, Reach. The past doesn't matter nearly as much as the future. Do you know what you'd like your future to entail?"

I shrug. I have a broad idea, but it's not hashed out into a workable plan yet. "I think so, but…"

"You need us to achieve your goals, I think. And we need you. We have to help each other, Reach. Although, I understand your hesitations. We have shown you who we are. We don't have things to hide. We aren't hiding continents or manufacturing babies. We don't send children to space to further our interests and hope that they die out there. We aren't obsessed with succession laws and power. Reach"—she puts her hand on my shoulder—"we need to work together. Please, don't fight us. I promise we know the pieces of the puzzle that will make things better here on Mars. In return, you'll get help from Souterraine, and probably Jezero, in making things better on Earth."

The Queen of Souterraine is shrewd. I scratch my ear, because I suddenly feel itchy all over. Llama just told me she wants what the Queen of Souterraine is implying. I don't have a choice. I'm outnumbered. "What do you need me to do?"

"First, you need to learn everything you can about Earth from our perspective. It will be enlightening. Then, we're going to stop Jezero from breaking the Code of Martian Law, and I suspect you'd like to return to Earth with assistance for overthrowing the government of Nation?"

I blink and nod. "Yeah. That sounds like our mission. The last part, that is. Learning about Earth and overthrowing Jezero is…not part of our mission."

"Well, now it is," Queen Eleanore replies cooly. "When would you like to be married?"

I cough. "Could we…wait a while?"

"Ahh. I see those trust issues haven't been resolved, and it seems to be my granddaughter who is untrustworthy. Well, Reach, my advice would be to not kiss someone until you trust them fully. There's danger in a kiss. A kiss is a wordless, but very real promise. It means something —something beautiful when done with respect and care— but it's also a way to usher in pain. Yes, we can wait, but you'll need to have a formal engagement ceremony before you return to Jezero. The only way Llama can ever return there is if she's protected under diplomatic sanctions."

The queen gathers her skirts and sweeps from the room in a dramatic fashion, leaving me to wonder about the future.

When I see Llama next, she's wearing a crown of twisted branches interlaced with soft pink flowers and white ribbons. She sits next to Pippa on a window seat in the library. Late afternoon sunlight streams in, and dust motes float in the air. Llama's hair is lighter than before, and her skin is beginning to take on a bronze tone, like Queen Eleanore's.

My breath catches when I see what she's doing with Pippa. She's holding chess pieces.

"The horse," Llama says, and I snicker at the wrong name, "can only move in an L-shape."

"Why?" Pippa asks, turning the white knight over in her hands. "I think it should move anywhere it wants."

I step closer and observe them, both with twisted branch crowns upon their heads, close enough in age to be sisters, although Pippa is technically Llama's aunt.

I stand just to the side of them before I speak. "That would make chess a very difficult game to play."

Llama jumps and puts a hand to her heart, her light brown dress billowing out around her feet. "Reach!" she shrieks. "You scared me!"

Pippa jumps up. "You didn't scare me!" She still has long pauses between her words, but she smiles, proud of her reaction to my words.

"It would take more to scare you, wouldn't it, Princess Pippa?"

She considers for a moment. "Yeah." Then she brandishes the knight at me. "Why only move… some ways?"

"It's the rules of the game. It wouldn't be a real game if there weren't rules."

She takes this into consideration.

My gaze shifts back to Llama, who is watching me, her eyes full of adoration, but she lowers her gaze as soon as I meet hers. I take the knight from Pippa's hands. "May I?" Pippa nods. "Is there a board here?"

Llama extracts the chess board from where she placed it and leans against the wall. I notice a box with the rest of the pieces behind her. She holds it out and I take it from her, her fingers grazing mine as I grasp the board. My eyes are fixed on her as she leans forward slightly at the physical contact.

"You are…in love?" Pippa asks.

Llama and I both startle. I don't know how to answer Pippa, but the simplest answer would be to agree. Love or not, I know Llama and she knows me. We're going to be betrothed, married, unionized…or something. Our futures are intertwined regardless.

"Yeah," I say.

Llama's eyes widen as she bites her lip.

Pippa nods in agreement. "Good." She slides off the bench and scampers out of the room, leaving Llama and me alone. The door slams shut, and suddenly Llama launches herself into my arms.

"I didn't know…" She sobs. "That you…" More sobs. "Love me."

I place my thumb on the corner of her eyes, the queen's warning against kissing Llama without total trust blaring in my ears. But I *do* love Llama. And if I'm going to marry her and do what I need to do for this mission, then I need to love her. Understanding clicks in my mind. Llama has wanted love her entire life. *Has she ever heard someone say I love you and had it directed at her?*

The depth of emotion in her eyes, the way she has interacted with the people here, her grit and determination…they are all admirable qualities, but they don't make me love her. I start to say the words, words I understand she has been longing to hear her entire life, but stop myself. I can't lie to her. I can't. I won't do it. She deserves more than a lie from me.

Instead, I wipe the tears away and smile down at her before pulling her into a hug. She places her cheek against my chest, right over my heart, and closes her eyes. I kiss the top of her head on impulse.

"So, why are *you* teaching Pippa chess, Llama?" I ask, pulling back and looking into her eyes with amusement.

"I'm trying to understand the game, Reach. But I'm still terrible at it."

"I think we have some time. Should we play?"

Llama's lips turn upward in a smile as she sits on the window seat and pats the spot next to her. I place the board in between us and settle on the cushion.

"I really wanted you to love me, Reach."

I swallow. I want that too. And that's when I realize what's wrong with Souterraine, with this whole marriage business: they are using Llama and me.

Will we ever truly be free?

27

Llama's new crown comes with an announcement made to all of Souterraine in the clover field. I slept fitfully, tossing and turning as I considered what to tell Queen Eleanore about using Llama. I stifle a yawn just as Phil finds me. I'm standing in the shadows of the castle with a good view of the king, queen, Pippa, and Llama, who are seated on a raised platform in the middle of the clover field.

"How are you, Reach?" Phil asks. "You ready for this?"

I chew my bottom lip. "Ready for what, exactly? Do you know what they're doing today? I thought it was introducing Llama as Princess Llama."

Phil flushes. "No one told you?"

"Told me what—"

But the microphone-enhanced voices of the king and queen calling everyone to order drown out my question.

Phil puts a hand on my shoulder and grimaces as if to prepare me for what's coming.

"Today," the king declares, "we want to share our joy with all of Souterraine."

"Many of you remember Prince Alec," the queen says, her voice wavering. There's a hush and a rustle as everyone who is able to stoops and touches the ground at the mention of the prince's name.

The king takes over. "Prince Alec was lost in the cosmos, lost on Earth, but his efforts to learn about Earth were not in vain."

Queen Eleanore gestures to Llama, who comes and stands in between the monarchs.

The king continues. "Prince Alec gave us a gift, one we did not know of until recently. And we have to thank several unlikely subjects for bringing this gift to our attention. The Jezero Colony authorities first made the connection and alerted us. Our guest, Reach, corroborates the story."

The queen grasps Llama's hand. "People of Souterraine, I present to you our granddaughter, Earth-born daughter of Prince Alec, Princess Llama."

The advisors had all been aware of Llama's heritage, but this assembly is for the general populace. A small rumble and then applause breaks out in waves across the crowd assembled on the clover field.

"Phil?" I elbow him. He looks over with surprise. "Is this the entire population of Souterraine?"

"No, but it's close."

I survey the crowd. The field is packed, but it's full of women, children, and older men. Although not entirely absent, the number of middle-aged men in the group is significantly lower than the number of middle-aged women.

"Where are all the middle-aged men?"

Phil's shoulders slump. "A lot of things have gone wrong for Souterraine. A disease that affected only the men thirty years ago, and then, of course, the ones that left for life in Jezero after Prince Alec didn't return. There were many who thought that Souterraine would fall without a succession plan in place, and Pippa's condition didn't inspire confidence in the future..."

The applause stops and the queen steps closer to the people. She appears to be teetering on the edge of the platform. "It gives us great pleasure to announce that our granddaughter, Princess Llama, will unite Souterraine and Jezero colonies through marriage when her wedding to our guest, Reach, takes place. Reach is the Earth-born son of Jezero's President McAllistair. Reach, where are you?"

Phil signals to her, pointing at me. I glare at him. There is no applause at my name, only a dull hum, like bees preparing to swarm. The queen motions me to the platform. I trudge through the clover as nearly the entire population of Souterraine watches my every move. I'm aware of the animosity between the two colonies. I'm aware of the tension that swept through the crowd like a derecho—a straight-line wind, dangerous and ready to destroy.

I climb the steps to the platform. Llama must have been given instructions because she greets me with a hug and a kiss on my cheek. "Smile," she hisses through clenched teeth as she slips her hand in mine.

I let her lead me to the front of the stage, where I now stand next to the King of Souterraine. He looks down at me disapprovingly. The population of Souterraine can all see how he feels about me. This is *not* helping my case.

I fix him back with a glare. Probably not the best thing to do, but his response is unexpected.

He smiles and addresses the crowd. "Remember, dear people, that Reach might have heritage in Jezero, but he is Earth-born. He is *not* our enemy. We have long memories on Mars, but Reach has had nothing to do with the Jezero-Souterraine feud. We look forward to celebrating Reach and Princess Llama's formal engagement ceremony at the Feast of Trees. Until then, we must work and be gracious to our guest, and remember he returned *our princess* to us."

The crowd roars and Llama waves, her free hand cupped slightly as she rotates her wrist from side to side, smiling. I don't smile. Instead, I find myself gritting my teeth under the scrutiny of thousands of eyes and the awareness that I'm going to be formally engaged in a ceremony, and not of my own choosing.

Llama finds me in the library after the assembly. It's my favorite room. The black cat that usually shadows the queen meows from atop a stack of books on the window seat next to me. I stroke its fur tentatively, and it thrums with a purr.

When Llama finds me, she's not alone. Pippa is with her too. Pippa is, I believe, a year or two older than Llama, but Pippa has formed an attachment and follows Llama around. It's rather endearing—or would be, if I didn't need to talk to Llama privately.

"Hi," Llama says, approaching me slowly and looking at the cat with a raised brow.

"Hi." Words are not working right now.

"That was a lot today, right?" There's a lost look in her eyes, and somehow it makes her even more beautiful. But they're using her. And I can't do that. If I marry her, then I'm using her too. I can like her, maybe even love her, but I can't *use* her.

I make up my mind to tell the Queen of Souterraine 'No' to the entire scheme.

Pippa slides across the floor. "Hi, Reach. Hi, Shadow," she says before grabbing my hand.

I look at Llama, surprised by the familiarity, but Llama just shrugs and gives a half smile.

"Come on," Pippa says, joining her other hand with Llama's and pulling the two of us out of the library after her. "Outside." The cat hops off the stack of books and presses its nose into my hand before stalking away. "Shadow likes you."

I'm glad to know the cat's name, even if it feels strange to have an animal want my attention.

One advantage of Pippa's determination to get us out of the castle is that Llama and I learn new routes around the castle. She leads us up a staircase, through a hallway, and down another staircase. She opens what I think is a broom closet, but is actually a concealed staircase. That would be startling enough, but this staircase doesn't have steps. It's a slide.

Pippa plops down on the slide and pats the slide behind her in recurring staccato taps. Llama sits down with no hesitation. I wait. I don't like not knowing where we're going.

"Reach," Llama whispers. "It's ok. You can come down with us. Pippa, you know where you're going, right?"

Pippa pushes off with Llama holding onto her middle and yells, "OUTSIDE!"

I'm turned around in the castle after Pippa's tour, and though I could go back and retrace my steps, I worry about finding Llama again. I need to tell her that I can't do this. That I respect her too much to use her.

I sit down on the slide, and my gut clenches as I realize that my mistrust of Pippa is foolish. I have been lied to and manipulated more than I can count, but Pippa won't do that. What I actually want is to have fun, and there's a slide here.

I take a breath and shove off, air whistling past my cheeks as I descend.

I emerge, blinking and sneezing in a heap of clover flowers at the foot of the slide. I'm outside, just like Pippa said.

28

I slip into my bed for the night when a soft knock sounds on the door. At first, I think I've imagined it, so I lie still, listening. When it comes again, I know someone's there. And I'm sure it's Llama.

I get up. Souterraine provided sleeping clothes, which I'm grateful for. A soft white shirt and long pants that aren't quite red but somehow still invoke the color of the rock cover my limbs. I tread to the door and open it a crack.

Llama stands there. Just as I thought.

"What are you doing?" I ask.

She slides past me and turns, her eyes blazing. "I came to ask what's wrong with you," she hisses.

I scrub my palm down the side of my face. I'm too tired for this. "What do you mean?"

"Today you said you loved me, but then at the assembly, and after, you seemed different. Like something was—I don't know—*bothering* you."

"Llama," I hedge, but I can't repeat her name, so I stumble into the next best hedge I can find. "It's really fast."

She blows out an *oh*.

"I…we…we are being forced into this." Llama's brows draw together as the skin above her nose wrinkles, and she tilts her head. "I mean, we should get to decide, right?"

"I guess…but Reach, when have we ever decided *anything*?" I stop and consider the question. It's loaded, but it's also…true. "Reach, what do you want?" She asks it so softly it sounds like the rustle of wind through the trees.

"I don't…I don't really know," I whisper back, and I hate the look my words bring to her face.

"So you don't love me?"

"That's not…I didn't…I do…I don't…" Llama's eyes are wide, her head hanging. I can't stop myself. I step to her and lift her chin. Then I place a light kiss on her cheek. "It's too fast for me, Llama."

She nods, pain, understanding, and something else flashing across her features. "I was hoping I'd been forgiven. But that's not…-possible." She turns on her heel and begins to stride from the room.

"Wait, Llama, please." She stops. "I'm going to tell Queen Eleanore I can't do the formal ceremony in a week. But that doesn't mean we can't…be together. It just means I can't…It's too fast. And they're…"

"They're what, Reach?" Her hands ball into fists at her sides. "Kind? Good? Gracious? Showing us care? Willing to help us with getting back to Earth and take down Nation and Jezero too?"

The attachment she has formed to Souterraine in such a short time makes it impossible for me to say the next words, so I don't. Instead, I lean down and peck her cheek. "Good night, Llama."

She doesn't respond except to stalk out the door without even glancing over her shoulder at me. The air is ten degrees colder when she leaves.

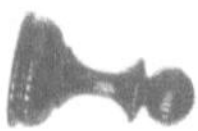

After Llama's midnight visit, my resolve is strengthened. I have to find Queen Eleanore. My stomach rumbles, but I can't delay, even though the delectable smells make me pause by the entrance to the kitchen. This is more important. Llama is more important. The castle is palatial, and I have no idea where the queen might be. This is a problem.

Pippa skips through the hallway, pausing when she sees me by the door. *Inspiration, thy name is Pippa.*

"Hi, Pippa!" She narrows her eyes and suspicion clouds her face. I have never been cheery with her, and my greeting was distinctly cheerful. "Could you help me find Queen Eleanore?"

Pippa stands there, as still as a statue. I tack on the word "please?" and she bolts down the hallway. I don't know if she's helping me or running away, so I take off at a sprint after her. She's fast, twisting and turning around corners, but thankfully I haven't lost all my fast twitch muscles from my sojourn through space.

Pippa rounds a corner and stops. I can't stop in time and end up plowing into both Pippa and Queen Eleanore.

The two royals topple to the floor as I bounce backward and collide with the wall.

"Pippa!" the Queen of Souterraine chastises from the floor. "Princesses do *not* run around corners. Princesses *slow* down around corners."

I'm panting from my run but immediately feel bad. This is my fault. "Sorry." My breaths are labored. "It's my fault."

The queen props herself up on her elbows and disentangles her skirts from Pippa's legs. Pippa pops up, unfazed. By the time the queen is on her feet, a glint of humor sparkles in her eyes. "Really, Reach. How is my daughter crashing into me, which is a daily occurrence, your fault?"

"I asked her where to find you. I said it was important, but I didn't mean to run."

"Ahh. Perhaps you should have clarified that."

Pippa watches the exchange with interest. "I was fast."

The queen turns eyes that are full of love on Pippa. "Yes, darling. You are very fast. Today is a school day, so please head to school. Phil is waiting for you. I think you're learning about deciduous trees this week."

Pippa's eyes light up at the mention of deciduous trees. She takes off at a run again. The queen raises her voice just before Pippa turns the corner. "Princesses *slow* down at the corners." Pippa slows for a visible beat and then is gone. Queen Eleanore looks back at me, her eyes shining with amusement. "She isn't going to slow down. Now, Reach, what is so important?"

The concern in her gaze shows she's shrewd, but she's not unkind. I know I can tell her. I know I can trust her. At the same time, I don't want to disappoint her. *Scratch that thought.* I don't want to disappoint Llama, and marrying her when I don't trust her fully…I don't want to use her.

I meet the queen's eyes with resolve. "I can't marry Llama."

"Is it the trust issue you mentioned?"

"No." *Yes*, but I can't tell her that. I'm curt and entirely less respectful than I ought to be, but I can't show weakness.

"What is it, then? I've been married for over thirty-six years. I know something about it."

"If I marry Llama here, I'm letting you use her."

The silence is so profound that I can't look at Queen Eleanore anymore. I shift my face away, then mutter, "I'd be using her too."

The queen steps into my space, her lengthy fingers tilting my chin up to look at her. "You have a conscience." I don't reply. "You understand, don't you, what love is? What love requires?" She waits patiently.

"Not really." *What is love?*

"Love is to want good for the other. Love is to protect, to honor, to defend. Love is to build up. Love is to sacrifice for the good of another." I stare at her blankly. "Reach. The very fact that you are concerned that Llama is being used, that you might be using her if you do this, is proof of your love."

I swallow hard and the whole truth spills out. "But I can't trust her."

"There are many marriages that have had to work at trust. It's not easy."

"She used me, and my mother was sentenced to death because of her." The words tumble out, and I stare at the air between me and the queen in horror.

The queen's eyes narrow, and she murmurs, "And they still sent the *two* of you to space. Together?"

I shrug, because obviously they did.

"What exactly happened?"

I don't particularly want to rehash this, but the queen did say she's an expert on marriage at this point, and I do really find Llama attractive, and there is a *rightness* about her and me. "Could we talk about this someplace more private?"

The queen glances around the hallway. "Of course." She takes a few steps. "We can go to my thinking gardens. The staff has an order not to disturb me there."

She leads the way through the building and out into the clover field. On a hill to the side of the castle a stand of trees casts long shadows across the ground. The trees are much closer than I'd originally estimated. The light and the curve of the dome must contribute to my depth perception being off.

We say nothing to each other the entire way to the gardens, but when I step inside the grove of trees, I am amazed. I let out an audible hum of appreciation.

Queen Eleanore turns to me and smiles. "It is lovely in here, isn't it?" I nod, my eyes raking in the greenery and the spots of colorful flowers that grow in the light. "Now, you can be assured this conversation is private. Please, Reach. Tell me." Her hand grasps my arm lightly, and she propels us over to a bench. She does it in such a way that if anyone looked at us, they'd think I was being courteous. She's a genius.

I wait for her pale yellow skirts to settle before sitting beside her on the bench. "Llama's family was betrayed by a woman known as Enforce back in Nation. Enforce was who…killed her parents." The queen says nothing, but purses her lips. "Enforce was named Llama's guardian by Llama's mother. Anyways. This is a lot. Maybe I shouldn't…"

"No, Reach," Queen Eleanore says. "You should tell me. But the history of how Alec died is history. I need to understand what happened between *you and her*. I need to understand your inability to trust her."

"Uh." My mind spins. "Enforce convinced Llama to get close to me romantically, and then to get incriminating information against my mother."

"Why?" The single word rings out.

"Because Llama wanted to get her mother out of Pen 1 in Nation. Her mother—she'd become…mentally unstable while in prison for years. Enforce agreed to let her out. But she didn't say how. Llama's mother was already dead."

The queen gives no sign of any emotion at my words except for the tiniest flare of her nostrils.

"So this…Enforce. She is a manipulator?"

"Yes."

"And Llama was manipulated?"

"Yes."

"And what happened to your mother?"

"She escaped. There was an incident when I wouldn't sign the papers saying I renounced my blood relation to her. She knew she was committing treason for years, and she'd probably be executed, but she had enough of a plan to escape."

"And where is she?"

"I don't know. They sent us to space pretty much right away after that."

"Nation is poorly governed." The words are surprisingly impassioned. "Reach. Llama was a girl searching for an opportunity to have a family. She has that here now. She won't betray you again."

"How can you be sure?"

"Because she still carries the guilt of it. I suspect you've forgiven her?"

"I…I think so."

"I know you have. You also know that I already had this conversation with Llama?"

I stare at the queen, mouth agape. "You did?"

"More or less. She told me she couldn't marry you because she already used you, then told me a little bit more in detail about how she betrayed you to someone who has a long history of betrayal and psychological abuse. I told her to look for signs you loved her because they were there, plain as day to anyone who looked closely. It's probably why Enforce concocted this plan."

My mind is stuck on a thought the way a cactus needle sticks to a fiber. "What signs?"

"Self-sacrifice for the other, kindness, friendship, romantic gestures…saying the word love… kissing…" She stops and winks at me. I flush. "Llama cares very deeply about you, Reach. And it's clear you care very deeply about her. You do not have to do anything you aren't ready for, but you should know that marrying Llama is the most efficient way to help with three unique objectives."

"What are the objectives?"

"Stop Jezero from manufacturing lifeforms that will deplete our resources faster and go against the primary Martian technology treaties." She ticks up her pointer finger. "Unite Jezero and Souterraine, which stops a war no one can win." The third finger rises. "Return to Earth with the support of two colonies who can help you overthrow Nation."

"You really think that me marrying Llama will result in…all that?"

"Yes, Reach." She smiles. "Not only are you deserving of happiness, but you also clearly have a mission. I'm fairly accomplished at game theory myself, although no one here plays chess the way you do. I can assure you, you are not using Llama. No one here wants to *use* someone in that way. But there is a way to further our objectives, where everyone wins. Including you and Llama. I don't think you've experienced that before. You don't have to marry her, but it would be very helpful to two colonies—and two planets—if you did." The queen stands, her skirts billowing out behind her. "Think about it, Reach. You'll have plenty of time on your own to consider. We'll make sure you have the time and space you need." She hums as she begins to stroll away, but stops and bends over a large purple flower. Her peace and countenance and leadership make me feel confident in myself.

Before I can overthink it, I call out, "Queen Eleanore. I'll do it. I'll marry Llama, but not right now. I think just an engagement for now."

"Excellent." The queen raises from her crouched position. She snaps the flower off and brings it to me. "Now, if you'll excuse me, I have a formal engagement ceremony to plan for my granddaughter."

29

Tᴿᵁᴱ ᵀᴼ ᵀᴴᴱ queen's word, I'm left to my own devices for the next week. It's excruciating. I miss Llama. I'm not sure if the queen planned to make me miss her, but the preparations for the Feast of Trees are underway everywhere in the colony. As soon as I agreed, the queen launched into planning mode. She spent hours and hours with Llama as different artisans traipsed a well-worn path across the clover.

I found myself wandering around Souterraine. Inexplicably, I would meander to the school. The students would ask me questions at first, but then I just sat and listened and learned. On the third day of attending the morning learning, Phil invites me to tour Souterraine. I learn that Souterraine is massive, and it's housed in lava tubes that make it hard to chart, but effective for zones. The network of lava tubes extends for miles, and is used to grow crops. There is an animal-growth zone, where animals are raised for their fur, meat, or other products, like milk and cheese. Souterraine only believes in the humane treatment of animals, so there are not nearly enough animals for everyone to be wasteful. Meat dishes are served only on special feasts, for medical purposes, and some are raised for Jezero. The population of Souterraine consumes a plant-focused diet. It's so much more palatable than the space rations Llama and I subsisted on that I didn't notice the lack of meat until Phil explained the reasoning.

Phil also gives me a small history lesson about Souterraine and Jezero. Tensions between the two colonies have been high since the beginning. Phil's role as a junior advisor is helpful. He sees things—patterns—that most people don't. He's worked with the king and queen, and delayed a full-out war despite simmering frustrations between the Jerezo and Souterraine. It's hard to believe Souterraine could have tension when you stare across an idyllic wheat field, but the anger at being forced to produce for Jezero is evident if you listen to the workers. Grumbles and scowls at the name of Jezero, or McAllistair, aren't uncommon. It would seem that Greg McAllistair isn't the most unliked person on Mars. That distinction belongs to his friend, Percy McAllistair. I can't say I'm surprised. I didn't like him much either.

Today, I finished touring the pea fields with Phil. Peas contain a significant amount of protein, so this is a crop grown to its maximum capacity. But I need to hurry back to the castle, because this morning I found a note tacked to my bedroom door. In an elegant script that was definitely *not* Llama's were the words 'geography in the kitchen today, four p.m.'

Bernard provided a clock when I mentioned feeling disconcerted about the time earlier in the week. I check it as I fish the note out of my pocket and hold it in my hand. It's 3:47, just enough time to shower and change before meeting whoever wrote that note.

When I arrive in the kitchen at 3:52, I am greeted by Lyle and a woman I vaguely recognize from the advisors meeting.

"Glad you're here," the woman says in a clipped voice. "I'm Etta. I believe you know Lyle."

I grunt. "Yes."

"Good. We're here to discuss what we know about Earth," Etta says.

I notice Lyle takes a secondary role in this conversation. Etta is also quite a bit older, with a head of pure white hair and wrinkles on her skin.

"Shall we?" She proceeds into the kitchen and then into the informal dining room, where maps are spread across the surface and books stacked on the chairs. There are four chairs available, so I sit in one after Etta and Lyle take their places.

"This," Etta says, "is Earth and its landmasses, many of which are populous."

Lyle nods in agreement. "This"—he points with a long stick to a landmass on the far left of the map—"is Nation. Do you have any knowledge of the other landmasses?"

I stare hard at the map. "No. Maps are highly classified in Nation. But I don't understand why because there's nothing on the map even remotely close to Nation."

A look of glee briefly passes over Lyle's face. He launches into an explanation. "The Scientific Revolution was preceded by natural disasters the world had never seen. These disasters shifted the landscape of the population centers. Just before the Scientific Revolution, the ruling powers of the world decided to shift the way the globe was organized into quadrants. A Northwest, Southwest, Northeast, and Southeast quadrant." He places sticks on the unfurled paper map, denoting the quadrants. "This new quadrant system, coupled with the disasters, led the country that would become Nation to be isolated from the others. Truthfully, each quadrant was already isolated and deep in disaster cleanup. Nation's original leadership pulled away from treaties with other countries and opted to keep their scientific advances to themselves. Instead of sharing the limited resources they had, Nation kept everything secret. This may have been a move of self-preservation. The turmoil of natural disasters weakened each of the quadrants and made for instability. As time passed, the landmasses continued shifting, and natural disasters continued to occur. Eventually, the Southwest quadrant became inhabitable, leaving Nation as the only populated landmass on this side of the prime meridian line."

I scrub a hand over my head. My scalp tingles and itches. "How many populated landmasses are there now?"

"Three," Etta supplies. She places a golden maple leaf on Nation, on the Northeast and Southeast quadrant landmass. The Southwest quadrant is left blank.

"Do the other landmasses have names?"

"Not that we're aware of," Lyle answers. "But we know from our technology that there are population centers on these three landmasses." Etta unfurls another map. This one is clear, and she places it on top of the first map. "This is the historical map of the landmasses of Earth. Before the Scientific Revolution."

I stare at it. The landmasses are significantly larger, and much more connected. It's easy to see how, after the disasters, Nation kept itself isolated. There's simply no one close by from a geographical perspective.

"What does it mean?" Etta asks.

I rub the pad of my finger along the contour lines of Nation's continent. "I'm not sure yet," I answer honestly. "It's a lot to take in." My finger continues tracing when a thought bludgeons its way out of my mouth. "Are the other places...like Nation?"

Etta's mouth twitches. "We don't know. Our technology has only been able to detect population centers and human activity from afar. We don't have an understanding of the inner workings of the other places. We only know what we know about Nation because of Prince Alec." Her mouth twitches again. "And you."

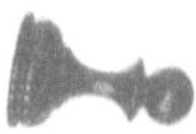

The queen glides into the kitchen after I've finished my evening meal. "Reach." She bobs her head and studies me. "We need to discuss the protocol for tomorrow."

The wooden spoon clatters into the empty bowl.

"Don't worry." The queen puts a gentle hand on my shoulder. "There's ceremonial clothing you'll need to wear. Mostly, you wait for Llama. Since she's the royal here, she plays a much bigger part in all this. You'll need to respond to the questions she asks with *respect*. The Feast of Trees is very important to our colony. I'll make sure

Alfred is with you tomorrow morning to assist with the clothing. That's the most complicated part of it all."

"Mama!" Pippa rushes through the door. "Shadow got out!"

"Oh dear." The queen sighs. "Reach, I need to go collect my cat. He has a propensity to climb trees. Hopefully I can get him before he reaches the grove. And the night before the Feast too!"

She rushes away, leaving me with more questions than answers.

What am I responding to?

How do I wear the ceremonial clothing?

And *why do I need the king with me tomorrow?*

PART 3

The Feast of Trees— my engagement ceremony day— is marked by several notable changes to the colony of Souterraine. The lights that power the colony have different settings designed to mimic Earth's natural day and night rhythms. Thus far I have seen dawn, daylight, dusk, and nighttime. What I have not seen yet is feast lighting.

The whole domed ceiling of the cavern is typically blue during the day and an inky black at night. It's artificial, but it feels real. Today, the entirety of Souterraine is bathed in a light so golden, so pure, so refreshing that it's like walking around in molten honey. Even the blue of the sky has taken on a honey-colored tint. All this lighting serves to make the shadows from the trees even more impressive. It's a heady juxtaposition of dark and light.

As the future *groom*, a word that sounds shockingly like broom, I am not expected to do much. Queen Eleanore said King Alfred would assist me, but no one has given me any instructions this morning. With nothing to do and no one to answer to, I wander. Souterraine is always productive, but today it's quiet.

I find Phil sitting on a bench by the river, the water swirling by in a hazy sheen. I am amazed yet again by the terraforming genius of Souterraine. How could Greg and Percy have called them weak? They have more here than Jezero could ever understand. And yet, the ache in my chest tells me that this place isn't home. That no matter how perfect it appears, Earth is where I belong.

"The light is different," I tell Phil.

His mouth turns up in a sad smile. "Feast lighting. It's different from normal, so our bodies respond differently to the environment. It's very effective."

"I noticed." Phil scoots down the bench, and I sit. "Have you ever been to…" I can't say it. My anxiety is flaring. Having tasks helps. But I have no tasks, and it's making my stomach knot as I think about what's to come. Unknowns are always the worst.

"An engagement ceremony?" Phil asks.

I shake my head, offering agreement that *that* is what I'm asking about.

"Yes, but it's pretty easy. You answer questions, and then you eat a feast. There's dancing too. Ceremonies like this are always held in conjunction with feast days here. The Feast of Trees is the only one where royalty can celebrate a ceremony though. What do they do for engagement and marriage on Earth?"

I dig my fingernails into my palm as I clench my fist. Memories of Dr. Etiquette's class surface, and I fight to stay grounded. "In Nation, there's a unionizing process."

Phil says nothing, just looks at me. He seems to sense I need some space to process what I'm going to say.

"Nation is…corrupt." I slump a little, the knowledge that I know *nothing* about the expectations of Souterraine and this process sinking in. "And in order to be unionized, you have to go through a process of learning your place in the world as a male."

"A male, not a man?" Phil questions.

"Correct," I agree.

Phil makes a small noise.

"And in Nation, you are only allowed to match with certain

people based on your aptitude and how you can best serve Nation. It's about science, and if you can further scientific discovery. If you're a male Citizen, you can only match with a woman who shows interest in you. There's a whole system, and the female Citizens are the ones who have the first and final say." I swallow down the bile that rises from my stomach at the injustice of that system. So far, Souterraine isn't like Nation in the least, but there's always fear lurking just below the surface that I'll uncover something and the idyllic colony I've been enjoying will be just as nefarious.

I sigh. "I don't know how the Nons do it. But Llama would. I haven't asked. Honestly, Phil." He turns his eyes to me. "I'm afraid of what she'd say."

"What's a Non?"

Talking about it actually eases some of my anxiety. I'm not sure why. Maybe it's just that Phil is sitting there, listening and giving me space to say words out loud. That's a freedom I've never had. The words are almost like birds. They seem to land at my feet, but then fly away before I can catch them. I know I'll never get them back, but I also know I'll always be chasing the freedom of letting them loose.

"A Non is someone with less status than a Citizen. They aren't provided with the same quality of life as a Citizen. They live in Wards separated from the Citizens, and they do menial jobs for the good of Nation. A Citizen can have their Citizenship taken away if they don't comply with the government. If you do that, you either are executed or demoted to a Non."

"And you don't know much about Nons?"

"I only know what Llama told me." I shrug.

Phil tips his head to the side as he studies me. "Llama is a Non? How is that possible if she's with you?"

"It's complicated. The whole rebellion thing, with her parents and Enforce. She grew up in what was considered "care of the state," since her parents were gone. She was technically not an orphan, but her mother was imprisoned, so she had no one else to care for her.

The government, who oversees the Wards, selects the most academically and athletically talented orphans and gives them a chance to show their loyalty to the government. If they do, they earn Citizenship status."

"Ah." Phil nods his head as he thinks for a moment, his lips turning down and anger radiating off him. "They weaponize the hope of something better for Nons against the fear of something worse for Citizens."

I blink. I'm shocked at how he summed up all of Nation's tactics in one succinct statement. "Would you fight against that?" Impulsivity is something I have indulged in since I left Earth. I'll need to rein it in, but I don't stop myself because Phil is *angry* at Nation. He's never been there. Never been subjected to their cruelty, their schemes, their power games, and he's here, *angry* at the injustice of it all.

Phil's hands ball into fists at his side. "Here or there?"

My answer is immediate. "There."

Phil's eyes narrow as he responds. "Would you fight against that here?"

"Yes. Llama will too." I close my eyes and breathe for a moment as I let my own anger wash over me, heating my blood. Anger that Nation is broken, and anger that Jezero is broken too. Anger that there is injustice on every planet in this solar system, and possibly other planets too. "We both want to."

Phil gives a quick nod. "Good." He stands and shakes his clenched fists out before inhaling a deep breath of the cool, sweet-smelling air. "I think, future groom, that it's time to get you ready for the ceremony. Would you mind if I helped?"

Relief spreads over me, and I gladly accept his offer. Phil has been a friend here—someone I can speak with honestly. That's something I've never had before. Which means that Phil is more of a friend than I've ever had.

We walk back to the castle in silence, but it isn't uncomfortable. What *is* uncomfortable is finding the King and Queen of Souterraine standing outside of my bedroom door wearing matching scowls.

"Where have you been?" the king asks in a hiss.

Phil pops around the corner at the sound of voices, and the king and queen visibly relax.

"I went for a walk to the river." I stand a little taller under the king's scrutiny. "Big day for some of us."

His brow furrows at my smart tone, but the queen sets a hand on his arm. "We didn't give you anything to do this morning, did we?" I shake my head. "I'm sorry, Reach." She elbows the king in his midsection, and he bends forward as a huff of air and an undignified groan escapes him. "Some of us were supposed to check in on you."

The king stands erect. "I'm sorry." His tone is not contrite.

The queen gives me a meaningful look. "Overprotective grandfathers aside, Reach, your ceremonial clothes are in your room. Get dressed and meet us at the tree grove in one hour. Phil, I'm glad you're here. Would you help make sure Reach gets where he needs to be? Someone *reliable* needs to help him," she says as she stares the king in the eyes with a deep frown.

"Yes, Queen Eleanore. The maple tree?"

The queen changes her countenance and beams in response to Phil. "Oh, and one more thing. Do not open this door until Bernard knocks on it. Then you'll know it's safe." She starts to shut the door, but then in, a moment of unregal majesty, she squeals. "I can't believe we get to have an engagement today!" She pulls me into a hug. She smells like flowers and…rust. The way everything on Mars smells like oxidized iron.

When she finally releases me and shuts the door, I hear her mutter to King Alfred, "I have *told* you. You don't need to be that way with him."

"But she's my granddaughter, and I have to protect her."

"Honestly, Al…"

Their voices fade, and I'm left with Phil and a stack of odd clothes I have no idea how to wear.

Phil tends to move with purpose, and this is no different. He marches to the pile of clothing and holds up each piece. The most confusing thing about the clothes is that there are so many garments. "Bathroom first, to fix your hair. Then you'll be able to get dressed." He speaks with the command of a teacher, and I obey.

I emerge, my hair freshly combed and my face clean-shaven. Phil hands me a shirt and a pair of pants. "Base layer," he says.

I put on the shirt and pants. They are soft, made of a material that has the same reddish hue as all the other fabric I've seen on Mars, but not coarse. It's like I'm wearing air against my skin. The base layers stop in cuffs just short of my knees and elbows.

"It's so..." I think for a moment. "Light."

"Yes, because you'll be in heavy ceremonial clothes," Phil says, holding up a crimson shirt. "Buttons in the back."

I shrug on the shirt, marveling at the brightness of the color. Phil does the buttons before passing me a heavy robe. Unlike the shirt, this one is a softer, deeper red color. Maroon, maybe. It's cut like a long coat with wrist-length sleeves and pockets in the seam at the hip. There's gold trim along the edges, and the collar is stiffened to stay popped up around my ears. It's rather like a cobra's hood.

Phil holds the robe open, and I place my arms inside the sleeves. As soon as he lets go, I am dragged down by the weight.

"Why is it so heavy?" I ask.

Phil grins. "The weight of leadership, I believe. Symbolic, but also, they sew rocks into the lining."

"And I'm supposed to walk in this?"

"Yes." Phil smirks. "Can you handle the weight of leadership?"

"Lift would love this," I mutter.

"Who's Lift?"

"A…" I start to say *a friend*, but the truth is, I don't know what Lift is to me anymore. The moment I recoded the mission and left Nation's carefully constructed lies behind, I burned bridges. I have no idea if Lift would consider me a friend or an enemy if he saw me today.

I swallow down the bile rising in my throat as I think of all the people who could choose Nation and see me as a traitor. I clear my throat. "The trainer who helped Llama and me get ready for space."

"Earthlings have the strangest names," Phil replies while handing me a wide green fabric loop covered in medals. "This goes sideways across your torso."

I can't move my arms high enough with the heavy robe to get the loop on.

Phil places it over my head, then eases my left arm through it. A glance at the medals reveals they are different species of tree, die-cast in metal. The light hits the medals and shining, shimmering patches reflect off the varnished wood floor. It's beautiful in a mesmerizing way. Phil gives a curt nod. "You're ready."

He turns me to a full-length mirror standing in the corner of the room. My eyes survey my own appearance, taking in my tall stature. In these clothes, you can't tell that I'm the son of a traitor. You can't tell from the way I hold myself that I met my father and found him disappointing. I meet my eyes and see a hardness there. A determination to do the next right thing. And also hope, because standing before me in the mirror is someone who has a commanding presence. *I look like a royal. I look like I belong. Maybe I'm not playing this game all wrong.* My gut lurches as I think of Llama. When she sees me, will she think I look royal? Will she think I belong here? Will she see this as only part of the game, or will she still have feelings for me?

Bernard knocks on the door. "Time," he hollers through the wooden door.

Phil swings the door open, and Bernard's amber eyes squint as he takes in my appearance. He gives one perfunctory nod that makes his white hair bob before he turns on his heel.

I attempt to follow, but my clothing drags me down. Each step must be intentional, and each step requires effort. I'm grateful for the perfectly climate-controlled environment of Souterraine because my back is sweating from the effort of leaving the castle.

Bernard leads us to a small vehicle. Phil opens the doors for me and picks up the robe so I can climb into the back seat. I'm ashamed of my weakness, and I briefly wonder if the king made sure this particular garment was extra heavy.

Did he sew hundreds of pounds of rocks into this?

Phil sits in the front seat with Bernard, leaving me alone with my thoughts for the ten-minute drive to the ceremony.

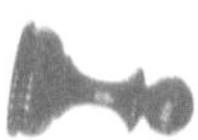

The maple tree is beautiful, casting leafy shadows that dance in the light. The bottom third of the enormous tree is covered in rich red and orange leaves, and the rich wood of the trunk stands out against the colors.

Phil directs me to stand under the canopy in the shade and in the shadow of the trunk. After requiring Phil's assistance to get out of the vehicle, I'm grateful I have enough strength to walk with my head held high to my spot at the tree.

I stand there, waiting. The tinkle of a small bell sounds while I survey the empty grove before me. At the sound of the first bell, more bells ring. The sound grows louder and louder as more bells join in, all coming from the same direction.

I turn my head toward the noise of what must be a thousand bells ringing and discover the people of Souterraine walking through the grove, escorting the king, the queen, and Llama to the maple tree. *To me.* The people peel off to stand in orderly rows in the grove while they continue on.

The light casts an ethereal glow over Llama. She's clothed in a wide dress that pinches at the waist before billowing out into a skirt that hides her feet. It's pure gold, with the same dusty red undertones that mark everything here. Across her torso, she wears a loop of bright red fabric. Metal ornaments adorn the loop, catching the light and casting spots on the ground. Her hair is loose, tumbling around her shoulders in a far different look than the braid she typically wears, and the woven crown on her head is interspersed with deep purple flowers.

I've known Llama on Earth as a beautiful, but odd, young woman. She has been a woman who didn't fit in. This moment—seeing Llama on Mars and dressed in finery—is like the final piece of a puzzle sliding into place. The clarity in my mind over what I want, what I *need*, startles me. Thoughts flow rapid fire. Llama is beautiful. Llama is a princess. Llama was odd on Earth because she didn't belong there. Llama belongs *here.*

A twisting feeling grips my stomach. *Maybe I belong here too.*

I shove the thought aside because Llama keeps coming closer, and she is mesmerizing. I want to belong with Llama. I want to belong *to* Llama. She's not a traitor. She was desperate to belong. And now that she belongs, she won't ever betray someone she loves again.

Llama's steps are marked with confidence. She arrives before me and holds out both of her hands to me, palms up.

I have no hesitation placing my own hands in hers before whispering, "You look beautiful."

She smiles softly, slowly, and her eyes meet mine in a question. I'm fluent enough in the language that is Llama to understand she's wondering if this is real. It's the same question I asked myself as I stood before the mirror in my room. I try to convey with my own eyes that it is. That I want to be with her, that I want to be united with her.

I never attended a unionization ceremony on Earth, and I certainly did not know what to expect in an engagement ceremony on Mars, but when Llama's voice rings out loud, clear, and commanding, I startle.

"Reach," she says. "I accept you as my future husband. My partner. My friend. My second hand. I accept you, Reach, son of Jezero Colony, as a worthy man. Do you accept me, Princess Llama of Souterraine, to be your wife after our engagement period?"

I nod.

You have to say yes, she mouths.

My brain doesn't want to supply the word because it's still stuck on her calling me a worthy man. *Am I?*

She digs her fingernails into my palms just a little and jars me back from my self-doubts.

"Yes," I say, hoping it was loud enough for everyone to hear.

"Do you accept the responsibility of leadership in Souterraine?"

"Yes."

"Do you accept the burden of care for the people of Souterraine, including me?"

"Yes."

"Do you accept me?" Her wide blue eyes show vulnerability at this question. She asked it earlier, but with the qualifier of her position here. This question isn't about her royal status, or even about Mars. It's about us.

I look deep into her eyes. "Yes."

The air is charged, and a chorus calls out, "Kiss!"

I'd like to kiss her, but the king steps forward, stopping the crowd from forming a chant. "Believe me, they have," he says dryly.

There's a murmur of laughter around the grove. When it dies down, he steps to my side. "You will never harm her." He lowers his voice to a threatening tone, staring at me with a dagger-like gaze. "You will be everything she needs you to be. And you will know that if anything, anything at all, *ever* happens to her, it will be your fault."

I meet his eyes with my own. Before I can form a response, the king breaks eye contact, turns, and announces, "The newly engaged couple, the Princess of Souterraine and her future husband, Reach. We will give the happy couple a moment of privacy. The banquet begins by the river now!"

There's a roar of thunderous applause followed by the people of Souterraine filing away from the maple tree and toward the other trees, touching the bark as they go.

The family trees, I recall.

Eventually, Llama and I are left alone under the maple tree. She bites her lip as she studies my face. I study hers, wondering if I could actually kiss her or if the king is going to pop out of the trees and threaten me again if I try.

"Do you really?" she whispers.

My forehead creases. "Do I really *what?*"

"Accept me?" Her eyes are downcast, her voice small. The insecurity in her tone breaks my fear of her grandfather.

Despite my heavy robe full of rocks, despite the jingling and jangling of the metal trees on my sash, and despite the fact that the king is a menace toward love, I reach my arm around Llama's waist and pull her to me.

I brush my lips over hers. "Yes. I accept you."

She leans into me, and we stand there in the golden honey light, holding each other and breathing in the promise of a future together.

Llama breaks our kiss, her eyes liquid and her shoulders shuddering as she steps away from me. She takes a deep breath, squares her shoulders, and grasps my right hand with her left one.

"We need to go to the banquet." She doesn't meet my eyes as she says the words. She straightens her crown, then looks down at the ground, that peculiar dusty red color tainting everything in Souterraine.

"Ok," I say, but I'd really rather not. I'd much rather stay here and continue what we were doing.

"It's this way."

I give her a nod, my heart racing as I consider having to face the king after kissing her. *He'll know.* I shove the thought aside. I can't be afraid of him.

Llama leads us away from the trees, out of the play of shadows, and into the honeyed ambient light of a Souterraine feast day. We crest the rise and turn toward the river. The same area of willow trees where I found Pippa the day she dropped out of the tree has been transformed. Under the tendril branches are plank tables made of sanded wood. Long benches line the sides. The tables are each made of a different type of wood, creating a patchwork effect when we see them from above. The sound of music floats through the air, hushed but present.

Llama exhales. "It's lovely."

She's right, it is. But when she speaks, my eyes are drawn to her, and there is nothing lovelier in the world, on Mars, in the universe, than Llama is in her finery at that moment.

"It is," I say, but my eyes are locked on her.

Llama turns her head slightly to face me and I look down, embarrassed to have been caught staring, but not before I see a flush form on her own cheeks.

She leads us down the sloping hill, covered in grass and clover, and approaches the river. In order to get to the river, we pass by the tables and into the stand of willows who guard the riverbanks. As we pass the tables, peals of laughter reverberate through the air. The closer we get to the river, the louder the sounds become. There is also, inexplicably, splashing.

I pull aside the last of the willow branches hanging before the bank like a curtain, allowing Llama to step through. I follow right behind her. When Llama stops short, I slam into her, nearly knocking her to the ground. I throw my arms around her waist to steady her, keeping her from falling face-first on the rocks. As my arms encircle her waist, applause rolls toward us like a wave.

The people of Souterraine are dancing on the banks, wading, splashing, and some are even swimming farther out in the deeper water. Every person has stopped and focused their attention on Llama. Every person's eyes are fixed on her standing in front of me like a shield.

I still don't like people. I don't like being on display, but something in my gut clenches, and I know that I need to face the people beside Llama as an equal. If I have any chance of convincing them to assist us with the Resistance against Nation, I need to be a leader too. Up till now, in Souterraine, I haven't been a leader. I have been a *follower*.

I pull in a breath and step to Llama's side, breathing the anxiety out through my nose, pushing down thoughts of the king attacking me with an iron frying pan for having a perfectly normal and also sanctioned relationship with his granddaughter, whom I've known longer than he has. I grasp her left hand with my right and raise our arms over our heads in a celebratory gesture.

The applause increases, the people in the river part, and the King and Queen of Souterraine are visible from the shore for the first time since we arrived under the willows. They walk forward through the waist-deep water until they stand in the shallows. They have changed into bathing costumes, still regal, but of a different material than their typical clothes.

The queen smiles, wrinkles crinkling the corners of her eyes, teeth gleaming brightly against her bronze skin. "The Feast of Trees commences!"

A voice calls out from the water, "KISS!"

A splash immediately sounds as another person pushes the heckler down.

The king stares daggers at me, his eyes flashing across the water. Unlike at the end of the ceremony where he intervened to give us privacy, he does not here. It's almost as if he's judging me by my willingness to give in to what the people want.

I look to Llama, whose eyes are on mine. She gives a small, barely perceptible bob of her head, and I close the gap.

It's a brief kiss, one that doesn't linger. But it's enough to make the point to the people and the king. Llama and I are together in this political alliance engagement, and I am not afraid of her grandfather.

I lift my chin defiantly in the king's direction and meet his stony gaze. He gives one nod, though his lips are curved into a frown. Llama drops my hand, bends to the ground, and hikes up her skirt to her knees. She pulls the full fabric through a loop at her waist, kicks off her Souterraine shoes, and steps into the water.

The people cheer, then the music resumes, as does the dancing and swimming.

"C'mon, Reach!" she calls over her shoulder, standing in ankle-deep water. Llama begins to spin in the water, spray misting from her steps. It's intoxicating. I want to join her, but even ankle-deep water will soak my clothing.

Phil hops off a boulder out of my peripheral and makes his way over. "Happy Feast of Trees, Reach!"

I smile and nod politely.

"You can take the robe off now," Phil says. "You can put it on a rock for the feast. And your clothes have loops too."

I slide the heavy robe off my shoulders and lay it on a large boulder before looking down and frowning. I don't see any loops, and I don't understand what he means. Phil interprets the meaning of my frown and sticks one of his legs out.

"See." His pants cuffs are rolled up several times to reveal a button. At the mid-calf of the pant legs are small fabric loops that the buttons can hook through, keeping the pants cuffs up from dragging in the water.

"Genius," I say, because it is. In Nation, we'd use elastic, but Souterraine is dependent on growable resources. The small buttons on my clothes are wooden, the clothing worn by the colonists is made of fibers, and despite being the opposite of Nation and Jezero, the people *here* are happy.

Pippa joins Llama, high-stepping into the water and watching as the spray comes up. Pippa laughs with delight as each droplet catches the light and forms a miniature rainbow. Once I've affixed my pants cuffs, I join them in the water. I extend my palm to Llama, who places her hand in mine with a surety that I can only hope she really feels.

I begin to spin her, matching the upbeat tempo of the music, watching as she smiles and laughs. The music ceases suddenly, and Llama is in my arms. I look down into her eyes and am about to tell her those three words I've known but haven't said aloud, when Pippa shoves her way between us, surprising me when she tugs my hand.

"Now. We are family." She says it with surprising smoothness.

I turn my face to Llama and find her gaze trained on Pippa. In reaction to Pippa's sweet comment, Llama's face shows shock, gentleness, and then a resolve I've never seen from her. Pippa doesn't notice Llama's reaction because she grabs Llama's hand in her other and begins swinging both of our hands, faster and faster until I'm afraid I'm going to lose my footing.

The Queen of Souterraine swims over. "Pippa, dear," she says. "That's too much."

"Oh." Pippa sighs, her shoulders slumping. "But we're family now."

The queen smiles. I smile back. "Not quite yet, Pippa, but soon. Today was the formal engagement. Reach will marry Llama next year at the Feast of Trees." She lowers her voice. "Or sooner."

I blink and drop Pippa's hand. I don't know how long I want to be here on Mars, but I intend to be on my way to Earth sooner than a year.

Llama stiffens beside me.

"What's wrong?" the queen asks.

Llama gulps and murmurs, "Not here. I can tell you later."

The noise of a motorized vehicle catches the attention of some children. "The food is here!" they shout.

Everyone begins to climb out of the river. Those in swimming costumes head toward a row of sheds to change into dry clothing, the king and queen among them.

Those who are mostly dry turn toward the tables, seating themselves in different groups based on which family tree they descend from.

Pippa leads Llama and me to a cedar table tucked against the willows and partially concealed from the other tables by the hanging branches. "We sit here," she declares, then plops down on the wooden plank bench.

I can't see through the thick green curtain across the table from me, but it parts, and a hand slinks through first, followed by a body in a silver spacesuit.

It's the last body I'd expected to see here in Souterraine on the day of my engagement.

"Reach."

Standing directly in front of me is Greg McAllistair, President of Jezero Colony on Mars. My father.

I STARE SLACK-jawed at my father. The man who shoved Llama into the back of a transport truck while she was in no shape to be moved because she discovered things they didn't want anyone to know. Because Llama was brave enough to pull a terrifying espionage device from the wall at the expense of her own health. Because *Llama* had the gall to show their weaknesses in spite of her, and my, own.

A surge of protectiveness rises, and I stand.

The King and Queen of Souterraine are not back from the changing tents yet. Llama stands frozen next to me. All the bold regalness she's carried melts away. I sense her terror in the face of the President of Jezero Colony. In this moment, I swear to myself that I will *never* ask Llama to return to Jezero.

"Why are you here?" I grind through clenched teeth as I shift to block Llama from his view. "What business do you have here?"

I'm startled at the way he flinches, a mottled red color flushing over his cheeks. "Reach, I'm breaking all sorts of protocols even being here. I need to speak to you, in private, immediately."

"Why?" I challenge, my palms flat on the wooden planks of the cedar table. "Why should I listen to you?"

"Reach…" he pleads. "It's imperative that we go—"

"Go where?" The King of Souterraine appears behind Greg, his eyes narrowed and face grim. "Where could you possibly be taking the future leader of Souterraine?"

"I don't want *her*, you old cod!" Greg snaps.

The king huffs in indignation. "Reach, perhaps you should tell him."

I don't actually know what to tell him. The queen stands at the king's side. Ever perceptive, she senses my discomfort, and answers in a cool voice, "Reach and Llama have been bonded in the formal engagement ceremony of Souterraine." She sounds haughty, and it's a timbre I haven't heard from her before. The tension between Souterraine and Jezero is obvious now. "So, the *her* you speak of is…" She gives me a slight nod.

I catch on quickly. "My future wife," I state, trying to keep my face blank as I consider the next move to make in this bizarre chess game.

I watch as Greg pales.

"Yes, isn't it a lovely predicament you find yourself in now, President McAllistair?" The king says, his voice low and menacing.

"And it is one hundred percent irrefutable?" Greg says.

"Formal. Public. In law. By law. For law. For government. For history. Reach assumed the weight of leadership of Souterraine today. And he bore it well."

I am surprised by the king's assessment. I do believe he still doesn't like me. An uncomfortable feeling floods my veins. It's one that's familiar. I'm a pawn in a game again.

Greg's shoulders slump. "You did that awfully fast."

The queen arches one delicate eyebrow. "You certainly made it known that you were no friend of Souterraine based on your treatment of a *known* royal."

"A spy," he corrects.

"Yes, and you didn't employ your own tactics on a potential heir, yourself?" Queen Eleanore retorts.

I flush, remembering Beatriz. It's strange—since seeing her for what she was, I haven't thought of her at all. Llama has been all my mind and heart have wanted.

Llama tugs on my hand, and I step aside as she stands and faces the man who threw her out of Jezero, bleeding and unstable, to ride for hours in a transport truck with only the hope of my limited medical knowledge, a loaf of bread, a canteen of water, and an extra oxygen tank to keep her alive. Her royal, bold demeanor has come roaring back. Pride fills me as she steps up to him, eyes narrowed and hands on her hips.

"President McAllistair," she says, her voice clipped. "You must have something you wish to tell Reach. Since he will tell me anyway, you might as well say it and then be on your way."

Greg steps backward at Llama's biting tone.

"Neither of us, Llama nor I, want to see you," I snap at the man who fathered me. The man I now wish I had never met but am glad I did meet, because I understand *what* he is. Just another power-hungry leader of a people.

The queen and king watch the exchange from a few feet back. They stand rigidly next to one another, anger etched on their faces.

"Please," Greg says. His voice drops lower. "Please, Reach. I can't *not* tell you."

"Tell *us* what?" Annoyance bubbles up in my chest when I see tears forming in Greg's eyes. His eyes flicker shut as he rolls them toward the top of Souterraine's dome.

When he speaks, it's in a whisper. "There has been a structural issue with Jezero's airlock system. The technology can't keep up with the population increase, and without filters, like these..." His breath hitches as he grimaces. "These *trees*. Our colony will die as the aircyclers in the airlocks begin leaching the oxygenated air out of the cavern, or...just explode. There's no long term fix. I came to say goodbye, Reach. And that I'm sorry."

The queen pushes me aside, passing me with fury. Her face reddens as she stands directly in front of Greg. "You mean to tell me that rather than ask for asylum for your people, you would let your entire colony die?" She jabs a finger in his chest. "You are no leader!"

"I don't have a choice," he mumbles.

"You *always* have a choice," Llama chides. "And you could have used that transmission center to contact us. Maybe buy your people some more time instead of wasting twenty hours driving over here."

Greg's head hangs and he stares at his spacesuit boots. "Percy is head of communications, and I couldn't arrange a transmission to tell you. He…has the biosecurity keys required to make a call, and I needed to see Reach."

"Human life has always been of the utmost priority here on Mars," Queen Eleanore says. "That is in *both* of our charters. Your people will be granted asylum here. What's the worst estimate of when the air won't be habitable in Jezero?"

"Three days." Shame laces Greg's voice.

"There is no hope of repair?" The king joins in the conversation, which has rapidly changed from personal to political, or perhaps from political to personal.

"No," Greg responds. "But you should know—your airlocks use the same aircycler structure. The same flaw is present in your system. You simply have more time because of the trees."

"How much time do you estimate *we* have?"

"Five years. Maybe more. It depends on the surface conditions and the strength of the individual components that were used in your air recycling system."

The king and queen fix each other with a knowing look, then turn their eyes to Llama and me.

"Llama, please tell President McAllistair about the medical center."

Greg closes his eyes as if exasperated.

"I saw the human reproduction technology center's *defective* persons area."

"Of course," Greg mutters. "Spies tend to find things they aren't supposed to see."

"Percy was angry, but he couldn't prove that I hadn't gotten lost. I was wondering if he'd tell you."

Greg's eyes flash. "Percy?"

"Do you trust your friend, President of Jezero?" the king asks, examining his fingernails as if an entire Martian colony isn't about to die from carbon monoxide poisoning.

"Of course, we've been friends for thirty years."

"Is friendship or power more important to him, do you think?" the queen presses.

Greg's face falls. "I can't answer that."

"Then you have your answer," Queen Eleanore responds. "You have people to care for. You may bring your living people, as spelled out in our charters. Life on Mars devoted to technology was your colony's calling. Yet, the one parameter expressly stated was that human life was not to be trifled with in any way. That technology could enhance, but never replace, the *human aspect of life*. Have your scientists created any…"

"No. I ordered that the project be stopped several days ago. It was taking too many resources and not helping the colony."

The queen nods succinctly. "Your people will find asylum here. But the additional load to our air systems will stress our own aircycler systems. We will enter our emergency protocols immediately."

Greg shakes his head. "They won't all come."

"Do they know?" the king asks. Greg remains silent. The king roars. "You, Gregory McAllistair, are a coward!"

Greg stares at the ground before he mumbles, "Percy knows. But he won't broadcast over the COMs channel, and he is convinced I'm overreacting. He has the biosecurity keys, and I can't force him to make the announcement."

"Does Reach have any power in Jezero as your son?" Llama butts into the conversation. She was with me when we spent time there, so I'm not surprised she sees a relationship between power and family.

"Yes. If I…abdicated…but he hasn't been announced as my son. He'd be up against Percy, and the people would support Percy over him. I'm not sure how to tell them everything about you, and

Percy refuses to share this information. The rules are clear, but it's an emergency."

"Reach," the king says. "You need to save your people. This coward won't do it."

Llama's hand grabs mine. "You're going to send him back there, knowing that the entire colony will be poisoned with noxious gas in a matter of days?"

"Reach is more of a leader than this fool." The king snarls at Greg. Greg's face pinches. "Reach, President McAllistair, and I will be returning to Jezero. Eleanore and Llama, please prepare our colony for the influx of people coming from Jezero and enter into emergency protocols. We need the aircycler technology tested in each of the airlocks immediately and our own longevity tests run. I don't trust this buffoon."

The queen's mouth sets into a thin line. Llama trembles, her hand shaking in mine. I don't think, I just do. I wrap my arm around her waist.

"Llama," Queen Eleanore replies, her own voice cracking while she looks at King Alfred with longing. "It is our duty to the people."

Llama's eyes well with tears, and I use my thumb to brush the drops off her cheek. "Please," she whispers to me. "Please come back."

"I will," I say. But I know there is no guarantee of that promise. Greg's estimate could be terribly wrong. Jezero could have hours, not days, and I'm headed into what is essentially a ticking Martian bomb.

Jezero may combust in more ways than one.

34

THE KING OF Souterraine has never been my favorite of people. Yet of the two men I find myself jammed into a transport truck with, he ranks far above my father. As soon as he understood the situation with Jezero's aircyclers, the king ordered that all of Souterraine's goods transport trucks be placed into convoy formation. Jezero doesn't have enough long-range transport vehicles to get everyone out of the colony, but quick math shows that if Souterraine supplies vehicles, life on Mars is possible for the doomed Jezero colonists. The linchpin of this whole plan is that the Jezero colonists must choose to leave. Greg is convinced that not all of them will.

Souterraine has enough supplemental oxygen to outfit the trucks, but it will be close. The other problem is that each person must leave at their assigned time. The colonists of Jezero don't even know they need to evacuate, and when they find out, there will be no time for waffling between staying or going. It's leave or die.

"McAllistair," King Alfred demands from his seat in the truck Greg drives. Unlike the trip from Jezero to Souterraine, this time I'm in the front of the cab. "You said three days. Was it three days when you left, or three days from today?"

Greg flushes scarlet. "From today. You might think I'm a coward, but the truth is we can't stay on this planet much longer. Our people are committed to Jezero's way of life." The truck hits a rut, and I'm flung against the side of my future father-in-law. The king pushes me off with one hand. I hold my core rigid, trying to keep myself still, trying to understand the power dynamics at play.

"And Jezero's way of life is clearly superior to that of Souterraine's."

Is the king being sarcastic?

Greg glares, then ignores King Alfred. "Reach," he says. I frown, but with less than a half inch of space between us, I can't *not* listen. "You didn't have enough time to understand the whole picture of Jezero, and I'm sorry for that. I hope you can see my coming to Souterraine to see you as an act of courage."

I bite down on my teeth, hard. *The courage of a coward.*

"I know it wasn't the best of partings," he adds.

I snort loudly. The king thumps me on the back as if I'm coughing.

"You threw a woman in need of medical attention into the back of a transport truck against medical advice," I grit out.

He snarls. "She was a spy."

"So was the *chef*." I stare straight ahead, my face granite. My father is a pathetic coward.

The king's eyes snag on mine for a moment as he contemplates my face.

"Should we let bygones be bygones? We have a colony to save," the king interjects. "Reach, I understand your opinion on this…specimen of Martian man…but you have a duty to your people, even the ones who are spies."

I clench my knuckles. I know this, but the people of Jezero Colony aren't *my* people. I have no connection to them except for the unusual circumstances of my birth. A thought forms deep in the recesses of my mind.

"What about Percy?" I ask.

Greg's neck cords and his Adam's apple bobs. "What about him?"

The king snorts beside me. "I believe what *your* son is asking, McAllistair, is what role does your fine friend *really* play in this mess? He certainly has one."

"He…is in denial, and it will require force to get the biosecurity keys from him to broadcast over the COMs channel. He's evading me, and he's stronger than I am. I can't physically overpower him."

"And when Reach and I appear, and Reach acts in official capacity because you have abdicated your post as President, Percy will…?"

I have a really good idea of what Percy will do. The man is all about power and authority.

Greg says nothing, just grips the steering wheel tighter.

"Reach." King Alfred turns toward me. "You need to be prepared to stake your claim to leadership."

Words bubble out before I can stop them. "How am I supposed to do that? They aren't *my people*! Percy is going to fight me, and he's been with these people for his entire life. I just appeared, and then disappeared when I was shoved into a transport truck." I turn my biting tone to Greg. "Are you going to tell the people? Or will I have to do it?"

"I'll…" He heaves a sigh. "I'll tell them when I abdicate."

"Very trustworthy of you." Sarcasm laces my voice as I continue. "*I'm abdicating my role as President of Jezero because our airlocks are going to combust, and this is my son, Reach, so follow him because I'm sick of having too much power. Also my second-in-command best friend wouldn't let me tell you this information, so I had to find a way to do it with Souterraine's help. Don't listen to him if you want to live.*"

Greg's eyes flash to mine for a moment, and I almost feel guilty at the pain in his. And then I remember what he's doing, and how he came to Souterraine under a guise, and how he shoved Llama and me into the back of a transport truck after first employing a spy of his own on me.

Really classy guy, my dad.

We travel the rest of the long hours in silence.

Jezero Colony is everything I remember. Sterile. Cold. Devoid of plant life. Barren. Greg drives from a small airlock along the side of the cavern that holds Jezero into the center of the colony. He keeps going, churning up the red Martian dust with every revolution of the wheels. I watch several cairns outside of residential buildings fall over from the vibrations. He drives all the way to the Tribunal Hall and parks next to the embassy. I shudder as I remember Llama lying in a puddle of blood.

Greg parks, throws the door open, stands on the running board of the transport truck cab, and slams his entire body weight into the horn. The resounding blast is so sudden and so loud that the King of Souterraine jumps and I press my hands over my ears. Supplemental oxygen masks deploy from the overhead compartments and dangle down in front of our faces.

Greg finally stops the accursed noise assault and slams the door as he stalks to the top step of the Tribunal Hall. It's exactly where he addressed the crowd when Llama and I first arrived. It's where the strange music was made. It's where he stood when I saw him for the first time. His shoulders slump, his face is worn, and his eyes don't shine. This is a man who has given up. This is a man I do not respect.

The people of Jezero file silently into the square, each of them wearing the silver government-issued clothes, and each of them fixing their eyes on Greg. Greg pulls the sash I saw him wear last time from a side seam pocket and loops it across his chest to make the *X* against his spacesuit. He straightens. A glimmer of something flickers in his eyes as he meets my gaze. He clasps his hands behind his back as he surveys the crowd. It's almost as if he's looking for someone. And then I realize he *is*. Percy.

The moment I realize this, I sense him more than I see him. The crowd begins parting at the back, and the low murmur of voices reaches my ears. Percy arrives at the head of the square, a little out of breath. His cold eyes snap.

"What is the meaning of this?" he growls at Greg.

Greg raises his chin and looks out at the crowd. It's now so big, the throng spills out into the surrounding streets.

"Good citizens of Jezero," Greg begins. "I am here in an official capacity to announce my abdication."

Percy steps forward, his hands outstretched. I watch from the edge of the group, my clothing conspicuous in the sea of silver. It's obvious from Percy's attention to Greg that he hasn't seen me or King Alfred.

Greg places his hands on the formal sash and meets Percy's gaze. "I am abdicating because our aircycler systems are failing." He speaks clearly, with confidence. "We have hours, maybe days, to leave before the colony is uninhabitable."

A murmur of panic flows through the crowd like a tangible thing.

Greg continues. "Our colonists have been offered sanctuary in Souterraine."

Percy's face reddens. "That's a lie!" he shouts.

Greg ignores him. "We will undertake emergency evacuation procedures. Jezero Colony, as it exists now, can no longer exist in the future. Life has been of the utmost importance on Mars, and I will not let our people die out if it can be helped." Greg yanks the sash over his head. Percy is at his side, hands open to receive it. Greg holds it away from Percy's outreached hands. "I appoint my son, Reach, who is now formally engaged to the Princess Llama of Souterraine, as the acting government official of Jezero."

The panicked murmurs cease as every person in the square loosens their jaws and gapes.

King Alfred shoves me forward. "Go, take that stupid sash that means so much to them."

I step out of the edge of the crowd and, feeling the eyes of thousands of people on my back, I stride to Greg.

Percy jumps around, trying to grab the sash from Greg's hand, where Greg holds the sash just out of Percy's reach.

"Reach McAllistair. Do you accept this position of government official?" Greg asks, passing the sash to me over Percy's jumping form. I attempt putting the sash on, but it's difficult with Percy's hands snatching wildly at the air around me.

"Yes," I say, my gaze stony as I ignore Percy and survey the colonists of Jezero. "I do."

Percy seems to have lost some of his fight for the sash and ceases his jumping and grabbing. He turns to the crowd. "You accept this *outsider* as your leader?" He scoffs. "You accept this? It should be *me*. I should be the one who's leading you. I have for the past twenty years. I'm the one who discovered the aircycler issue. I'm the one who—"

The people of Jezero scratch their heads in confusion.

A subtle nod from the king tells me what I need to do. "This man"—I indicate Percy—"is the one who decided *not* to tell anyone about the aircycler issue until it was nearly too late. Rather than broadcast the emergency, he hid himself and his biosecurity keys and—"

"I had a plan! The whole colony wouldn't have died out. We could use the emergency bubble and save ten percent!"

Anger thrums through the crowd.

"He was going to let ninety percent of us...*die out*?" a voice seethes from the crowd.

I nod.

"What about our children?" another voice calls.

Then another voice: "What about the Martian law charters about life?"

I hold up my hands in the universal stop gesture. I look to the king, and he nods again. Relieved, I swallow hard and then say what needs to be said. "The King of Souterraine and I are here to assist with the evacuation to Souterraine. We can discuss politics another time. The evacuation plan begins now. You have an hour before we will need to send the first transport trucks from the airlock ports."

The king steps to me, shouldering Percy out of the way from where he has stood open-mouthed and glaring. "For those of you who do not know me, I am King Alfred. And I assure you, you are all welcome in Souterraine. Our first group of evacuees will be mothers and children. You all have one hour, then arrive at your designated transportation port."

The crowd disperses in a shockingly orderly fashion, but the thrum of anxiety hums like cicadas at the end of summer.

The crowd is gone, leaving Greg, Percy, myself, and the king standing in the square.

"You," Percy spits in my general direction.

"President Reach," Greg snaps in correction.

"You have no business being here. You have no business leading this colony. I'll make you pay for it, Greg. I'll make—"

"You'll make me pay for it, how? Reach is my heir. He gets everything, not you. You showed your true colors a long time ago, Percy. I've been a coward in the name of keeping our friendship and peace for Jezero, but you are no friend of this colony."

"You know the law! You know that isn't how it works on Jezero! You know that I cannot do anything different than what is stated in the Martian Charters."

King Alfred steps between the two yelling men, extending his arms and separating them.

"That is enough!" He exhales loudly. He turns to Percy. "You two will be the last to evacuate, with both Reach and myself. Clearly, you need someone to keep an eye on you."

Greg sighs.

Percy sputters. "But the people need someone they can trust. I should be in the first group."

"No. I need you to do one good thing in your life and go and make the announcement over the COMs system to sector six that evacuation is underway. You know it takes hours for the biosecurity keys to update, otherwise I'd do it myself." Greg snarls at his previous confidante, the man he trusted to be second-in-command.

Percy stares at me, his eyes beady, his gaze stone cold. There are no depths in them. All I see is his boiling rage, controlled behind a crumbling façade. "There's no point." Percy glowers back, but he walks down the path in the direction of the COMs transmission building.

The king shakes his head. "Do you think he'll do it?"

"Percy!" Greg bellows. "That's an order!" Then, quietly to the king and me, says, "If it's an order, he'll do it."

The king shakes his head. "Reach? You're the government official here. When should these selfish cowards be evacuated?"

I stare at Percy's retreating back as I issue my first decree as President of the doomed colony of Jezero. "The single men of Jezero with no children will be the last group of people to leave this colony."

And with those words, I cement my place in Martian history.

35

THE PEOPLE OF Jezero are orderly. The plaza empties in minutes. I'm not surprised. They have a propensity for rules, regulations, laws, and preparedness. The evacuation plan was known in advance, and even if it has never been enacted, every person in Jezero understood what Greg meant down to the tiniest detail when he stood on the steps of the Tribunal Hall and told the people to leave their home.

The plan always included evacuating the most fragile and vulnerable people first. On a planet where resources are scarce, the fear of dying out has governed the entire colony, at least on a subconscious level. No one offered any rebuttal to me, Greg, or the King of Souterraine. No one except Percy, my father's friend and second-in-command.

I stand in the plaza with a red sash crossing my chest. It's a bizarre combination of Soutteraine's dress clothing and a symbol of Jezero leadership. King Alfred stands next to me, absorbing some of the tension. He claps a hand down on my shoulder.

"Let's go to the checkpoints and make sure everything is working as it should, Reach," he says. "And let's hope that Percy does his job."

Greg's eyes flash, the blue of his irises expanding and contracting in less than a breadth as his eyes widen and narrow. "He was given an order. He'll follow it." His voice drops lower. "He has to follow it." It sounds more like a wish than a certainty, and I wish I could confirm Percy's actions. The foolishness of letting him go with no one to account for his warning to sector six hits me like a rocket blast in the heart. My hand flies to my chest, trying to still the rapid thumping of my beating heart.

Greg looks at me. "I am no longer in charge, but if I were, I would not let..." Greg swallows. "I would not let him evacuate with us if he doesn't warn the sector. He is a threat to Martian life. What do you want to do with him, Reach?"

I swallow hard. How did I go from kissing my betrothed to evacuating a colony and *now* considering exiling—which, in this case, would be an instance of execution—a man that my father trusted for years to help him lead a colony?

I look to the king, because at this moment, he's more of a mentor than anyone else on Mars.

King Alfred raises a brow. "If you choose to keep him here and not evacuate him, what would happen?" The question is directed at Greg.

"With the reduced load to the aircyclers, there would be more time, but eventually he'd die. It would take a while. Starvation isn't a great way to go. Of course, the airlocks could explode and he could suffocate or freeze to death. That would be preferable to the loneliness, I imagine."

The king doesn't say anything. He gives no sign he has a preference. I am completely unencumbered by the weight of other's opinions, and I hate it. Being told *what* to do in situations like this would be extraordinarily helpful. At the very least, it would make it easier. I think of Percy's face as he walked away. He wasn't remorseful, he was enraged. He didn't care that he was going to let ninety percent of the colony die out. He was celebrating the ten percent he thought he could save. Part of me wants to simply throw him out of the airlock now and say, "Good riddance."

The King of Souterraine bends over and picks up a fistful of the Jezero dirt. He lets it sift through his fingers, the iron oxide dust falling to the ground in a visual reminiscent of blood. It is the visual I need, one seemingly innocuous movement that reminds me of the blood on the hands of Enforce, Leader, Legislate, and Litigate. It's the same way people are expendable in Nation.

I do not want blood on my hands, least of all Percy's.

I grip my fists into tight balls at my sides and grind out words that anger me, but are necessary. "He comes with us but will answer to the regular law of his people after the evacuation is complete." I stalk off, leaving Greg, Percy, and the King of Souterraine to figure the rest of whatever *that* means out.

The women and children of Jezero wait in a neat line outside of the first checkpoint I find. I don't fully understand how the transportation system to Souterraine will work, but a child with blond curls sees my sash and begins hopping up and down.

"Look, Mommy! Look! It's the Present-erdent!" His mother smiles down at him and nods. Worry is evident on her face, but genuine concern for her son is there too. She also finds humor in his childish speech. I do as well.

I stop and crouch down to meet the child's eye level. "Hello. I'm Reach."

The child blinks solemnly. "I'm going to a new colony."

"Yes, I know."

"Have you been there?"

I smile. "Yes."

"Is it red?"

"A little. It has lots of colors. It even has trees."

A collective gasp sounds from the children, who all tug free from their mothers' hands and surround me. There are not many here, maybe only thirty children at this checkpoint, and they range from babies in mothers' arms to young teens.

"Trees!" A gasp escapes a young girl, maybe three years old, with dark hair and darker eyes. "I sawed pictures once!"

I bite back a laugh. "You'll see them soon. They make a breeze that tickles your hair." I ruffle the blond boy's curls and he giggles. I turn serious. "I'm new to Jezero—"

"No, you're not. You've been here before! We saw you with that girl."

I sigh. "Yes, well…" I meet the eyes of the mothers, and they give me an encouraging nod. I can't tell these children that their government threw me and 'that girl' out after accusing her of espionage while hypocritically conducting espionage of their own. "I was getting things ready for you in Souterraine. Do you know what you're going to do next?"

"Yes, Mister! We're going to get on the special trucks, and we're going to wear funny masks, and we're going to drive through big dark rock tunnels, and it's going to take a long time, but when we do, we'll be in Sewer-terrain." The blond boy hops up and down while holding his mother's hand.

A few older children snicker.

"Souterraine," I automatically correct.

"Yeah, there."

I'm fishing for information from children, and that's not great leadership, so I straighten and smile at them all while turning to the adults and continuing down the line of refugees.

"Hi," I say to the nearest woman. She bats her pale eyelashes. *Oh no.* "Uh. Could any of you adults explain the evacuation plan? I'm a little fuzzy on the details."

"Sure." The woman puts her hand on my arm. I bite back a grimace. "We're going to go through the transportation airlocks. They are emergency-use only, but there are about ten of them throughout Jezero. There's the main airlock that leads to the surface and is the key to the air recycling program, but the emergency airlocks are almost never used. When they open, they can't reseal fully, so they only open them when it's a true emergency and never all at once, like they're doing today."

The dire state of Jezero Colony is made apparent right then. I shrug out of her grasp, but give her a kind smile. This woman is being forced to leave everything she's ever known. She can't hold a candle to Llama anyway. The least I can do is be kind.

"And then you'll wear oxygen masks?" I ask as I begin walking slowly down the line, away from the woman with groping hands.

"Yes," says a woman holding a baby in her arms.

"And how many children in Jezero are being evacuated?" I ask her. "What about babies? What about your things?"

The woman with the baby shifts. "There aren't many. There are around one hundred children in total in Jezero." Her throat bobs as she swallows. "Kaden was the eighth baby born this year, and that was two months ago. We usually have one a month."

The baby begins to fuss and she looks away, swaying and shushing the baby.

Another woman says, "Our things are going with the people in the household who don't have to evacuate with a child. We can only take one bag per household."

The rapid mental math doesn't take long to calculate. Jezero Colony was going to die out without the aircycler issue anyway. Maybe not with this generation, but within two or three at the most. This level of population decline is not sustainable.

A thin green light appears over a metal gray swirl in the rock wall of Jezero. Each woman and child clutches a mask as the swirl spins open, revealing a large silver transport truck that looks in much better shape than the one Llama and I used. The driver stands in front of the truck, an oxygen mask on his face. He's wearing the clothes of Souterraine.

As soon as the doors are fully open, he rips the mask off his face. It's Phil.

36

Phil has a calming presence. That much is an irrefutable fact. He's a successful teacher because nothing seems to ruffle him. Phil and I are *not* cut from the same cloth, because everything ruffles me. Right now, I am beyond overwhelmed. It's like my body is a rubber band wound too tightly, and my emotions are fraying as my skin waits for the tension to release. My very bones itch.

I'm the President of a doomed colony. My father is a coward. Percy is…a word that I can't even say aloud.

I'm not a hugger. I'm not big on any physical contact with most people—Llama excluded—but when I see Phil, I step forward and pull him into a hug.

Phil startles, but regains composure and claps me on the back. "Reach," he says as he pulls away. His eyes take in the crisscrossed sash over my chest. "Woah. You're the President here?"

I shrug. How can I explain the whole succession ridiculousness that led to this? "Yeah. And we need to get these people out of here."

"That's what I'm here for." He gazes down the line of Jezero colonists waiting.

"Are all the drivers from Souterraine?" I ask.

Phil bites his lip. "No." He's silent for a beat as his eyes continue down the line. "I counted thirty-four people at this transport station."

"Yes, sir," says a woman standing nearest us. She holds a small child's hand in her own and balances another child on her hip. "Forty people are assigned to this transport station. Once the airlock is used a second time, it won't be functional again, and we only have thirty minutes now that you've used it."

Phil frowns. "That's not much time." Under his breath, he mutters to me, "Who designed this escape plan? Where are the missing six people? It's terrible."

I frown. "I have no idea, but we have to get them out of here."

Phil steps forward and adopts his instructor voice. When he speaks in that tone, with his unflappable demeanor, everyone listens. "Hi everyone, I'm Phil. I'm going to drive you to Souterraine. Does everyone have their oxygen masks?"

I'm pretty sure I see several of the women fan themselves with their masks and swoon. Phil is an attractive man, and at this moment, he's definitely a hero.

"Children," Phil says. "We're going to put on our masks now. The truck we're going to ride in isn't really made for people, so let's get our masks on and then we can get into the truck." He demonstrates how to put the mask on, and each child follows as best as they are able. For the infants, Phil walks along the line, conversing with the mothers and making small adjustments.

When Phil reaches the end of the line, he looks at me. The concern in his eyes is remarkable. Unflappable Phil is *flapped*. He drops his voice. "I don't know where the missing people are, but they should be here. I don't want to leave with empty seats. This is the *one* chance they have to get out. And since this is a checkpoint for families..."

The gravity of the situation hits with full force. It's likely that the missing people are children and their mothers.

"What should I do?" I whisper to Phil.

He grimaces in response. "You need to ask about the missing

people, and if you can, *get them on this truck*. I have to leave in…" He consults his watch. "Twenty minutes. I'll load the people here."

I give a quick nod and determine the best way to figure out who's missing is to ask the adults. I find the woman who knew the number of people assigned to this checkpoint. "Ma'am?" I ask. "Do you have a roster of who is assigned to this checkpoint?"

She frowns. "I wish, but I only know the number of people assigned. I'm not even sure how many children are in the missing group. It could be any combination, or a family with…" She trails off, considering, before her eyes mist over. "Oh *no*…" she whispers. "It's the VanPools. They're one of the only families in Jezero with five children, and I don't think anyone would have told… They probably wouldn't have heard…"

"What do you mean they wouldn't have been told? They wouldn't have heard?"

"They live by the main airlock, and it's really far away from the Tribunal Hall Plaza. There wasn't a COMs announcement. They're not…" She looks down, embarrassed. "They're not the most well-to-do citizens of Jezero, and they are sometimes seen as a…"

"They live by the main airlock?" I ask, looking the woman in the eyes but all the while seeing the image of a small child in worn clothing in a crumbling structure as Llama and I entered Jezero for the first time.

"Yes. But it's…far," she whispers. "And we can't endanger everyone here by sending someone for *them*."

The rubber band in me snaps. Actually, it melts as rage boils up. I draw myself to my full height, almost a foot taller than this woman. "No one told them. And no one wants to tell them *now*."

She shrinks away. I know I intimidated her, but she just admitted that she'd rather save her own skin than do anything to attempt to help a family with *five* children. The cowardly attitude is so reminiscent of Percy that I nearly gag.

Phil has loaded a group of people into the truck, but I call out to everyone still in the line. "The VanPools. Is that who we're missing?"

Shock and understanding dawns on each person's face, but no one moves.

"They live…" I prompt.

A child, maybe eight years old, interjects. "By the surface airlock."

"And which way is the fastest way?" I ask.

Fingers point in one direction down the street.

I don't think.

I sprint.

The streets of Jezero curve, so I am running full throttle along the road when the curve cuts off my vision. I round the bend and slam directly into a woman carrying a baby. She had time to move, but I didn't. I get a good view of the group from my prone position as I stare up at the red dome of Jezero and they all come into view. The woman has three older children next to her. The tallest of the children carries a slightly older baby than the one the mother holds. Their clothes are patched and faded, slightly too short at the cuffs.

"Sorry, President…" the woman stutters. "No—no one told us. And no one came to let us know…"

I catch my breath and prop myself up on my elbows. "How did you find out that something was wrong?"

"Isla went to ask a friend to play, but when six friends weren't home, I knew something was wrong. We're on our way to the Tribunal Hall Plaza. What's wrong?"

My jaw drops. She's here on intuition that will save her life. "Evacuation," I say in a low voice. I try to keep my tone even, trying to act like Phil. "It's the worst case."

The woman blanches. Her children begin pulling on her clothes, the baby fussing and the older baby whining. "Stop it!" she commands. "Stop it this instant!"

Her commands are not followed.

"Here," I say as I stand. I scoop the older baby out of the oldest child's arms. "We have to hurry. Your transport truck leaves in minutes."

The oldest child must have some idea of what's about to happen because tears well in her eyes.

"Isla," the mom grits out through clenched teeth. "We do not have time for a meltdown."

"Are you fast walkers or runners?" I ask Isla and the other two children. The younger children shake their heads. "Should we run?"

"YES!" shouts the youngest, like I just offered her a prize.

"Miss VanPool?" I say. Her gaze jerks away from the baby in her arms to meet my eyes. "I'm sorry. Things are different in Souterraine."

She swallows hard. "Ok."

"But we really do have to run."

She's shaking, but manages a quiet "Ok."

My back smarts from where I hit it on the hard red ground, but it's a matter of life and death for the children.

I shove the pain down, adjust the baby in my arms, and begin to run—again.

The airlock doors are beginning to close, whirling blades spinning back into place. There is no stopping, no thinking, nothing except action.

Anyone caught by the blades will be sliced through.

This really is a terrible escape plan.

But we have nothing else to work with.

"PHIL!" I shout as I careen forward. "PHIL!" My breathing is labored, but the children have kept pace with me. They haven't been carrying an additional human being though.

Phil stands next to the transport truck, his eyes wide. I can't go in there, or I'll risk not being able to be here in Jezero for the rest of the evacuation. The only thing I can do is literally throw the children through the airlock grates as they spin, closing into a tighter circle.

Phil understands. I have to hope he does. I kick my pace into a sprint and throw the child through the door. I linger for a moment to watch Phil catch him, then pass the child to another woman. The three older children, all girls, have fallen behind after my mad sprint. Miss VanPool is behind them. I have less than two minutes to get them all through before it's too dangerous.

I make a decision, scooping up two girls, holding them like baggage under my arms, and running again. When I'm close enough, I drop one child, launching the other straight to Phil. I don't even make sure he's caught this one before picking up the child on the ground, murmuring a 'sorry,' and throwing the next child into the airlock.

Isla is gaining on me. She's a smart child. I'm not going to toss her into the airlock.

"Isla!" I yell. "RUN! RUN STRAIGHT THROUGH THE DOORS!"

She runs harder, her feet kicking up the red dust as I run for Miss VanPool and the young infant. Metal creaks and gears whine, and I know we don't have much time. When I reach her, I wrench the baby from her arms and scream, "RUN. YOU HAVE TO RUN," all while running to the airlock doors. There is less than three feet of space between the blades now.

"PHIL!" I throw the baby, watching as he arcs through the blades and into Phil's waiting arms. The baby lets out a wail.

Miss VanPool twists her body to the side, losing one of her shoes as she flings herself through the rapidly closing space.

The doors thunk closed and the screech of metal gears grinding ceases, leaving me heaving, bent over, wondering if the last thirty minutes were real.

I catch a glimpse of a single spacesuit boot, a stark reminder of how dangerous it is to evacuate an entire Martian colony on short notice.

37

THE AIRLOCK DOORS slide shut. The technical system in place takes the port out of service. A red light illuminates the metal and projects the words "DANGER. WILL DESTRUCT IF TAMPERED WITH" across the sliding door plates. There's nothing else for me to do here but hope those children and their mothers make it to Souterraine. If I imagined this, I might feel good about saving lives, but I don't. Not really. This is real life, real *lives*. A rock has fallen into my stomach, and I have nothing to counter the anxiety with.

I turn, wondering where I should go next, when a small sound catches my attention.

A child, roughly five years old, comes into view. His clothes are pristine, the blond curls across his crown are neat and orderly, his green eyes wide. It's obvious this child is cared for. This begs the question, why is he alone?

"'Scuse me, mister." The child sees my sash. "Are you the *Present*?"

"Yes," I say, crouching down to his level. "What do you need? Where are your adults?"

"I don't have a mom. And my dad doesn't want to 'vaccutate'."

"What do you mean your dad doesn't want to evacuate? It's not optional for families."

The boy shrugs. "I don't know where to go."

I frown. There was bound to be some confusion regarding the sudden evacuation orders, but I had not considered people *not* wanting to go beyond Greg's brief comments that not everyone would. I certainly didn't think that attitude would extend to people with children.

"Do you know which checkpoint you're assigned to?" The boy shakes his head. I blow out a breath. The children should have all evacuated by now. "Do you know where your dad is?"

This time, the boy brightens and nods. He grabs my hand and says, "I'll show ya."

I'm not sure what I'm going to do when I get there, but the little boy's steps are purposeful. I let him lead me along.

"I'm Reach," I say, breaking the silence.

The boy's eyes widen. "Your name isn't Present?"

"Uhh. No." The boy digests the information, marching doggedly down the street. "So," I say, "what's your name?"

"Efan," he lisps.

"Efan?" I ask.

"No, E-T-H-A-N."

"Oh. Nice to meet you, E*th*an."

"Here." The little boy lets go of my hand and bounds up to the door. The cairn at the front has only two stones, but a smooth red stone lies just to the side. I remember what the boy said about not having a mom, and the way the cairns represented the families who lived in each dwelling. That stone, lying off to the side of the others, makes my chest tighten.

"Dad!" the boy calls. I wait just outside the door. "I brought a Present!"

"Ethan, you did not need to go get a present," a stern voice responds.

"No, Dad, he's right here." Ethan reappears and pulls me inside the home, where I come face-to-face with a man whose face abruptly changes into one of intense dislike. He surveys my Souterraine clothes and the Jezero Presidential sash.

"Why are you here?" he growls.

I level him with a stony gaze. "Ethan found me at the checkpoint. He didn't make the children's evacuation schedule. He says you don't want to go."

"By the surface, I don't." Ethan's dad spits at me. "Government puppet, I am *not.*"

"I can appreciate that, sir, but this is a matter of life and death."

"I'm not going! That's final!" Ethan's father shakes with rage.

"You don't have a choice in the matter," I return. I keep my voice level, but my blood boils at his refusal to follow orders and put his son's life on the line. "It is not optional for families. You are going to die if you stay here."

"Better be a dead man than a *sheep.*"

Ethan lets out a hiss and covers his ears. I imagine fuzzy white creatures frolicking in fields of green grass. It's apparent the word does not mean the same thing to me as it does to them.

I meet his unflinching stare with one of my own. We're locked in a staring match while I try to determine *what* to say to him.

Heavy steps sound behind us. I turn and see the king and Greg jogging up to me. The king pulls an oxygen mask below his mouth and calls out, "The last evacuation trucks are leaving the checkpoints in eighteen minutes. We have to be on them. Our last tech advisor monitoring the air quality showed that there's already significant damage to the air quality in Jezero. It's exponentially worse than we feared. This colony won't last another day."

Greg stops when he sees the little boy. "What's the problem here?"

"He won't leave." I jerk my thumb in the man's direction. "Which means Ethan won't leave either."

Greg mutters something under his breath. "Frank. You've known who I am for a long time. There is significant air quality damage here in Jezero because the aircycle technology is failing. I can't force you to come to Souterraine, but you will die here."

Frank clenches his teeth. "Better to die a free man here than be a *sheep*."

Greg rolls his eyes.

The King of Souterraine crouches down to Ethan. "Do you have an oxygen mask?"

Ethan nods. "I'll go get it." He scampers off.

The king stands to his full and impressive height. "We can't force people into a transport truck, can we?" He looks to Greg, who shakes his head in agreement.

"By Martian law, we cannot."

"What about the boy?"

"We can." Greg bites his lip. "Emergency in the case of minors."

"Listen," Frank says, scrubbing his hand down his weary face. "I don't want to leave Liza. Our life was here. I'd rather be with her than anywhere else. And I'm not the only person who doesn't want to evacuate."

Ethan returns, clutching a mask in both hands. "Brought you one, Dad."

Frank turns to Ethan and frowns. "Nothing's been good for us since Mom died. You're going to go with these people. But don't ever forget you need to think for yourself."

Ethan flings himself at Frank's legs. "Please come too, Daddy."

Frank gives Ethan an awkward pat on the back. "No."

"We don't have time for a lengthy goodbye," the king says. "We have to go—now."

"Ethan," Frank says in a deep voice. "You have to go now."

"But will I see you?"

"No."

And then Frank pushes us out of the entryway and slams the door.

Ethan stares at the door, two oxygen masks in his hands. King Alfred bends down and says to the boy, "Ethan, we need to hurry to our checkpoint. Do you understand?"

Ethan's eyes well up with tears. Tears form in mine. I look at Greg, feeling my jaw harden. "He just…"

"Yes," Greg interrupts me. "But we can't force him. We have to leave the colony now."

"What about the others who aren't leaving?"

"They've all been warned."

"But have they?"

Greg fixes me with a look.

"A family with five children wasn't warned," I say.

Greg's nostrils flare. With anger or disgust, I'm not sure. "Did they get out?"

I nod.

"That's more than we'll be able to say for us if we don't go. This way, *now*."

Greg takes off at a jog, leading us through the deserted streets and to an airlock by the embassy. There are twelve people waiting in a line. Each of them wears the sash of leadership. I grimace. At least some of Jezero's leaders understand what it means to be in this position.

Greg slows, and a shadow passes over his face.

"President McAllistair," a woman calls out.

I don't respond. McAllistair isn't *my* name.

"President," she repeats, louder this time.

Greg elbows me in the ribs, hard. The King of Souterraine and Ethan follow behind. King Alfred whispers loudly, "You have to talk to them, Reach."

Oh.

"Greg…I…don't know anything about what's supposed to happen right now," I admit.

Greg steps forward. "Are all your sectors evacuated?"

Each person nods as Greg fixes them in his gaze one by one down the line. The last person in the line is Percy.

"And you accounted for children in your sector?"

Again, each person nods. Except Percy.

"Percy. You were asked to act in an official capacity and warn people to evacuate through the COMs system. Did you warn sector six?"

Percy doesn't say anything.

Greg swears violently. "It was an ORDER!" he roars.

"You don't give orders here anymore," Percy responds smugly.

Greg hisses. "Margot, have you updated the biosecurity keys yet?"

A woman with blue-framed glasses steps forward. "I didn't think there was much point…but I can do it now."

Greg shakes his head while his lip curls. "There is no point now. Did you get the archives?"

The woman nods and points to a large black bag on the ground near her feet.

Greg scrubs his hand over his short, shorn hair. "Reach, who is Jezero's current President, took it upon himself to assist that sector. Because of your mismanagement of time and resources, Percy, five children from that sector were nearly…*not* evacuated."

The entire line of men and women turn to Percy and stare him down, hard. I shift uncomfortably.

"Thankfully, those five children were evacuated, and a sixth child is with us now." Greg steps back and gestures to the king and Ethan. A murmur, a drone of angry hornets, grows.

"This is the last transport truck out of Jezero. We don't have room for another person," the lady with the blue glasses says.

Greg shifts. "I know."

"What are we going to do, then?" a man with dark brown skin and darker hair asks. He's calm about it, and his demeanor reminds me of Phil.

"Ethan is a minor. He has to leave. We invoked state emergency power to take him. His father is Frank DiCusso."

A collective *oh* sounds from the group of leaders in front of me.

"Anise?" Greg asks. "How many chose not to evacuate?"

"Seventeen." She thinks for a moment. "Eighteen, now that we are including the defacto from sector six."

Greg nods. "Good. Beatriz is driving this transport truck. She'll see you all to Souterraine safely."

My brow furrows in confusion. Why does it sound like Greg is saying he isn't coming? And Beatriz? *Oh no.*

I look at King Alfred, and he gives a small nod, confirming something I didn't think would happen.

"No!" The word tumbles out. "You can't stay."

Greg looks at me with something like fondness. "There are a few systems we could try. The failsafes aren't perfect, but we might not totally lose the Colony if I stay. And with a smaller load of people to support, we could have more time. There's one thing we can do. An emergency bubble with airlock technology…but it can only house so many people, and it takes a while to inflate. I… We can try."

I don't believe it, especially not with the air quality report from earlier, but before I can argue, Greg jerks his head slightly in Ethan's direction, and I understand.

Greg is giving up his seat on the transport truck for Ethan. Ethan, a five-year-old child, who didn't make it to his own seat because of his father's choice.

I feel many things about Greg, but at this moment, I feel loss. I feel pride. I feel conflicted. I understand that everything he just said to me were platitudes. I'll never see my father again.

I break every social rule I've ever followed and pull him into a hug. The weight of his sacrifice is crushing, but also right. For every moment I thought my father was a coward—despite every moment my father *was* a coward—he's being a leader when it matters.

Percy starts to step out of the line, and it's clear he'll suggest staying here, especially since he could have all the power he wanted among the eighteen people left, especially if the bubble works.

The man next to Percy drags him back into the line. "No. You are coming with us and will be answering to Martian law regarding your actions."

Percy scowls.

The airlock door spins open.

Beatriz stands next to the truck. "Let's go, everyone," she calls.

The queue moves forward.

I turn to the king. "I don't trust her. She… There's history."

The king rolls his eyes. "Then don't trust her. But I'm rather sure you're her boss right now."

Greg bites back a smile. "Beatriz is one of our best field operatives. You'll be fine. Also, you'll have to ride in the front with her. There are two seats there. What happened before was…a job for her."

The king holds Ethan's hand as they walk to the back of the transport truck. I walk with them. This one at least looks like it was made with the idea of human transport in mind. There are seats, tubing to connect the oxygen masks to the truck's supply, and even an enclosed small area off to the side to function as a toilet. It is *nothing* like mine and Llama's drive to Souterraine. For Ethan's sake, I'm glad.

King Alfred meets my gaze, then jerks his head to the back of the truck. I understand his meaning. He's going to stay with Ethan instead of coming up front with me. Ethan hasn't said anything since we left his home.

I trudge up to the front of the truck, my heavy footfalls kicking up red puffs of Martian dirt as I drag myself into a situation I have zero desire to be in.

I climb into the front of the transport truck cab and shut the door.

Beatriz flips buttons on the dashboard and stares at me. "We meet again, President Reach. Buckle up."

All I can think as I secure my seatbelt is, *Llama will not like this one bit.*

38

Beatriz toggles switches on the dashboard, then pulls a lever. The truck lurches forward. "Great," she says, the sarcasm in her voice evident.

My plan of riding to Souterraine in silence and not looking at her is shattered. I look over at her. The doors to the Jezero airlock are closed, while the doors that lead to the tunnel road to Souterraine are opening. "What's wrong?"

Beatriz laughs. "Nothing. But I could tell you were going to sit there and not look or talk to me. It's a *long* ride, sir."

I scoff at the title, but then remember King Alfred's words about her. I don't have to trust her. But I am her boss. I bite my lower lip and roll it under my top teeth while I consider what I want to say.

"You can just ask, Re—err, sir," she says. Her hands look comically small on the steering wheel, but she's relaxed against the seat while the airlock grates grind and clank as they rotate. "It's a *long* ride."

I sigh. "Fine. You know that Greg McAllistair abdicated his position and named me as the acting President for the evacuation, right?"

"Yes," Beatriz answers. The doors open fully and she grabs an intercom device from the dashboard next to the wheel. "One second." She presses the large gray button on the side and speaks into the intercom. "This is Beatriz and President Reach McAllistair"—I bristle at the use of Greg's name as my own—"letting you know our destination is Souterraine. It's a long drive, so make yourself comfortable. The transport truck is equipped with a temporary seal for the air mix that will be flowing through the back, but due to the emergency nature of the evacuation, it's better to keep your oxygen masks on. It's ok to take short breaks, but no more than five minutes at a time. If you start to notice any lightheadedness, or feel a sudden change in temperature, place your masks on and call me with your intercom device. Over."

Beatriz shifts the truck into drive and pulls through the open airlock doors. The headlamps illuminate the rocky red tunnel. She punches a few buttons on the dash, then, after twisting the steering wheel ninety degrees and navigating a turn, she looks at me.

"Don't you need to keep your eyes on the road?"

She shrugs. "Not really. It's got automatic driving along the route, but it's best to have a driver to override if...there's debris or a collapse in the tunnels."

"Oh." The idea of this transport truck driving us through a passage of collapsing tunnels does not make me feel confident. *Claustrophobia is just a self-preservation instinct. I'm safe. I'm safe. I'm safe.*

I force myself to breathe slowly and fully.

"So," Beatriz prompts. "What did you want to talk about?"

I study her in the dim light. Her face is blank. She looks different than she did when she was actively spying on us in Jezero. She looks almost like a blank page waiting for a sketch. She is any number of things, and I get the sense she can be anything I need her to be. She gives nothing away with her posture, her body language, or her eyes. She's robotic. I remember the near sentient beings from Nation. I know Beatriz isn't one. I've had enough interactions with her to know for certain. *I think.*

I swallow the uncomfortable thought away. "So you calling me *sir* is because…?"

She laughs brightly. "Because you're my boss. I take it you weren't briefed."

"Nope."

"I'm one of the field operatives for Jezero's Data and Information Retrieval Force. It's an elite group of operatives who can conduct any number of technical missions for Jezero. We give our lives to the colony, but more than that, we give our lives to the President of Jezero."

I don't like how that sounds. "What do you mean?"

"President orders it, we go, no questions asked."

"But who oversees what the President does?"

She tsks. "No one, really."

"Oh," I breathe, because there is not enough oversight for this type of power. "So how many people are with you? In the…Data Force thing?"

She shrugs again. "About sixty. But age and ability vary greatly. Some operatives are only on the technology side of things, and others have more intensive training and can participate in human subject missions." Her eyes dart away from me briefly as she says *human subject missions*. It would appear she may feel guilty about that.

I might as well ask the question that's been burning since I climbed into the truck with her. "What was your mission with me?"

She looks ahead, placing her hands back on the steering wheel. It's only when her eyes are locked on the tunnel that she speaks. "Sometimes we have to do things that are…more…unethical than the code of Martian law would ordinarily permit."

"So you were breaking the law with what you were doing?"

"No, not exactly. It was more of a gray area."

"And what were you doing?"

Her eyes snap to mine briefly. "Sir, you're an attractive man, and I'm an attractive woman. There are lesser reasons people have spilled secrets."

"I thought so," I say. "It feels terrible, you know."

Her brow furrows. "What?"

I don't know how to describe what she did. How does one sum up a woman attempting to get close to you romantically in order to get potential state secrets? The phrase comes to mind. "Being used."

"I know," she murmurs. "Believe me, I know."

There's an undercurrent of heartache in her tone that brings my memory back to Nation. "I suppose being used comes with the territory when you're into espionage."

"Yes."

"So, what next? What's your mission here?"

"Former President McAllistair decreed that the Agency would fold if we ever were in need of an emergency evacuation. Most of the agents are disbanded, but several of us are in charge of transport trucks. You'll remember Cait from your stay before. She's driving one too. Once we reach Souterraine, we'll have to figure something else out. Since there isn't a Jezero to serve anymore, our oaths are rather useless."

"So what do you want to do?'

"I don't really know, but I'm good at a lot of strange things. I really do love to cook. Maybe repairs. Maybe…" She trails off, and I can't help but feel her tension. She's on the cusp of revealing something big.

"Maybe, what?" I prompt after a beat of silence.

"Well, I don't have a family. The Agency prohibited that for people in my position. But that means, I'm free to really do anything. I think I'd…"

I wait.

"I think I'd like to go to Earth."

Her face pinches in embarrassment, like the words are shocking to hear uttered aloud. I smirk. Saying you want to go to Earth is probably the Martian equivalent of a child on Earth saying they want to go to Mars. "You know," I reply. "I did come from there."

"But are you going back?" Her words come fast and in a single breath. The hope in her question brings me to the sobering reality of how to leave this planet, and what I'll do once I'm back on Earth.

I swallow before I nod. "Yes. Yes, I plan to go back. But it will be a fight."

"I can fight," Beatriz says, and I don't doubt her. It seems I've just found myself an ally in the fight against Nation, an ally in the quest to return to Earth.

Ally, not friend.

39

The ride to Souterraine is blessedly uneventful. Beatriz peppers me with questions about Earth, and I'm only too happy to answer them instead of thinking about being trapped in an underground tunnel between two colonies. Each breath requires me to shove the fear of enclosed spaces and the memory of the cave training implosion away. It's exhausting. When Beatriz asks me about Earth, she asks about phenomena like *snow* and *outside*. Sometimes I forget that people raised on Mars have never truly been outside.

Fresh air is something I can't take for granted, not for a moment. Not after my time in Hub, the scientific research center of Nation. For years, I was trapped inside a building, my every move dictated by scheduling software that tracked my movement through biosensors in the tile floors. When I was finally permitted to leave the building, feeling the sun on my face was a shockingly emotional experience, but it was seeing the outside, natural habitat that brought me peace. Jezero, with all its sterility, reminds me of Hub, and Souterraine, with all its nature, reminds me of freedom.

I explain Earth's weather systems and Nation's topography and geography as best I can. There are still glaring holes in my knowledge of Nation and the entire planet, but Beatriz doesn't need to know that. Instead, I focus on telling her what I do know.

The headlights catch a carving etched into the side of the tunnel, and Beatriz grabs her intercom device. "How's everything going back there?"

There's static, and then a familiar deep voice answers, "Are we there yet?"

I have to laugh. Intercolonial travel is *not* something anyone on Mars enjoys, and the king and I have made this journey twice in mere hours. I can attest that sitting in the front of a transport truck is significantly more enjoyable than the back of one, but it's unpleasant just the same.

"Yes," Beatriz says. "Thirty minutes and we'll be in the Souterraine airlock. Prepare for some bumps as we're coming in though. This airlock isn't the most common port."

My eyes are drawn to Beatriz's. Her face is mostly hidden in shadow, but her eyes contain something hopeful. The bland look of before has been replaced with something else. *Could it be a dream?* Something about the new expression on her face makes me think of Llama. The two of them are...*alike.* Which brings my thoughts back to Llama.

"Beatriz..." I begin, unsure of what to say.

"Hmm?" she hums, her eyes focused on the tunnel road ahead and her hands at the ten and two o'clock position on the wheel.

"Llama..." I squeeze my eyes shut while I think about what to say.

"What happened with you two anyway?" Beatriz asks.

I blow out a breath. "We're engaged. In Nation, they call what happens next a unionization ceremony, but in Souterraine, it's called a marriage."

"Oh." I sense the tiniest deflation in her shoulders, but she pops up again. "Well, that's exciting. Congratulations. Marriage is a big deal in Jezero. And Souterraine. So I guess marriage is a big deal on Mars. Is it not on Earth?"

Her question takes me by surprise. "Uh. I can't speak for all of Earth, but in Nation, unionizing is a big deal. On Earth, unionizing is about power—it's still different here. The King and Queen of Souterraine had us celebrate our formal engagement with a feast."

"A feast?" Beatriz scoffs. "Sounds wasteful. That would never happen in Jezero."

I resist the urge to roll my eyes. "It became very apparent that there are differences between the Martian colonies as soon as we stepped foot in Souterraine."

Beatriz flushes. "I'm sorry." She sets her jaw. "I was just doing my job and following orders."

"Of course," I say, because I can't think of anything else. I know what it's like to be in the service of a corrupt government. That thought stops me short. My father was in charge of a corrupt government too. "Do you think…" I swallow. "Do you think they'll live?"

Beatriz seems to know exactly what I'm referring to. "I'm sorry, Reach," she says. She reaches over the empty middle seat and places her palm on my leg, giving the space just above my knee a squeeze. It's too familiar and entirely strange given our circumstances. I consider that for a moment, and Beatriz removes her hand.

"No, Reach, sir," she says. "They won't live for very long."

"How do you know that?" I ask.

"There are airlock breach measures in place, but with all the airlocks from the evacuation sealed, they only have one way in and out. It's the main airlock, and it's the one that has the most wear and tear. It's also the one that is the weakest due to sheer size."

"What's going to happen to them?"

"They'll try to extend their lives, I'm sure, with the emergency bubble and protocols. They might not be able to get it up and running before the worst happens. If they do nothing…eventually, they'll just fall asleep—and they won't wake up."

I frown.

"It's not painful. And it's not…" She pauses and clears her throat. "That way is not sudden. They know. They can prepare."

"How long?"

"Depends on when the aircycler finally breaches fully. It was only thirty percent effective when President McAllistair went to Jezero. It was at about eleven percent effective when the evacuation was underway. I would imagine that it would be soon."

My eyes water. Greg McAllistair—coward, hero, leader, father, selfish, and selfless man. I don't know what to think. With thoughts of Greg come thoughts of my mother. She never said as much—and how could she have, given the weight of her secrets—but the reunion she must have dreamed about with him will never happen.

The truck jostles and jolts over pits in the road. I have no words.

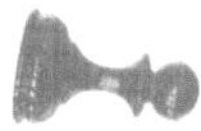

The few minutes it takes to cycle through the Souterraine airlock are blurred. Beatriz says nothing to me directly, but does announce to the back of the truck, "Entering Souterraine territory." She must sense the weight of my emotions. Or perhaps she's kind enough to ignore the tears trickling down my cheeks.

King Alfred snarks back, "About time." With the king's voice, I startle back into the present moment and wipe the tears from my face.

The airlock door to Souterraine opens fully, and I find myself blinking at the sudden change in light after hours in the dark tunnels. It's blinding in comparison.

A throng of people stands in a semicircle around the door.

"We can disembark safely now," Beatriz says into the intercom device. She presses buttons and flips switches on the dashboard. The gentle roar of the truck's machinery stops and silence assaults my ears.

Beatriz turns to me. "It was nice having company on the ride. I'll…see you around, I guess."

"You're leaving?"

"You're very important here. I'm not. So I'll go find my place in this colony and try to earn my way to an Earth mission…" She stops herself. "I mean an Earth assignment. Good luck with your fiancée. I think it might be for the best if I wasn't here for that reunion."

I frown, not liking her insinuation. "I'm a gentle—"

"I know you are, Reach. You didn't give into the training I've had—training specifically meant to exploit weaknesses and attraction. But I get the sense that Llama won't forgive easily. And also, she's coming this way."

Beatriz slips out of the truck door and disappears into the throng of people.

Llama barrels through the crowd as it parts for her, her face creased in worry. She clasps her hitched-up skirts in her fist, showing her knees and lower legs. I'm momentarily stunned at the beauty of the woman running toward me. And then I realize she's running *to me*.

That thought is all I need to jump out of the transport truck and run to her, forging my own path through the throng. Our bodies collide as our lips meet.

With each moment, I feel the truth of who we are, together, etching itself deeply in my soul.

"Reach," Llama breathes, resting her forehead against mine. "I was so worried. Don't leave me again."

"I won't," I breathe in return, knowing full well I can't promise that, but not caring because I will do everything in my power to not leave her again.

It's not enough. Empty promises won't fill the gaping hole of loss and pain and anguish that the last few days have wrought. Only one thing will.

I press a kiss to her lips again as applause erupts around us.

40

AN ELBOW FLIES into my ribs, dragging my attention away from Llama. I scowl, a guttural noise escaping my throat until I realize the elbower was Pippa.

"Reach!" she yells, yanking on my arm. Reluctantly, I let her pull me away from Llama.

"Hi, Pippa." I force a smile.

Llama's hands are crossed over her chest, and I suspect that if I could see her heart, it would be beating just as fast as mine.

Pippa smiles, her joy palpable in the simplest of actions. She grabs my hand, then snags Llama's arm with her other hand. "This way."

I turn my attention to Llama, looking over the crown of Pippa's head. Llama flushes red. "We were supposed to go right to the ceremony," she whispers.

"Oops," I mouth, not feeling at all sorry that we didn't follow orders. Sometime I'd like to *not* be anyone important to *any* government. It's rare to think of my childhood of obscurity as ideal, but I can see now that it was. Leading revolutions, *leading people*, is exhausting.

Pippa bobs and weaves her way through the crowd to a platform where the King and Queen of Souterraine sit properly in chairs behind a podium. "Reach."

Queen Eleanore nods primly, but her eyes twinkle knowingly as she takes in Llama's disheveled hair and flushed cheeks.

King Alfred snorts, but I notice the queen's own slightly disturbed coiffure and swollen lips. It's clear that the king and queen love each other, and though they don't give in to physical displays of affection often, they obviously just did.

"Reach," King Alfred acknowledges as I raise a brow toward him and slightly incline my head toward the queen with a scowl indicative of his own. And then perhaps the strangest thing that has ever happened to me occurs. The king *laughs*. "Yes," he says. "I kissed my wife. I would imagine that you and Princess Llama have enjoyed that pastime lately too. It tends to be how things work after surviving something so harrowing that you not only saw, but walked the very fine edge of what lies between life and death."

I stare, stunned. The king is being *friendly*. He was assistive in Jezero, and helpful, but so much was happening I couldn't make sense of it. "I…" I start to speak, but the queen holds up her hand.

"We know, Reach. And welcome to the family. You really are a great leader." With those words, she stands and begins walking across the platform to the microphone. On her way, she passes Llama and me. She touches my shoulder affectionately. "Welcome home," she whispers, then shoves me down into one of the chairs.

I let out an 'oof' of surprise as I find myself seated, and I have to laugh. Llama's grandparents are unexpectedly wonderful.

Llama lowers herself into the chair next to mine, but it feels too far away. I pick up her hand and tug her closer, wrapping my arm around her shoulders. Something about touching her makes me relax. I feel grounded. I feel *safe*. But more than safe, I feel *home*.

That thought shocks me, and I'm pondering it when Queen Eleanore begins speaking, dragging my attention away from my own internal reactions and over to the needs of Souterraine as they absorb the now-defunct colony of Jezero.

"Welcome to Souterraine," she says, her voice calm, clear, and composed. "We are so very glad you are here. The evacuation of Jezero Colony was truly a heroic undertaking. Each person who participated in the event risked their lives in the name of the Martian code of Law. Lives were risked for the greater gain of protecting life on Mars. Here in Souterraine, we value life, agriculture, and ingenuity. We are peaceful. We have prepared housing for our newest colonists. The children will attend school. We will help you in any way we can with your adjustment."

There's a roar of approval, but it's not hard to see the happy noise is coming only from the Souterraine colonists showing support to their leaders. One of the Jezero political leaders steps forward, still wearing their sash.

I look down at my chest where I see that I, too, still wear my sash. I move to take it off, but Llama places her hand on mine and says, "Don't." My eyes search hers, looking for a reason to continue representing the highest power of a now-defunct colony. "They need a leader, Reach. You'll have to be one for them."

My hand cramps with an itching urge to rip off any signs of leadership as quickly as possible, but I don't. I still my body and count my breaths.

The Jezero leader approaches the platform. King Alfred bends over and listens to the man as he speaks into the king's ear. I can't see the king's face, but the Jezero man talks for a long time. Long enough that Queen Eleanore leaves the podium and joins the king and the leader. From her stance, I can see her side profile. I watch as her countenance changes from joy to one of abject determination. The Jezero leader looks at me and points. King Alfred and Queen Eleanore nod, then turn around and summon me over.

I can tell that this small conference happening at the edge of a stage is *not* going to be something I want.

"Yes?" I grit the words out through a grimace as I crouch down to hear what the Jezero man needs to say.

"We want you to represent us as President here. And we also need to remind the Queen and King of Souterraine that *your* aircyclers may have a few years left because you have trees, but we're running out of time. The code of Martian Law has always been clear about what to do when the planet will not support humankind any longer."

I don't say anything because I do not know the code of Martian Law beyond that human life is to be protected but never trifled with.

"Yes," King Alfred says. He turns to me. "Reach, the code says, *'When Martian soil becomes inhospitable for human life, be it in ten years or ten thousand, the resident Martians will return to Earth, having given the planet time to heal, and successfully undertaking the greatest of all human experiments'.*"

I bite my tongue.

"Reach," the king says. "Is Nation run by a hospitable government?"

He knows this, but he's asking me in front of this Jezero leader because it helps *me* with *my* chess game against Nation. "No."

"Reach." The king says my name again, and I sense it's to make a point. "As the most recent person to arrive and reside on Mars, you have the most experience regarding Earth matters. What should we expect when we return to Earth, specifically to Nation?"

I swallow. "A fight." I think about Beatriz and her desire to go to Earth. "But I think…" I frown. Llama is also aware of Earth matters, maybe even more than I am. "I think Princess Llama should be part of these conversations." I survey the throng of people shifting nervously. "But not now. This has been too much for everyone."

The Jezero leader stands and gives a small, stiff bow. I nod. The queen steps forward to the microphone. "To assist with the transition from Jezero Colony to Souterraine, the Jezero leaders will maintain their positions of leadership and will work with the Souterraine advisory council to determine the best course of action for all Martian colonists. Reach McAllistair, son of the former President McAllistair, will remain as a figurehead for all things Jezero Colony-related."

I toy with the edge of the sash crossing my abdomen. *So much for getting rid of this stupid thing.*

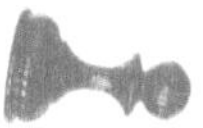

All I want is to collapse into a bed, or a heap, or on the ground. And yet, the people of Jezero are *all* staring at me. The eyes of an entire colony burn into my being and singe my conscience. They've lost everything. I know that I am the last link to life as they knew it. Even if I'm unfamiliar, it's all about the stupid sash and succession laws for power. Who am I to deny them?

I swallow, the stark realization that they do not care one bit about *me* but about the *sash* almost making me walk away and leaving them to figure it out on their own. It's Llama who doesn't let that happen.

"Reach," she whispers, effectively breaking my stupor. It would appear that being sleep-deprived makes me forget to move and act. "I'll come with you to show them the place we prepared for Jezero."

I crinkle my brow in confusion but bob my head in agreement. She sounds sane, and at the moment, my own thoughts do not. Llama tugs my hand, and I follow her obediently to where the Jezero colonists stand, shifting uneasily in the Souterraine sunlight. In the haze of my own confusion, I find the queen leading the king over to the colonists in a similar fashion.

Llama steps behind me just as we arrive at the grouping. "Tell them we have prepared a village for them," she murmurs.

"Jezero colonists." My voice comes out rough. I shake my head, trying to clear the pressure building in my ears. "We have prepared a village for them."

Llama's hand is on my arm and she narrows her eyes at me. "Reach. Focus on my nose," she hisses. The queen's voice enters the fray, but my eyes stay locked on Llama's nose. I wish my own nose could detach and move around the way hers is.

"We have prepared a village for you. It is near the Souterraine school, and there is work to be done in the sectors. It might not be what you're used to, but it is good work, vital to the health of your people."

"How can anything *here* be vital to the health of our people? Our people don't exist anymore," a gruff voice gripes. It might be Percy, or maybe someone who sounds like him.

"Shut up, criminal!" a man retorts.

"You'll find," the queen answers with her songlike voice, "that your colony does not make your people who they are. Souterraine does not wish to take away your heritage. We simply ask that you contribute to the good of this colony, which you are now residing in. We ask nothing more than children to attend the school and for the adults to assist with work in the sectors where it is needed. As we adjust, I am sure you will find the proper place for your talents to be utilized."

A MUV drives up to the group and startles my gaze away from Llama. The ground rushes at my face and then slaps me. I'm not sure how that happened. Ground is supposed to stay stationary. Llama crouches next to me. "C'mon, Reach." She pulls me up and opens one of the half doors of the MUV. I feel a push on my lower back as I tumble into the vehicle.

It is blissfully dark under my eyelids, and the gentle rocking of the vehicle makes me fall into a light sleep. I'm aware of movement, of Llama beside me, and then suddenly, the car jerks to a stop.

My eyes fly open, burned by the brightness of the day light overhead.

The queen stands in front of the MUV, which she was driving, and announces with a sweeping gesture, "This is the Jezero Village Sector of Souterraine."

Curiosity is stronger than my need to sleep. I take in the scenery. A row of wooden cottages with thatched roofs and brightly painted doors curves out of sight. The river runs to the right of the cottages, hidden by a bank of weeping willows. Piles of small red rocks from the riverbed sit next to the MUV.

It's for them to make cairns. I shake my head to clear away the tears forming. The rulers of Souterraine shock me at every turn. They are the kindest people I have ever met. A piece of stone that I cemented over my heart chips and cracks.

"Please, settle in," the queen says. "Jezero leaders, if you could please assist with this task, we'd be most grateful. You would know best how to assign the cottages."

"Ma'am," a woman I recognize but can't quite place speaks. "What about the…orphan?" she whispers.

The queen frowns. "Orphan?"

"His father elected to stay."

Ethan. My eyes fly open and I'm wide awake. *What will happen to Ethan?*

"Where is he?"

The woman gestures and the queen, despite silver streaks in her hair and apparent age, hops off the MUV and follows the woman into the crowd.

It takes only a moment, but then the queen is back, with Ethan gripping her hand.

"Ethan," I say.

The queen looks at me in confusion. "Ethan, do you want to stay in the village with a family here or come to the castle with us?"

The child bites his lip. He's trying so hard to be brave, but he trembles. How can a child make the choice of who to live with when he's so young?

"Ma'am," a different voice calls from the crowd. It's one of the Jezero advisors. He spins a tablet in his hand and holds it up to the crowd. "Jezero is…gone."

The group hushes, and any excitement over the idyllic village melts away into oblivion. An otherworldly noise breaks the silence. One by one, the Jezero colonists begin to sing their strange, wordless music. This time, I understand what it is. It is a lament. They mourn and grieve, tears streaming down their faces as they sing. It's the music of my father's people that breaks me.

I climb over the side of the vehicle and find Ethan, tears cutting a path in the grime on his cheeks, with his hand in the queen's. I kneel to his level and hug him. The two of us, orphans in an unfamiliar place.

"Ethan, will you come to the castle with us?" I ask.

"Yes." His tiny voice fills the pulsating sorrow.

The music ends, the silence encompassing even more brokenness than the music.

Queen Eleanore wipes tears away from her eyes with the back of her dress sleeve. "We will take the child to the castle. Thank you for sharing your grief with us. We will leave you now to mourn and adjust to life, as is your custom. You are welcome here in Souterraine."

The queen opens one of the half doors and helps Ethan into the back. He sits between Llama and me as the queen reclaims her place in the driver's seat. Soon, his small head presses against my arm, and I catch Llama's gentle gaze on his sleeping form.

41

AFTER THE JEZERO village, Queen Eleanore drives back to the castle. She pulls the MUV to the side once we reach the clover field. When she's finished parking, she turns around and takes one look at me before she whispers something to Llama. Llama nods her agreement, which I barely see because everything has taken on a hazy quality again. Without understanding how, I exit the vehicle and lean against it.

Llama leaves the queen and approaches the king, who wobbles just a bit as he stands. We've been without proper sleep for at least fifty hours. Ethan wakes and stays by the queen's side, holding her hand.

Looping her arm through the king's, Llama starts toward me. She extends her other arm, and I squint my eyes while I rise. The lights are too bright. Everything is waving.

"C'mon, Reach," Llama murmurs, and I follow the sound of her voice. All I want is to lie down and listen to her voice. Maybe she could read to me. She loops my arm through hers, and I force my body to take steps that match her own. Each step is akin to trudging through sludge.

I'm vaguely aware of Bernard approaching the king and leading him off somewhere. Llama walks me to my bedroom. She stands at the threshold, wringing her hands together in the folds of her skirt. "Do you want to change…"

I should, but the very idea sounds too difficult. I flop onto the bed and close my eyes. I sense the moment when Llama starts to back away. "Stay?" I whisper.

"Ok," she whispers back.

I open one eye and watch as she props the door open with a vase full of red flowers from the dresser. With a scraping noise, she drags a chair from the corner of the room over and sits next to my bed. "Go to sleep, Reach," she murmurs.

I relish the feel of her hand gently stroking my forehead, her fingers tunneling through my hair, and then I'm blissfully aware of nothing at all.

A blanket covers my chest when I wake up. The sun streams through the window, dust motes dancing across my vision as I experience that momentary disorientation that comes from awakening after a deep sleep.

I run my fingers along the blanket, feeling the grain of the weave. It's as if the sensory input kicks my brain into gear, and honestly, I'd rather go back to being oblivious. The crushing weight of Jezero Colony, the evacuation, the leadership role I never asked for, the expectations on me from the King and Queen of Souterraine as a leader here, my relationship with Llama…all of it settles on my chest. The anxiety I've worked so hard to manage flares, sending tendrils of heat across my skin, making me itchy from my scalp to my toes.

I lie quietly, breathing in and out, practicing a double inhale, counting each one. I get to eighty-three when the door opens gently and Llama steps through, Pippa, Ethan, and the queen on her heels.

"Are you hungry?" the queen asks softly. "You've been asleep for a full Martian day."

I don't really know, but I haven't eaten in days. Martian days on the surface are called Sols, and they are longer than an Earth day. Underground, the technology allowed the original colonists to keep to the twenty-four-hour schedule, but the queen's use of "Martian day" means I've been asleep for more than twenty-four hours.

Pippa bounds over and sits on the bed, narrowly missing my shins. At least I'm alert enough to move my legs out of the way. Queen Eleanore fixes Pippa with a stern look. Pippa scoots off the bed with a pout.

"Pippa," Queen Eleanore says. "We do not sit on other people's beds."

"Sorry," she says, but not looking sorry at all.

Llama smirks from behind the queen's shoulder. "I brought you some broth." She holds a wooden tray by the rounded handles at the side. A steaming bowl and a hunk of crusty bread sit on top. I try to look at Llama's beautiful face, a face that I love, but my eyes keep wandering to the food. Now that I know it's here, my empty stomach rumbles.

Llama carries the tray and sets it across my lap. I can't resist the urge to place a kiss on her temple as she stands. My mouth won't form any words because all I can think is, *eat this food*. But Llama deserves some acknowledgment, even if it's brief. She sinks into the chair next to my bed and spreads her skirts out around her.

I tear the bread into pieces and dunk it into the broth. The flavor explodes on my tongue, and suddenly, bite by bite, things don't seem quite so dire. It's not until I'm sopping up the last of the broth with the bread that Queen Eleanore speaks.

"So," she says. "We have a few things we could use your help with regarding the Jezero colonists, helping them understand the way of things here."

I blink at her. "I don't really understand the way of things here."

"Oh, I know, dear. But we can tell you what to say. It's just that it needs to come from someone with Jezero authority, or else they… might not believe it to be in their best interest."

I catch a glimpse of Llama rolling her eyes. I resist the urge to do the same. My authority over Jezero is ridiculous, given what I know about that colony. Their rules about being an heir were absurd.

"Ok." I sigh, feeling the tension rise just under my skin again.

"Excellent." Queen Eleanore smiles. "Also, we need some assistance with refurbishing our communication station. You both saw Jezero's station while you were there, correct?"

"Yes," Llama says tersely.

"Good. Our station has the capability of contacting and receiving messages from Earth, but it hasn't been used in that manner since Alec was…" The queen looks off into the distance, then catches Llama's gaze. "Anyway, we need to update the station. Jezero took over interplanetary communication, and we simply related news and transport shipment schedules. Things are changing now. Alfred won't be pleased."

I scan the room at the mention of Alfred. The king is…confusing to me.

"Where is he?" I blurt.

Pippa laughs. "Still sleeping!"

"We wanted to talk to you first," Llama explains.

"Why?"

"Because we think…that Percy had communication with Nation…and Dr. Jog is…" She mumbles the last words, but at the mention of my mentor, I shove myself up using my elbows, wondering why she sounds distraught.

"We think he's…dead." Llama's jaw shakes as she clenches down on it. Tears well in the corners of her eyes.

My own jaw locks. Dr. Jog can't be gone. He can't be. The single word I utter in response comes out harsher than I intend. "Why?"

"Margot—she is the leader who took over communication management for Jezero after Percy was disgraced—followed the evacuation protocols perfectly, meaning she brought transcripts from the last archives with her," the queen explains. She looks down fondly at little Ethan. "There are some people who, despite being part of Jezero Colony, have been quite helpful. Margot is the one who requested we get our communication station up and running for interplanetary connections."

"Why do you think that Dr. Jog—?" My voice catches on the 'g,' and I cough.

"Here." Queen Eleanore reaches into the pocket of her dress and extracts one of the black spinning top tablets. She turns it counterclockwise several times, then taps the top and passes it to me.

I recognize the strange device from Jezero. As I look down into the glass surface, I see the words *"Jog executed. Be aware of rogue space travelers. They are coming to coordinates…"* The message continues past the confines of the screen, but I can't bear to look at anything else. The words *Jog executed* cloud my ability to read further.

"Wait," I mumble, forcing the tears *not* to come. "Does this mean Nation knows about all the things here on Mars?"

Llama bites her lip and nods.

"It appears they knew about Jezero," Queen Eleanore supplies. "Margot is looking into her archives, but it's not an easy thing to search. Percy was rather…underhanded."

"But what about Souterraine?" I ask, hating the feeling of Nation's tentacles expanding across planets and into space.

"As far as we know, they do not." The queen levels me with a look. "We have worked hard to build our own world here, away from the conflict and struggles of places like *Nation* and Jezero." I don't miss how she places Nation and Jezero in the same category. "But again, Margot is digging into the Jezero archives. I need to go wake Alfred, so we'll leave you two. But, you should know, our council is meeting tomorrow. We need to discuss all our options. Mars has been a hospitable home to us for many years, but I fear the time of our welcome on this planet is running out. Pippa, come, please."

Pippa skips off to meet Queen Eleanore, leaving flower petals floating in her wake. While we were speaking, Pippa systematically removed each petal from the red flowers in the vase. They pool by the door, reminiscent of all the blood on Nation's hands.

Ethan stops by the door, his wide brown eyes sadder than any five-year-old's has a right to be. "I'm sorry." And then Ethan slides away from the door and the pitter-patter of little feet disappears down the hall.

Llama hangs her head and reaches for my hand. "Reach," she says, her voice shaking like glass at a high frequency. "I think they… I think he's gone."

I grip her hand tighter with mine, squeezing all the words I can't say into this one gesture. "He was a good man."

We sit in stony silence while our tears fall on our hands. Neither of us makes any move to wipe the water away, a vigil of tears for a mentor, ally, and friend.

42

The gurgling protest of my stomach breaks our vigil. Llama laughs at the absurd loudness of my hunger, and I join her. Grief is a strange concept. It's a weight bearing down on your shoulders for an unspecified amount of time and then lifting for a while. At first, a moment, and then lifting for longer, but all the time, you know that the weight is there, hovering, and that it can come crashing back down at any moment.

Llama swipes her tears away with the backs of her hands. "I think we should get something to eat."

My voice cracks as I answer her. "Yeah. Are you hungry?"

The corner of her mouth quirks up in a small smile, and she shakes her head affirmatively. "I'm going to wash my face. I'll meet you in the kitchen."

"Sure. That sounds good." I start to remove the blankets from my body, but as I do, I catch a whiff of an odor. The cold tentacles of horror descend on me as I realize the smell *is me*. "Uhhh." I stop abruptly. "I'm going to shower first."

Llama's nose crinkles as she stands, nods, and leaves the room with a swishing of a dark green skirt. Once she's gone, I spring out of bed. I feel disgusting and grimy and repulsive. The air in my room tastes stale.

I fling open the wooden shutters to let the light and the freshness in. I need more plants in here to purify the room of my stench. I stare down at the reddish-colored bed sheets. I don't know where the laundry is, but I know they need to go there. Before I shower, I decide to pull the sheets off my bed. The problem is that while I know how to ensure the sheets get to the laundry—I simply place them in the woven hamper by the door—I don't know where to get replacement sheets for later. The smell is so strong that I don't want the sheets in my room overnight. I suspect they might need to be burned.

Leaving the bedding in a heap on the floor, I pick a soft, pale green-colored shirt and tan pants from the dresser drawers, along with fresh underthings. The Presidential sash of Jezero Colony sits rolled into two tight loops with a single star visible. It looks very proper and formal, and I certainly didn't bother with anything other than throwing the sash off my body. *Is there a protocol for how to store this thing?*

I shake my head before heading to the shower.

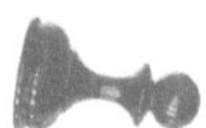

Clean-shaven and smelling like the eucalyptus soap left in the showers, I return to my room. The open shutters have made a difference, and already the air feels brighter, cleaner, fresher, but the clothes I was wearing for my sojourn to Jezero and the sheets still need to be dealt with. Scooping them into a large bundle, I leave the room. I'll find the laundry, and then I'll go to the kitchen. Bernard will have something delicious. My stomach rumbles in anticipation.

The castle is an odd place because while it can be bustling with advisors and Pippa's running, it's also often quiet. I'm so hungry I'd like for Pippa to crash into me so she can show me the fastest way to the laundry. As it is, I do not have that luck.

My instincts tell me that laundry would be on a lower level of the castle, but I can't be sure. I wander past the kitchen, following the corridors past rooms with small plaques outside the doors that say things like *Parlour A* and *Sitting Room, Hospitality*, and *Ballroom E*. Ballroom E's door is cracked slightly open, and I hear voices from within. I ease the door open with my toes, wishing for something a little more substantial than just open air between my toenails and the solid wooden door. *If there's anything I miss about Nation, it's proper shoes.*

It takes effort to maneuver around the heavy door while holding a pile of dirty laundry, but I manage to squeeze inside Ballroom E without dropping the bundle in my arms.

My eyes adjust to the dim light in Ballroom E, and I stand frozen in memory. This room feels familiar. It's a lengthy rectangle, and at the end of the room is a short set of stairs that disappear into darkness. The polished floor gleams and chandeliers cast sparkles onto the ground. The pale curtains surrounding the windows on the long wall dance in the breeze.

I take a breath. This room is *not* the banquet room from when I first went to Hub City. *I am safe.*

I have to tell myself that three times before my feet unstick and I can move again. The voices are fainter, but I can still hear them. I can't tell if they're up or if the room continues beyond the stairs, but I do need to catch up to them if I'm ever going to find the laundry.

I try to walk quickly, but the shoes make a clack-clack-clack as they flop against the floor, and the floor is slippery. I hurry as best I can to the stairs, but something catches my eye from the dark corner next to the wooden stairs.

It's a beast with black skin, a wide body, three gold-colored feet, and a startling monochromatic line of teeth. I feel the compelling urge to touch the teeth. I don't know why, but my feet carry me to the behemoth, and I drop the bundle. With one finger, I reach out and press down. A sound reverberates from the belly of the beast and I step back, startled. When the beast doesn't move, I look closer.

Under the teeth is a black bench. I pull the bench out and sit. My fingers arch over the teeth, and one by one, I press down in order from the left to the right. White and black. White and black. The sounds begin deep, and they bellow before ending in twinkly high strains.

"What are you doing?" a small voice asks from behind the body of the beast.

I jump up and feel a flush creep down my face. My eyes rove the room and find Ethan, in Souterraine clothing, and Pippa standing at the back of the *thing*.

"I'm…" I struggle for words.

"Play piano?" Pippa asks, pointing at the teeth.

My brow furrows. Pippa doesn't wait for a response. She slides next to me, pushing me to the right edge of the bench as Ethan follows and plunks onto the left edge. With a gracefulness that surprises me, Pippa begins to press the teeth. Her fingers fly as music fills the air.

My eyes widen. The *thing* is an instrument. It makes music.

"You do," Pippa commands as she slides toward Ethan. Ethan stands up and takes Pippa's hand in his. I slide into the middle and place my hands as I saw Pippa's.

I envision the way her fingers moved, but I can't see where she started. "Which one was first?"

Pippa leans over my shoulder and presses one white key.

Inexplicably, my brain knows what to do. My fingers move and press the keys in a replica of Pippa's movements, but mostly I hear the sounds she produced and how each one blended into the next.

"Wow," Ethan whispers from where he sits next to me. I didn't notice him sitting down next to me while I pressed the *piano's* teeth.

"You're good," Pippa says. "Lessons?"

I shake my head.

Her eyes widen. "By ear!" Pippa grasps my hand and smiles, but then she wrinkles her nose. "Smell?"

I look down at the sheets rolled into a ball on the floor near the piano as my stomach gives another tremendous rumble.

"I need to go to the laundry and then the kitchen. Would you help me find the laundry?"

Pippa looks at Ethan, grins, and takes off running. I only have a moment to grab the smelly laundry from off the floor, but I sprint after her and Ethan, ducking around the stairs and into another hallway.

Pippa's dress is a shade of pink that looks unintentional. Almost as if something red was washed with something lighter, and the colors ran together. It's not a color seen anywhere else in the castle, and I'm thankful for that because as Pippa turns corners and disappears down hallways, the flash of her skirt keeps me on track. This castle is a maze, and there is no one who knows it better than Pippa.

Ethan's smaller legs can't run as fast as Pippa's. He stays near me, gamboling along in a half gallop.

Finally, Pippa stands still outside a small door marked *Laundry*. I have no idea where we are, or how we got here, but Pippa opens the door and ushers me into a brightly painted room. The floor is white wood, the walls are white, the ceiling is white, and there are rows and rows of white cabinets along one wall while along the other is a bank of windows with machines under them.

Ethan steps through the door with me, but Pippa does not.

Three people stand in the back of the room at a table, folding and sorting clothes. They all wear Souterraine clothing and a white apron over the reddish-hued cloth. An older woman with stick-straight gray hair, an older man with no hair at all, and a familiar younger woman. The second our gazes meet, I recognize her.

Beatriz.

Something about her being here in the castle irks me. She's too close. I don't trust her. I know we parted amicably after our ride to Souterraine and she helped evacuate Jezero, but my hackles rise all the same.

Ethan sneezes, and the man and woman look at us.

"May I help you?" the woman asks, her voice deeper than I'd expected.

"Yeah. I…had some clothing and bedding that needed washing."

"And you couldn't put it in your hamper and wait for our staff to care for it, President Reach?" The suspicion in her voice cuts through the bright air with a clinical precision.

I want to explain, but Beatriz rolls her eyes at the woman's snarky attitude. That little act of defiance stops me from explaining. I rescued a colony, I don't need to explain.

"Where should I put them, Miss…" I wait for her to respond, but she doesn't. She frowns, likely from the stench, and gestures to a machine under the windows.

"Any of those will do. Separate by color." She turns her attention back to the man and Beatriz. "We do not usually have visitors in the laundry room. It's not a place for spying and secrets. It's a place where we maintain the cleanliness standards of Souterraine. Beatriz, go assist him."

I bite back a laugh of irony. Miss Laundry is being cold toward me because I might be spying for Jezero? *Does she even know what Beatriz is?* Of course she doesn't.

"Sorry about her," Beatriz whispers as she stands next to me. Her nose scrunches. "Yuck."

"Yeah well, I kind of was dragged from my engagement ceremony all the way to Jezero and then had to help with an evacuation and then back to Souterraine, and that meant I wore the same clothes and was awake for roughly…" I do some mental calculations. "Fifty-nine hours, and then I collapsed into bed and slept for another twenty-eight."

"Oh. You can sort the things by color and put them in different machines." She strides over to the white cabinets and begins pulling small vials out, as well as a jar of white powder.

After I finish shoving the different colored items into the machines, Beatriz marches over and flips dials and knobs. The rush of water sounds and she scoops powder inside. Then, she opens a small vial and shakes tiny drops of something into the water before closing a lid.

"Behold the great mystery and highly guarded secret of how we wash things in Souterraine," she says.

"Why are you here?" I ask bluntly. Because *why* is she here in the castle doing laundry? I know she's a highly trained operative. And while no one runs around spilling secrets here, it is suspicious.

"The king and queen asked us to help the colony. And since Jezero colonists need to get used to Souterraine clothing and systems, I figured I'd learn how. I'm not out to unearth secrets or spy, President Reach. And if I was, you'd know because you would have reinstated my agency and given the orders." She blinks at me, a challenge in her eyes, but I can't understand what she's challenging me to do.

"Oi! You two!" the man calls while he snaps his fingers. I can't tell if the man and woman are ignoring Ethan on purpose or just haven't seen him. "You can go." The woman points at me and then points at Beatriz. "And you need to stay. Your laundry service training is just beginning."

Beatriz gives Ethan and me a wry smile. "See you around, sir."

Ethan and I leave the room, but I'm aware of the piercing glares the man and woman direct at my back and confused by Beatriz's comments.

One interaction in a laundry room showed better than anything else that centuries of distrust and disagreement between Souteraine and Jezero won't be undone in a single day.

"C'mon, Ethan," I say loudly enough for the man and woman in the back of the room to hear. "Some people are too suspicious to spend time with."

Ethan looks at me questioningly, but follows me out the door where Pippa awaits in the hall.

"Why didn't you come in?" I ask.

She points to her dress. "Bertha said I can't…help…anymore."

That explains the color.

My stomach rumbles, followed by Ethan's. Pippa grins. "Picnic! With Llama too!"

She's off running through the castle, and Ethan and I take off after her.

43

Pippa leads us through the castle, flowing through the labyrinthian passages with a skill only she possesses. Ethan and I keep up a bit better this time. It's easier for me when I'm not holding a bundle of laundry in my arms.

Pippa darts through the door into the kitchen and gleefully exclaims to a surprised Bernard, "Picnic!"

Bernard bends over and extracts the spoon he dropped at Pippa's exuberant greeting from the cutting board of vegetables. "A picnic, Princess Pippa?" His voice is gentle, his eyes kind. It seems everyone but Bertha has a soft spot for Pippa. "How many guests this time?"

Pippa's mouth purses. She points at herself, Ethan, and me, and then says, "Llama!"

Bernard looks at me.

"Four, I think," I answer.

Bernard shakes his head and rolls his eyes heavenward, but I can see he's smiling.

"Hello, young man." Bernard crouches down to Ethan's level. "What is your name?"

Ethan ducks behind my leg, but peeks out and answers, "Efan."

"Ethan. How lovely to meet you. I hear you'll be living at the castle now?"

Ethan shakes his little head, his brown curls tumbling like waves at the motion.

"Well, how lovely. I'm Bernard. I cook. We'll have lots of fun together. Princess Pippa will keep you entertained by finding every shortcut possible in this castle."

Ethan smiles shyly before Bernard stands to his full height. "Princess Llama is outside. I believe she said something about the clover field and the main door. I'll make this picnic up and then send it with Princess Pippa."

Bernard passes us a hunk of crusty bread slathered with butter.

"For the wait," he says, winking at Ethan.

"Thank you, Bernard." I smile at the older man.

Ethan repeats my thanks and we step away from the kitchen.

I do know how to get from the kitchen to the clover field, and the idea of a picnic sounds delightful, especially now that the warm, crusty, buttery bread has stopped my stomach from rumbling.

Beside me, Ethan licks his fingers and then looks embarrassed. "Sorry," he says. "That wasn't good manns."

"Manners?" I ask. I haven't quite figured out all of his speech idiosyncrasies, but I'm getting a little better.

"Yeah, those."

"It's ok," I say. "You were hungry."

"Yeah, I was." His eyes widen as we step through the wooden door into the clover field.

Llama stands by the side of the door facing away from us. She holds a smooth red rock the size of her hand, and there are several other rocks lying on the ground around her feet. She places the rock on top of another and groans as it falls over.

"What are you doing?" I ask in a low voice and she jumps, placing a hand over her heart.

Ethan walks over to her and tugs on her dress. "Can I help? I'm good at cairns."

Llama's gaze slowly, sheepishly returns to mine, and I understand that I caught her in a moment of vulnerability and she's not entirely secure in that yet.

She kneels in the clover next to Ethan and hands him the stone.

"I thought that, since you're living here, you would like to have a cairn outside the door, just like at Jezero."

Ethan's eyes light up. "Yes!" He turns the stone over in his hands before he places it gently on the first rock. "Could I have another one?"

Llama hands him another one.

I sink down into the clover with them.

Ethan places each rock until Llama says, "That's it."

Ethan counts, "One, two, three, four, five, six… Six people in my family?"

Llama nods and points to the two bottom stones. "Yes. In the castle, there are more than six people usually, but you get to be part of the family with the queen and king,"

"I do?" Ethan asks, hope shining in his eyes.

I cock my head and look at Llama. "Are they adopting him?" I ask over Ethan's head.

Llama smiles a yes, and I'm glad of it.

"And then there's also Pippa." She points to another stone. "There's me and Reach." She points to two more, and then she gently touches the little stone on top of the cairn. "And you."

Ethan smiles. "I like this one better than the other one. The other one was sad. Momma's rock was never put back."

Suddenly, I have an idea. Cairns might be a Jezero tradition, but we could certainly honor Ethan's family of origin too.

"I think we should add two more for Ethan's…" I almost say *parents*, but I don't know what to call them.

"Ethan," Llama asks tenderly as Ethan slips his hand in hers. "Should we add a rock for your momma? And your dad too?"

Ethan's eyes are solemn. "Can we?"

"Of course. But we'll need to go to Jezero Village to get two more stones from the riverbank pile."

Just then, Pippa comes out of the castle swinging a woven picnic basket vigorously along her arm. "Ethan!" she shouts and runs to him like she hasn't seen him in years, even though it's only been minutes. He gives Pippa a hug, and the two of them walk away from me and Llama before sitting in the clover.

"So, did I miss anything else while I was sleeping after Jezero?" I ask Llama as she brushes a stray tendril of hair off of her face.

"No. It was just…too much to tell you with the news about Dr. Jog…" She bursts into tears. "And Ethan's parents…" She gasps, and I do the only thing I could possibly do in the moment. I step forward and tug her into my arms. Her cheek rests on my shoulder, and I feel the wetness of her tears seeping through the fabric of my shirt. Her tears brand my skin. The knowledge that we belong together and I don't want to wait to marry her singes deep into my soul.

I rub circles on her back and let her cry.

Ethan comes running over. "Why are you sad, Llama?" his tiny voice asks.

"Sometimes I'm just sad because sad things happen in the world." She frowns. "And on Mars."

Ethan's arms wrap around Llama's legs, pulling her off balance. I stabilize her and keep her from falling on the little boy at her side. When Ethan lets go, Llama straightens and shifts away from my embrace.

"I'm sad too, sometimes," Ethan says with seriousness. "But sometimes I'm happy." Then he runs to the picnic blanket he and Pippa spread out and skids to a stop before flopping down onto the red-and-white-checkered fabric.

Llama's hand reaches out and grabs my own. "I'm glad we're here. Together," she says, giving a pointed look in Ethan's direction.

"It bothers you? That he's here?" I ask.

Her shoulders slump. "Yes. But not because he's here. Because he's an orphan. And I grew up practically an orphan. For all intents and purposes, I was one. I just hate that his father made that choice. That he couldn't try to live for his son."

"Llama." I tip her chin up so her eyes meet mine. "People make wrong choices every day. People make big mistakes, people make small mistakes. People do things that eat us up inside. But when we forgive them, we can move forward."

Llama blanches. "You're talking about me, aren't you?"

I feel a tender smile creeping across my cheeks. I bring her hand to my lips and press a kiss to the back of it. "Yes. Because I love you." I press another kiss there. "You can forgive Frank DiCusso for abandoning Ethan, and you can forgive your parents for what happened to you, because you know deep down that they didn't choose this for you. And you can forgive Dr. Jog for giving his life to save ours."

"Grief doesn't make any sense, Reach."

"No, it doesn't. But I'll be here with you through all of it." I smile gently at Llama before tugging her hand. "Now, come on, Ethan is waving us over, and Pippa looks like she's eaten an entire pie."

Llama looks at Pippa and giggles as she sees sticky blue all over Pippa's cheeks and down the front of her pink dress. She lets go of my hand before she runs across the field to the picnic blanket, and I can see that she feels lighter.

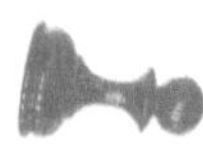

I slide down to the checkered blanket as Llama hands me a sandwich wrapped in wax-coated fabric. I'm sitting next to her, and our shoulders brush. I remember Queen Eleanore's words about love and wanting the best for the other. All I want for Llama is her good. I've never understood it until now, but watching Ethan and seeing his father's selfish choice to abandon him to strangers brought home the point of choosing the good for another, even when it's hard for yourself—choosing the good, that's real *love*. Ethan needs a lot of love. Thankfully, I know that the Queen and King of Souterraine will give it.

I take a big bite and sigh. "Bernard is a genius," I say around bites.

Pippa laughs. "You play…by ear…you…genius."

Llama lowers a brow. "What does she mean?"

I'd explain, but Ethan surprises me by telling Llama all about the piano.

"An instrument?" She whistles sharply through her teeth. "And you just *knew* what to do? Did you have training?"

I shake my head no. "No, I just…heard the sounds. And I watched what Pippa did, and I tried to do that."

"Well, what song did you play, Pippa?"

Pippa scrunches her nose, but Ethan answers, "*Für Elise*. It's ancient. Did you really come from Earth? Do they not have music there? Only people here have instruments, but in Jezero, we sing a lot. Music is culture."

The line *music is culture* sounds ridiculous coming from a five-year-old's mouth, but is delivered with such sincerity that I bite my cheek to keep from laughing.

"We did come from Earth," Llama answers. "And there wasn't much music there. We learned more about science and progress than anything."

"What's progress?"

Llama shrugs. "It's an idea people made up. Something to keep us unhappy and always working toward the next thing, I guess."

Pippa unearths a napkin from the picnic basket and begins wiping her face, but it's hard to get all the smudges of blueberry without a mirror.

"Here," Llama says gently. She pours a little water from the canteen onto the napkin and wipes Pippa's face free of the blueberries. I watch, in awe of her tenderness. Greg said that the leaders of Souterraine were weak because of their tenderness. More and more, I see tenderness as strength.

Ethan's brown eyes bounce between us. "You look at her the way my dad looked at my momma."

Ethan's words, coupled with thoughts of my own father, break the fissures of composure I've held onto into full-fledged cracks.

The weight of grief drops heavily on my shoulders, and a tear leaks out from my eye. Ethan sees me wipe the tears away.

"I cry too," he says as he scoots closer and grasps my hand. The sticky feel of his palm in mine pushes clarity to the forefront of my mind. Nation and Jezero and their determination to use science or money and power as the only means of worth were wrong—*are* wrong.

It's startling to understand what's at stake. The Resistance has never been about me and my future, it's always been about *his*. A world for children—for my own children, and their children, and generations to come.

Ethan deserves more than what Mars has given him, and the children of Earth deserve more than what Nation is willing to provide. It's time to start preparing. It's time to make moves.

Ethan deserves someone to fight for him. It's time to fight.

44

THE FRONT DOOR to the castle creaks and groans open. Bernard stops a moment by the cairn and shakes his head. It's impossible to tell if he's pleased or displeased by it, but I sense it's positive. He crosses the clover field with heavy-set footsteps, and when he speaks, his voice a low rumble. "The council is convening. You are both required to attend to your various civic duties."

Ethan scowls at Bernard. "The picnic is over?"

Bernard sits on his haunches among the clover. "For Princess Llama and Reach. But it doesn't have to be over for you and Princess Pippa."

"But I *like* Princess Llama and Reach. Reach is the Presernet."

"President," Bernard corrects.

Ethan's brow crinkles. "That's what I said."

"Well, sometimes adults have to do things that would be no fun at all for children. But I can think of something that would be fun." He waves a wooden spoon in Pippa's direction.

Pippa bounces over with glee. "Cooking?" she asks with a combination of joy and questioning hope. I can tell that when Bernard allows Pippa to cook with him, she enjoys it.

Bernard shakes his head and winks. "Yes. I was thinking about making some fresh bread and some…" He drops his voice low in a conspiratorial whisper. "Macarons."

Pippa jumps up and claps her hands.

Ethan jumps up too, thrilled by Pippa's excitement. "What's a macaron?" he asks.

Bernard groans and mumbles just loudly enough for me to hear, "Jezero, you failed at the most basic task of humanity. How can a child not know what a macaron is?" He begins cleaning up the picnic, but as he gestures Llama and me away, he pulls something red from his pocket and thrusts it in my direction. The Jezero Presidential sash. "Go, you two. You have a council to attend."

I stand, stretching my back and feel the warmth of the Souterraine lights hitting my face. Llama's warm hand finds its way into mine, and we wave to the three others before turning back to the castle.

"You know," Llama says once we're out of earshot, "Ethan has made me think. He needs someone to show him what love is. He needs someone to fight for him. But not just him, all the children from Jezero and Souterraine and even Nation need us."

I nod, my own thoughts exactly the same.

"It's time to think of how we're going to make Nation a better place. Reach, I love it here, but…"

When she doesn't speak again for a few moments, I say the words to finish her thought. "…but we have a duty to Nation."

"Exactly. You need to put that sash on."

I groan but slide the crisscrossing loops over my shoulders, the weight of grief and leadership pressing me into the Martian soil.

The king and queen are in the long hall where Llama and I first met with their advisors. People mill about, with elderly advisors sitting in rocking chairs and the more spritely chatting freely with others. The leaders from Jezero stand in an awkward group to the side.

"Oh good, Reach," the queen says, "you're here."

"Yes, Your Majesty." I barely remember to adopt the formal address, but am glad I did when I catch Phil's nod of approval.

I walk to the Jezero advisors and offer what I hope is a comforting smile. I'm not sure if they can see how fake it is, but at least it's something. None of them smile back.

"Well, now that we're all here," King Alfred drawls, "we can commence our meeting of the council. First order of business: Phil, how are the children adjusting to Souterraine?"

Phil steps forward from the throng. "Well, today is not a school day, and the Jezero children only had two days of school this week, so it is difficult to say for certain. Jezero had a robust school system. The students required ten minutes to get used to the concept of recess and play as an important part of our day, but they have all reported that the experiential learning and play is their favorite."

Everyone in the room nods. A Jezero leader steps up next to Phil. "Yes, the children seem to be adapting well, but it has only been a few days. The experiential learning is concerning for us, given what we need to prepare for."

"And what's that?" an older woman with spectacles calls out in a crackling voice.

The Jezero leader's cheeks flush, and he tucks his hands into the pockets of his silver Jezero spacesuit before answering. "The aircycler failures. It's only a matter of time before…" He trails off, eyes darting wildly around the room. I get the sense he's looking for something familiar to bolster his courage but not finding it. And then his eyes land on me—specifically, the Presidential sash. He visibly loses the stiffness in his limbs. "Before Souterraine collapses. We're on borrowed time here. The aircyclers can't complete the conversion cycle process with optimum efficiency. Especially with the increased population!" With each statement, his voice grows more and more shrill.

"That's enough now, Ian." A woman with dark red hair places her hand on Ian's shoulder.

Queen Eleanore nods as Ian melts back into the group of Jezero leaders. "Margot? Do you have findings for us?"

Margot nods, her jaw clenching as the hollows of her cheeks show the prevalence of bone in her thin face. "I do. And it's as I both expected and feared."

A hush falls over the room as we wait in anticipation. "Percy was in communication with Earth, specifically Nation. He had contact with someone who signed the messages with a stylized *E*."

Llama's eyes meet mine in a flash of concern. *E*—most likely Enforce.

"These transcripts hint at a plan to help *E* in return for power and riches on Earth. It's unclear to what end Percy was intending to help *E*. Though I believe it had something to do with discontent at the succession plan for Jezero."

I scratch my head. That doesn't make sense. "When were these transcripts dated?"

Margot pulls her spinning top tablet from her pocket and taps it, sliding her finger around the screen counterclockwise. "It was months ago. They started while you were in space and heading here. It seems perhaps right after you overrode the code to go rogue."

I have been a pawn for so long that this should not surprise me, yet it does. Enforce suspected what I was years ago. Llama's betrayal wasn't necessary, it was only a way to drive division between us. Enforce wanted... *What does Enforce want?*

The answer comes to me as quickly as the question fades. *Power.* The same thing Percy wanted.

Enforce is playing her own game of political chess, trying to force hands and manipulate the board. The true surprise to Percy wasn't me, it was Llama and her royal connection to Souterraine. I've never been the metaphorical queen on the board the way Dr. Jog said I was. No, I've been a rook. Important, sure, but only capable of lateral, predictable moves.

I clear my dry throat. "Did Percy ever communicate with *E* about Souterraine?"

Margot smiles, the skin around her eyes crinkling. "No. No, he did not."

A whoosh of air moves through the room as the advisors release the tension from their lungs in a collective breath.

"So," Queen Eleanore says, "I'm sure we're all wondering, what does this mean for Souterraine? Perhaps President Reach or Princess Llama could you give us some insight into who this *E* might be and what that might mean for our colony here."

I start to speak, but Llama raises her hand and steps forward. "Let me," she mouths, and I do.

"*E* is most likely a woman named Enforce," she explains. "She's the head of Nation's Punishment and Retribution Department. At the time of our departure from Earth, she was in trouble with the Three Powers for her actions involving excessive use of force on Reach during his mother's execution."

A collective shudder emanates from the Souterraine advisors around the large room.

"Reach's mother was able to escape during the chaos of Enforce's actions against him," Llama continues. "The timeline is suspicious. But it appears that Percy wasn't terribly surprised by Reach's visit to Mars. However, he was definitely surprised by both Reach's connection to the Jezero Presidency and my Martian connection to the Souterraine royalty."

Brows crinkle as people try to work out all these secrets and lies and who knew what and *when*. I'm even confused.

"I think we all were rather shocked by that, dear." Queen Eleanore pats Llama's hand. "This is quite the mystery, and sadly, I don't know how much it matters anymore. Percy is here in Souterraine awaiting trial by his Jezero peers. It appears that treason is a reasonable charge. In Souterraine, we do not condone the taking of human life. That much has always been clear to us in the Martian charters." She worries her bottom lip. "A sentence of a life of hard labor is certainly well within the rights of sentencing though."

The Jezero advisors shift uncomfortably behind me.

King Alfred wraps an arm around his wife's waist. "I think, my dear, that we can leave our Jezero residents to decide this at another date. There are more pressing matters we need to understand." Queen Eleanore looks up into the king's eyes and nods in agreement while the king smiles fondly down at her. "Now." He snaps to attention briskly. "We need a report on the agricultural sectors. We require more agricultural output with the Jezero Village residents."

One by one, different Souterraine residents step forward to give a report. They drone on about different crops, and I start to lose focus. My head still spins from trying to make sense of the information about Percy and Enforce.

"Ah, Edith," King Alfred intones, bringing me back to the room and out of my spiraling thoughts. "Beans. The farthest sector of agriculture. How are things going there?"

Edith wears a pair of blue overalls, her hair in a long braid down her back. The outfit is reminiscent of the student uniform I wore on Compound. Edith jams her hand in her front hip pocket. "It's not good, Your Majesties."

King Alfred's face sets into a hard frown. "Come on then, Edith. Please give us your report. How bad is it?" he asks.

"It's..." She takes a breath. "It's blight."

Something akin to a whistle echoes around the room as a sharp intake of breath is pulled into each advisor's lungs.

Queen Eleanore brings her hands to her face before regaining composure. "How bad?"

"We have the area contained, and the protocol is in place, but it's...it's spreading regardless."

"How?" King Alfred asks.

"We don't have any way of knowing for certain, but it may be related to the aircycling filters. If they aren't working optimally and scrubbing the spores from the air, then an airborne blight will eventually take over."

"What are the consequences of that?" Llama asks, and I'm surprised by her decision to jump right in and ask questions like a ruler.

Edith fixes Llama with an incredulous look. "If we can't grow food, we can't live. If we can't live we..." She trails off.

"Leave Mars," Llama whispers.

"How much time do you estimate we have based on the rate of spread?" Queen Eleanore asks, her voice eerily calm.

"Best-case scenario," Edith replies, "three to seven years. The worst-case scenario: twelve months."

"Advisors." King Alfred stands. "Please pair off into your groups and consider any suggestions or concerns regarding this problem. Bernard, please lock the doors while we deliberate. We don't want to create any rumors and cause a panic. Jezero leaders, please discuss, and if you have any ideas, this is the time to voice them. Your thoughts and ideas are welcome here."

I stand awkwardly next to the Jezero leaders as they all look to me. Truthfully, I don't know how the advisors split up, but I suppose this grouping makes enough sense. "Right. So, blight here is bad… Do you have any ideas for…solving it?"

Margot spins her tablet clockwise and begins tapping furiously. Everyone watches her, entranced. "Right," she says, stopping and looking up. She rolls her eyes to the ceiling and mutters numbers, then resumes typing. After a moment, she stops. "Ok. Mars is showing signs of being inhospitable to colonists. It's been over three hundred years since the original founders arrived on Martian soil. The way I see it, we can stretch the worst-case scenario into a more manageable one quickly."

"What do you mean?" I ask. "How can you stretch one year of food into more?"

"It's simple, really," she says. "We leave."

I stare. "And go where?"

"Earth." She shrugs. "With the communications channels open for the first time in hundreds of years, we could go to Nation."

I clench my jaw. "I don't think you understand the scope of what Nation is."

A shout erupts from across the hall. It's Phil's group, and it includes Llama. "We have a solution!"

Everyone stops, everyone stares.

"Yes?" Queen Eleanore asks. "What do you propose?"

Phil steps to the center of the room. "We did some calculations and discovered how to stretch the worst-case scenario another three years. In order to do this, we would have to break the colony into thirds and leave Mars. Essentially, we would take three waves of colonists back to Earth. The first group would go as soon as they are prepared for space travel. The second group in the next year, and finally, the third group the year after that."

"What is the likelihood of the best-case scenario, Edith?" the queen asks.

Edith's shoulders slump in response. "Agriculture is a fickle science, Your Majesty. I can't say for certain, but erring on the side of caution is the best practice."

"So the three-to-seven-years best-case scenario was…" The queen fixes Edith with a glare.

"Truly the best-case scenario. If the blight is contained and nothing else happens, then yes, that is within the realm of statistical possibility. But it's more likely that it will *not* be the best-case scenario."

"Thank you, Edith," King Alfred responds. "As always, the discussions of the council are confidential. We have things to think about. I think it is safe to say that we do not want to raise the alarm among the colonists yet. We have enough food for now, and we have stores as well. We will take this idea under advisement.

"Margot, please assemble a team and immediately begin developing a more robust communication center for transmissions to Earth. Preferably without biosecurity, since we've seen how *that* can be mishandled. Phil, please begin adding instruction in necessary subjects for space travel to the children's curriculum. Let the afternoon learning teachers know what the expectations are. You are dismissed, but we will reconvene in twenty-four hours to discuss the plan further. Adjourned."

45

THE ADVISERS LEAVE in groups of three and four, a low, hushed whisper among them. Finally, all that remains in the advisory hall are the King and Queen of Souterraine, Llama and myself, and Margot.

Llama stands by the window, her forehead pressed against the pane. The king and queen whisper for a while, then hold each other in a tight embrace. Margot spins her tablet idly in her hand. She's waiting for something, but I don't know what it is.

Margot breaks the silence. "I think you might like to read some of the transmissions."

Llama's head jerks away from the pane, and I catch her gaze. I don't know why we didn't think of that.

"Since you most recently came from Nation, perhaps you could help make sense of some of these exchanges, President Reach and Princess Llama?" Margot says.

The king and queen look on from a distance, interest evident on their faces.

I swallow. Communication with Enforce sounds terrible. I've enjoyed time away from her sadistic tendencies. To willingly open up words written by her, it's too much like being sucked back into the never-ending political drama of the Three Powers. Of course, it also means that we can have an advantage. We can maybe glean information about our opponent, and it's looking more and more like we will actually have people to return to Earth with us. That was the whole idea of us *going* to Mars in the first place.

Llama leaves the window and slides her arm between my elbow and my torso. Instinctively, I grasp her hand. *She knows too*, I marvel. She knows what opening a communication from Enforce means. And this time, we do it *together*.

I can do anything with her by my side.

With the thought bolstering my courage, I find my voice. "Yes, please." I sneak a glance at the king and queen. The tension is still evident in their body language, but there's also a relief there. I sense that they would not force us to look at the transcripts. The stories Llama and I have told must have been dark enough.

Llama's hand tightens in mine, but while she stands rigid, I feel the tremor that runs through her as Margot approaches with the tablet. Margot places the tablet in my palm with a nod.

"It's set to the first transmission. Simply swirl your finger around the edge in a clockwise direction to move forward, counterclockwise to move backward. Spinning will take you to a different application, so don't spin the device."

I force myself to breathe.

"Would you like to look with me?" I ask Llama, my voice low and quiet.

Llama closes her eyes, then meets mine with a resolve that I find remarkable. "Yes."

I tug gently on her hand and she walks with me and the tablet to the window seat. I place the tablet in the center of the seat, then sink down on one side. Llama joins me on the other.

The first transcript is not what I expect.

Be advised, rogue scientists from Nation attempting contact with Greg McAllistair via Jezero Colony base. - Σ

Llama inhales a sharp breath through her teeth. I read the next. There's a series where each line follows a significant time lag. Mars and Earth are light minutes away, and Percy's clandestine messaging means that each line of communication took days.

Rogue scientists confirmed. Heritage? -JZC

Advise on health of scientists. -Σ

Healthy, girl claims Martian heritage? -JZCP

Alec, colonist returned to Earth, is her father. Will you help us? -Σ

What do we get if we help you? -JZCP

Nation needs you to return. -Σ

Why? -JZCP

Government weak. Place for colonists to return and make life better. Opportunities for better, for all. -Σ

What would I get if I help? -JZCP

Positions of government, fresh air, sunlight, resources… -Σ

What do I need to do to ensure the primary leadership role in the new Nation? -JZCP

Help them. Convince people to return to Earth. -Σ

How? -JZCP

Colonists return to 46.5436° N, 87.3954° W ASAP. The time is near, we move if you send soldiers. -Σ

I slide my finger clockwise along the tablet, but there are no more messages.

"Reach," Llama whispers, her face ashen. I brush a lock of hair out of her eyes with my thumb. "Yes?"

"Reach. That's not from Enforce."

I blink. "Who else could it be from?"

"I think…it's from someone outside of Ward 11. But those coordinates would tell me for sure. Can you find the location on Earth? I think…" She bites her lip. "I'd rather be sure before I say who I think these are from. I might be wrong…"

"Queen Eleanore?" I call. She walks over from where she has been hovering like a hummingbird a few feet away from Llama and me. She was pretending to look at books on the shelf, but I sensed that she was more worried about the possible distress Llama and I might endure with these communications.

"Yes, Reach? What is it?" she asks, a slight hitch in her voice.

"I need an older, pre-Scientific Revolution map of Nation with latitude and longitude lines. Do you know where I could find one?"

"Yes. I'll be right back." In one of the most uncharacteristic displays of royalty I've seen, Queen Eleanore hitches up her skirt and runs from the room. It is the exact mannerism that she chides Pippa for on a daily basis. I would laugh if I wasn't concerned about the coordinates and Llama's vehement refusal to consider that these messages are from Enforce.

Minutes pass, and I sit next to Llama, staring at the door, waiting for the mystery of the coordinates and the mystery of the author of these messages to be revealed. Llama seems certain that the coordinates will confirm her theory.

The queen bustles back in, holding a canister the size of half her body. "Here," she huffs, thrusting the canister at me.

I wedge the cap off the top and slide the map out. Unrolling it, I lay it on the floor, placing anything I can find on the edges.

It's an old map of Nation—one of the ones Dr. Geo showed me during my geography training at Hub. I follow the latitude and longitude markings until I find the intersection of the lines.

"Here." King Alfred hands me a pencil.

"Thank you," I say. Then, I draw a large X on the coordinates. "Llama?"

Llama's eyes grow huge and she plops back down on the window seat, a tremor overtaking her body.

"Llama?" I question, moving to sit by her as my concern ratchets up.

She leans over and buries her head into my shoulder. "It's not from Enforce, Reach." She squeaks her words out between sobs. "It's not from the Three Powers or the government."

I stare at her, my brain trying to make sense of her words.

"Reach. That's outside of Ward 11, but I know it. And that's not an *E*, that's a *sigma*."

Understanding dawns like pinpricks of light just before the first rays of the sun creep over the horizon. These messages aren't from Enforce. *But who was communicating with Jezero, then?*

"Reach, did you ever learn what your mother's codesign was when she went to space?"

I shake my head no, because code signs aren't used after a space mission is served. They are only used in the official logbooks. There's a lot about my mother I don't know. I don't even know her real name. I only know her as *Dr. Impart*, or less formally, *Mom*.

"Reach, these transmissions are from *off grid*."

I blink hard and fast.

"Reach, these transmissions are from *your mother*, code sign Sigma, on her space mission."

Margot, the king, and the queen have gathered around, shaking their heads.

"What does it mean, though?" Margot asks.

I interject because some questions are more pressing than others and best answered immediately. "How do you know about my mom's mission? I don't know anything about my mom's mission. They wiped it from the records after she returned with me."

Llama grimaces but answers me first. "The Ward schools are always the last to receive new technology, resources, and curriculum. Since children in the Wards never grow up to be important, they can get by with learning outdated materials. We studied about the famed scientist who was *going* to Station 15, and who was a symbol of progress and pride for Nation every year for four years."

After she answers my question, Llama snaps her eyes to her grandparents, something blazing in them I can't quite understand. "It means that humankind has a duty to help other humans. That you might be Martian colonists, but Mars is failing you, and we have an opportunity to remove tyrants from power in Nation. Reach's mother is telling us exactly what they need. What *we* need."

"And what is that, precisely?" the king asks, his voice gruff.

"Soldiers," I reply. "A Martian army to return with us to Earth prepared to take down despots."

"But surely not...both of you...will return to fight." Queen Eleanore's eyes brim with tears.

I think for a moment about what leadership has cost her. I think of her sending her beloved son to Earth to scout conditions there, and him never returning. Sending her beloved husband into a doomed colony with no guarantee he will return. I think about her waiting, being left to wonder while preparing for any and all outcomes. I don't want my future wife to wait for me. I don't want to be separated from her.

I stand, extending my hand to Llama, who grasps mine as she rises. Her eyes meet mine for a fraction of a moment. "We're going—together," we say in unison.

They all consider us for a lengthy moment.

"Eleanore," the king breathes into the silence. "It's a chance to start over and make things better for all. Isn't that what we promised when we rose to this throne?"

The queen bows her head, but nods.

"I had hoped our return to Earth would be peaceful," Margot offers.

The king grins wryly. "Margot, when is change ever *truly* peaceful?" Then he directs a firm look at Llama and me. "You two are the most unlikely of change agents. Yet, I believe in you. Souterraine does not have an army, nor did Jezero, but we will help provide the soldiers you need. Margot, can you please try to transmit and ask how many soldiers this *sigma* wants us to provide?"

"Yes, Your Majesty."

"Now, Margot," the king prompts when Margot doesn't immediately recognize her dismissal.

"Oh, yes!" Margot hurries from the room.

"My dear," the king says, wrapping his arm around the queen's waist and dropping a kiss to her forehead. "For the first time in history, Souterraine must prepare for war."

War is an ugly word. I set my face into the stoniest mask I can muster, but images of the war before the Scientific Revolution cross my mind. I close my eyes against the imagery, knowing that I must fight against Nation and the Three Powers, and hoping that war today does not look like the war of the past.

"Reach." Llama tugs my shoulder down so that she can whisper in my ear. "Reach, whatever happens, we will face it *together*."

I shake my head and smile at her. I can't help but marvel at this woman who's been a friend, a lover, an enemy, and now so much more. She's everything.

And we're going home.

For better or for worse, we'll be together.

THE END

Want to know more about Reach, Llama, and the world they escaped? Read the beginning of their story in REACH. And remember, in chess, even a pawn can checkmate.

amazon.com/dp/B0D8FSGCXN

Will Llama and Reach succeed, or will Nation win once and for all? Find out all this and more in RETURN, available for preorder today.

amazon.com/dp/B0F564S2MY

AUTHOR'S NOTE

All glory and honor to God.

Publishing a book is a process that is impossible to do alone, which is strange because writing is such a solitary activity.

I need to thank Caitlin Miller, editor extraordinaire, for her hard work with this manuscript, not only helping me find my crutch words, but also fixing my comma issues and deleting my too frequent em dashes.

Benita Thompson, of Kairos Design, thank you for the beautiful cover, and knowing how to format books, and staying with me on the phone as I'm uploading manuscripts to KDP and Ingram Spark.

To all my online friends who have cheered me on, Rachel, Madelyn, Ursi, Andrea, Paige, Leah…and everyone who has been there for me on this wild journey, thank you for your support.

To my in person writing crew: Mary Kreger, Lily, and Julia. You make me a better writer. Thank you.

To my family: Patrick, who's support of my dreams is a gift I cherish. To Gabriella, Maria, Pascale, Blaise and Paxton who have all the questions about books and think it's cool that I write them. Thank you for cheering me on. Being your mom is the greatest adventure.

O. McCarthy took the overactive imagination of her youth and decided to put it to good use. She lives in Michigan with her husband, children, and to the disappointment of her five children, no pets.

When she's not writing, O can be found running, baking fresh sourdough bread, folding epic amounts of laundry, or chauffeuring her children around town to various activities. Thankfully, her best thinking is done in the car.

This is O's second book of many.

You can connect with Olivia on Instagram:
@oliviamccarthyauthor